THE ICING ON THE CORPSE

Stan knelt next to Char, who leaned over Betty. The musical notes faded as the rest of the crowd caught on to the drama unfolding nearby. People lined up on the sidewalk, watching apprehensively.

"What happened?" Stan stared at Betty's white face. She felt sick, remembering Sarah Oliver's words. *Something's wrong.*

Betty stirred and opened her eyes. Stan and Char exchanged a look of relief. When Betty's eyes landed on Char, she burst into tears.

"Now, Betty, don't be upset." Char leaned over her friend as approaching sirens grew louder and an ambulance careened into sight. "The ambulance is here. You're going to be fine."

"It's not me," Betty whispered, struggling to sit up. Stan grabbed one arm and Char took the other, and they helped her to a sitting position. "It's Helga!"

Char looked around. "I don't see Helga anywhere."

"Inside," Betty whispered. Her next words were so soft Stan strained to hear them. "I think . . . I think she's dead. . . ."

Books by Liz Mugavero

KNEADING TO DIE

A BISCUIT, A CASKET

THE ICING ON THE CORPSE

Published by Kensington Publishing Corporation

The Icing on the Corpse

LIZ MUGAVERO

KENSINGTON PUBLISHING CORP.
http://www.kensingtonbooks.com

KENSINGTON BOOKS are published by

Kensington Publishing Corp.
119 West 40th Street
New York, NY 10018

All Kensington Titles, Imprints, and Distributed Lines are
available at special quantity discounts for bulk purchases for
sales promotions, premiums, fund-raising, and educational
or institutional use. Special book excerpts or customized
printings can also be created to fit specific needs. For details,
write or phone the office of the Kensington special sales
manager: Kensington Publishing Corp., 119 West 40th Street,
New York, NY 10018, attn: Special Sales Department,
Phone: 1-800-221-2647.

Kensington and the K logo Reg. U.S. Pat & TM Off.

ISBN-13: 978-0-7582-8482-2
ISBN-10: 0-7582-8482-9
First Kensington Mass Market Edition: April 2015

eISBN-13: 978-0-7582-8483-9
eISBN-10: 0-7582-8483-7
First Kensington Electronic Edition: April 2015

10 9 8 7 6 5 4 3 2 1

Printed in the United States of America

In memory of Bill Stanley, Sr.,
whose history lessons and friendship
will always be in my heart

Chapter 1

Groundhogs invaded the basement of the Frog Ledge Unitarian Universalist Church. They came in all shapes and sizes, at least sixty of them—tall, short, fat, skinny, fluffy tails, flat tails. Some stood around drinking coffee, others chatted in groups, still more milled around the makeshift podium at the front of the meeting room, waiting for the festivities to begin.

"This is surreal," Stan Connor said quietly.

"You just feel out of place because you don't have a groundhog costume like the cool people." Jake McGee, her sort-of boyfriend, gazed solemnly at her. "I told you I would've gotten you one."

She elbowed him. "Oh, be quiet. You don't have a costume." Not that he needed one to stand out. He was easily one of the best-looking people around, in his own jeans, baseball cap, and stubble kind of way.

"I'm not cool." He winked.

"Good morning!"

All eyes turned to the podium now commandeered by Betty Meany, Frog Ledge's librarian. Betty was so short you could barely tell she stood two steps above the crowd. But the tangerine-colored scarf she'd tied around her spiky white hair, combined with her bubbly energy, made up for what she lacked in height. A drop-down screen lowered behind her. Not surprisingly, a smiling groundhog image appeared.

"Happy Groundhog Day," Betty continued. "I'm so thrilled you're all here. We have such a great program planned for you today. Before I give you a sneak peek, I'd like to introduce you all to this year's Groundhog Gift-Giver: Stan Connor, owner and chief baker at Pawsitively Organic!" She led a round of applause. "Stan has been chosen to present Lily-pad, our groundhog guest of honor, with her annual gift. Stan, can you please come up?"

Stan felt her face heat up. She'd never been asked to give a groundhog a gift before. That alone was stressful. And a groundhog named Lilypad took it to a whole new level. Couple it with being on display for the whole town's critical eye, and it was worse than her most contentious media face-off at her old corporate job. The situation was exacerbated by the continuous replay of the *Ally McBeal* theme song in her head—because certainly, this could only happen on a nineties TV show. She still hadn't lost her old habit of assigning most things in her life a soundtrack. She mentally shoved the song out of her head. Jake gave her a gentle push forward.

"Go! You don't want to miss your moment in the sun," he said.

She didn't have time to glare at him as all eyes turned toward her. She took a deep breath and squeezed through the crowd until she reached Betty.

Betty beamed at her. "Congratulations! Would you like to say a few words?" She moved aside, giving Stan room at the podium.

Luckily, thanks to her past life in public relations, Stan could recite a good quote without even thinking about it. "I'm absolutely honored Pawsitively Organic has been chosen as the gift-giver for Lilypad. I can't think of a better way to spend my first Groundhog Day in Frog Ledge." She smiled brightly, showing plenty of teeth.

A flashbulb went off from the front of the crowd, nearly blinding her in the dim room. Cyril Pierce, publisher and lone reporter for the local newspaper, the *Frog Ledge Holler*, called out. "Is the gift edible?"

"The gift is edible," she assured him. "But that's all I can tell you before the unveiling."

As the "chosen citizen"—the one who presented a gift to the town groundhog—Stan had a tradition to uphold. Namely, no one could see the present before Lilypad. Many citizens had been vying for the honor of gift-giver for years and had never even been considered. At least that's what her friend Char Mackey had told her in awed tones when she'd heard the news. Who knew? But the whole town had been speculating like crazy about what Stan would do for Lilypad. Which had resulted in a whole lot of pressure over the last two weeks since the mayor had tapped her as "the one."

"Thank you, Stan." Betty led the round of applause as she stepped down. "We can't wait to see the gift. In the meantime, we'll continue social hour right here, with refreshments, stories, a slideshow of our past events"—she indicated the screen behind her—"and then we'll move outside around eleven. Lilypad will arrive shortly thereafter. We'll have live music and our town historian, Helga Oliver, will start the ceremony with a history of Groundhog Day in Frog Ledge. Mayor Tony Falco will present Lilypad with a citation. Then Lilypad will offer her verdict and hopefully, we'll bring winter to a close!" Betty smiled and nodded as the crowd offered up another round of applause.

"Stan will present the gift in closing. Lastly, I just want to remind everyone what an honor it is to have Lilypad the groundhog here. Lilypad's handler told me when she accepted our invitation that Frog Ledge is the only celebration she would consider, because our programs are so classy. So thank you all for your help in making our town's celebration *the* go-to event! We'll see you outside in an hour!" And she hurried off the podium. Behind her, the slide show began to flash across the screen as "We've Only Just Begun" began playing. The Carpenters? Really?

Stan looked at Jake. "Do other towns really do this? I thought it was just that little town in Pennsylvania where the media always converges."

"We're the only ones in Connecticut who do it up this big," a voice from behind Stan chimed in.

They both turned to find Cyril Pierce behind them. He wore his typical outfit—a black trench coat over black jeans and a button-down shirt—and his short, curly hair stuck out every which way, thick glasses askew. He carried a steno pad and the offending camera. He nodded at Stan. "Congratulations."

"Thanks. Is there a reason we do it up big?" Stan asked.

Cyril shrugged. "We like to celebrate random holidays."

It was as good a reason as any. Stan had gotten to the point where, almost a year after moving to Frog Ledge and despite still feeling sometimes like she'd gone down the rabbit hole, she was much better at accepting the way things were done.

"I'm going to go see if Betty needs help." Jake leaned down and kissed her cheek. "I'll find you." He walked off. She watched him go, not sure if her cheek was really burning from his lips or if she was having some weird flashback to sixteen.

"Hello? Stan?" Cyril waved his steno pad at her. "I have a couple more questions."

"Hmm? Oh, sure. Shoot." She focused on him. "But I can't give anything away about the gift."

She spent the next few minutes dodging specifics while explaining that, based on her research, groundhogs were vegetarians who enjoyed an occasional bug. Those findings had given her pause considering her occupation—baking healthy, natural, organic pet treats—and the task before her, but she figured she could make it work. She'd spent all day yesterday baking a special, full-sized, carrot-shaped cookie flavored with nuts and berries, resting on a bed of grass. Organic, homegrown cat grass, to be specific. She hoped Lilypad liked it.

"Excuse me." A groundhog-costumed man tapped her on the shoulder. "Do you have any treats here? I promised my dog I would bring some home. I hope you do. He'll be real upset if not." He looked anxious.

Stan glanced at Cyril. He seemed about to protest this diversion of her attention when a portly old man with an unlit cigar clamped between his teeth materialized at his elbow. Stan noticed their resemblance to one another immediately. Namely, the same thick glasses and unkempt curly hair, although the older man's was gray.

Cyril looked startled. "Dad. What are you . . ." He turned so Stan couldn't hear him and said something. The old man looked annoyed. Cyril glanced back at Stan and flipped his notebook closed. "I'll need comments and a photo after the presentation."

"Absolutely," Stan promised. She watched them walk away, the faint smell of stale cigar following. Cyril had a dad. Funny thing to be surprised about. She'd never actually thought about Cyril as a real person with a family. Mostly he was Frog Ledge's prickly newsman.

"So what kind do you have?" the groundhog man asked, dragging her attention back.

She focused on him. "I have broccoli and cheese, peanut butter and banana, and blueberry vanilla barley. Three sizes—large, medium, and small."

The man pumped his furry fist in the air. "Awesome! Are they . . ."

"Groundhog shaped?" Stan finished. "You bet." She smiled as she led the delighted customer to her display set up on one of the folding tables Betty and her team had dragged from the storage room and dusted off that morning. She was catching on to this group of quirky townsfolk and their preferences. It had been a mad search for three sizes of groundhog-shaped cookie cutters, but her persistence had paid off. She'd even made salmon-flavored cat treats in the same shape.

She packed up some cookies, collected her money, and sent the guy on his way, then scanned the crowd for Jake. Nowhere in sight. If he'd offered himself up to Betty, she was sure to keep him busy for the rest of the event. He might even miss her gift presentation.

"Hey! You ripped out my *fur!*" The ear-splitting shriek jolted Stan. Two kids faced off, one with a clump of fake fur from the other's costume in his hand, an evil smile on his face. The kid unfortunately missing his tail burst into tears and began screaming for his mother, who didn't seem to be anywhere in sight.

In the midst of the chaos, Stan heard the shrill voice behind her loud and clear. "*You're* the pet food lady!"

She turned automatically at the title—she was used to it in some form or another these days—to find a woman with long, frizzy platinum curls, dressed like Stevie Nicks from Fleetwood Mac. Her flowy purple skirt was accented by a lacy top and high-heeled boots. All that was missing was a top hat and a microphone with a scarf tied around it. She smiled eagerly at Stan, waiting for her response. Her right front tooth was smeared with Corvette red lipstick, a color that remained only in faded tones on her lips. Immediately, the opening bars of "Gypsy" floated through Stan's head. She half expected the woman to break into a signature twirl. Another woman who seemed to be accompanying her stood a couple of steps behind, a slightly mortified smile on her face. By contrast, she looked like an affluent soccer mom, sporting a North Face coat, expensive-looking yoga pants, and carefully messy, salon-streaked hair. And a very nice Louis Vuitton bag.

"That's me." Stan offered her hand, clamping down on her runaway mental activity. "I'm Stan Connor."

"Sarah Oliver. I have heard delightful things about you." Sarah took her hand, clasped it between both of hers, and closed her eyes.

What the heck is she doing? "Oliver. Are you Helga's daughter?" Stan asked, delicately trying to tug her hand away.

Sarah didn't say anything for a long minute and continued to hold on to Stan's hand, her grip like a vise. Finally, she opened her eyes. "You have strong energy," she said.

"Uh, thanks."

Sarah smiled and nodded. She finally dropped Stan's hand. Stan swore it felt hot. "I am Helga's daughter. Do you know Mum?"

"I do. I'm—I know her through Jake. McGee." Four months in and she still didn't know what to say about Jake. Were they dating? Was he her boyfriend? As much as she liked him—heck, she really liked him—did she *want* to put a label on it? This stuff shouldn't be as complicated in your thirties as it was in your teens and twenties.

But the recognition dawned as Sarah put two and two together. "Of course. Jake's new gal. We've heard all about you. But *I* knew about you because my mum is a fan of your cat treats. Her Benedict is a picky eater."

Heard all about her? Was Jake talking about her to Helga? She knew Helga was a very close family friend of the McGees, basically a surrogate grandmother to Jake and his two sisters. The thought of Jake confiding in her about his sort-of relationship made her blush.

The other woman finally stepped forward. "Hi. I'm Carla Miller."

"Nice to meet you, Carla." Stan shook her hand, too.

"Carla's my sister-in-law," Sarah said. "I drive her crazy."

Carla flushed. "You do not. Hush."

"She's a politician's wife," Sarah told Stan. "That's why she's so polite. And a little snobby." She elbowed Carla playfully, but Carla did not look amused. She shifted her bag to her other shoulder, adjusting it so the Louis Vuitton tag was unmistakable.

"Politician?" Stan asked.

"Don Miller. Town councilman," Sarah said. "My big brother. Different fathers," she added.

Carla looked like she wanted the floor to open up and swallow her. Sarah was oblivious to the discomfort she appeared to be causing her sister-in-law. She leaned closer to Stan. "Are you giving the groundhog a dog cookie?"

Stan glanced around to make sure no one else was paying attention and answered in her own stage whisper. "It's not a dog cookie . . . it's a groundhog cookie."

Sarah's lips formed an O. "Can I see it?"

Stan cringed at the question, hoping no one had heard. Too late. Betty materialized at Stan's elbow, and the look on her face could've crumbled the cookie into a million pieces. "Sarah, what do you think you're doing? You know better than that!"

Stan opened her mouth to intervene, but Sarah suddenly closed her eyes and swayed, grabbing the edge of the table. Alarmed, Stan reached for her.

"What's wrong?" She looked at Betty. "Is she okay?"

Betty's look of disdain said it all, but Sarah's eyes flew open. "Where's Mum?" she asked urgently.

Stan looked around. "I haven't seen her."

"Neither have I," Betty said, still sullen. "Why?"

Sarah's flighty demeanor was gone. In its place, Stan read fear in her eyes. "Something's wrong. We need to find her."

Chapter 2

"She's just a drama queen. She was trying to divert my attention from her inappropriate question about Lilypad's gift." Betty stormed outside and scanned the crowd huddled in the parking lot, braving the cold and waiting for the event to start. The green itself was still covered in at least six inches of snow, so they were relegated to the smaller concrete area for the festivities. Stan hurried to keep up with her.

"Everyone knows you can't peek at the gift! She doesn't bother with her mother that much anyway. All of a sudden she's worried about her?" Betty made a hand gesture that Stan wouldn't expect from a librarian.

"Are you sure?" Stan asked. "She seemed pretty serious." After her near-fainting spell, Sarah had rushed off, Carla in tow, presumably to look for her mother. Stan didn't know where they'd gone.

"Trust me. You don't know Sarah. She's trouble with a capital *T.* Raymond!"

Ray Mackey turned from the group of people he

huddled with. "What can I do for you, Betty? Hello there, Stan."

Stan gave him a hug. Ray and Char Mackey, owners of the Alpaca Haven Bed-and-Breakfast, were her first and most trusted friends in Frog Ledge. They knew all the gossip, were always supportive of her, and the fact that Char was from New Orleans originally didn't hurt. She made the best food and strongest drinks in town, though Stan wouldn't tell Jake that. As the owner of McSwigg's, the local Irish pub, he would find that assessment offensive.

But Betty was in no mood for niceties. "Where's Helga?"

Ray, in his usual slow and steady manner, thought about that long enough that Betty looked about ready to pop. "I'm afraid I don't know, Betty."

"Aargh," Betty muttered. "She's got to be around here somewhere."

"Do you need a replacement historian?" A man with a scraggly beard and tiny eyeglasses appeared behind Betty. "I'm happy to jump in if Helga is neglecting her duties. I'm quite an expert on our town's Groundhog Day legacy." He smiled at Stan and held out a cold, thin hand. "Dale Hatmaker. I'm—"

"We'll be fine, Dale," Betty cut in, stepping in front of Stan before she could shake his hand. "Thanks for offering."

Despite Betty's curt tone, Dale Hatmaker didn't look offended. Instead, he smiled at them both, clasped his hands together, and bowed his head at Betty, then walked away.

Stan looked from Betty to Ray. Both were glowering after Hatmaker. "Who was that?"

Betty rolled her eyes. "That's Dale. Self-elected historian. He wants Helga's job and doesn't make it a secret. Shameless, if you ask me."

"Completely shameless," Ray added, snapping his suspenders. "As my wife would say, he ain't got the good sense God gave a rock."

Stan smiled at the southern phrase so common to Char. "Her job? You mean you get paid to be the historian?" she asked.

"Well, of course you do!" Betty looked at Stan like she was slow. "It's not a fortune, but it's a small salary. Dale just wants the title. He knows some things, sure, but he's not a lifer in town like Helga and her family. He's only lived here about fifty years." Betty sniffed, as if that were equivalent to about two weeks. "He just wants his name in the paper. Anyway, I must go find her. If you see her, please find me right away." She hurried off, leaving Stan and Ray staring after her.

"What's Betty so frantic about finding Helga for? The ceremony isn't in danger of starting without her." Ray looked at his watch. "Although we are getting close. Holy smokes," he interrupted himself. "Is that Arthur Pierce?"

Stan turned to see Cyril and his dad engaged in a serious discussion under a tree. "I think so. Cyril called him dad."

"Well, of course it is. It's wonderful to see him. They just had some devastating news." He leaned close to Stan, and whispered, "Arthur has terminal cancer. Diagnosed just last month."

Stan made a sympathetic noise. Poor Cyril.

"Anyway, I apologize. I sidetracked you. What's got Betty so up in arms?"

"There was a strange episode with Helga's daughter. She said something was wrong and we had to find her," Stan explained.

"Ahh. Sarah?"

Stan nodded. "What's her deal? She seemed a little . . . spacey."

"She does tend to appear that way," Ray said. "But, actually, she's a medium."

Stan's eyes widened. "A real one?" That explained the energy comment.

Ray pulled a pack of chewing gum out of his pocket, unwrapped a stick, and offered it to Stan. She declined. He popped it in his mouth, chewed slowly. "She thinks so. I don't think it's her day job, but she considers it a talent. What's the fuss about? What's wrong with Helga?"

"Sarah didn't say. She looked like she was going to pass out. Then she said something was wrong and we had to find her. Betty shrugged it off, but now she seems concerned." Stan huddled deeper in her coat. Now she knew why people were wearing groundhog costumes. The day was cold, overcast, and damp. She was freezing and wished for a hat. At least she'd had the foresight to bring gloves. February was not the best time of year for an outdoor event in New England.

"Hmmm." Ray stroked his own beard. "Well, I'll take a walk around. Anyone seen Gerry?"

Helga's companion, Gerry Ricci, was ninety-two to her eighty-seven. Despite their advanced ages, they were one of the most visible couples in town, always out and about, participating in some historical event or other town gathering. Gerry had bad knees and Helga had a bad hip, but they got around swimmingly. They reportedly met for breakfast twice each week and dinner on the weekends, but both maintained their own households in that true old-fashioned mind-set. Stan hadn't seen him either and told Ray so.

"I'll put an APB out." He winked at her. "We'll get to the bottom of this. Don't you worry. I'll get Char on it. You know my wife. She can find out anything."

He wasn't kidding. Char Mackey had a gift for gossip. There was nothing she couldn't get people to tell her. Part of it was a gift, and part of it was her Southern heritage.

Before he could walk away, a shout from farther down the green distracted them.

"She's here!"

They both turned to look. Stan hoped it was Helga, but realized the pseudo-groundhog making the announcement pointed to a woman unloading a pink carrier from an SUV parked on the road next to the green.

"Lilypad's here," Ray said. "You better run in and get your gift. Don't worry, I'll keep looking for our errant historian. She probably just got tied up at the museum. You know how she is when she's working."

"Hope so. Thanks, Ray. Speaking of missing people, have you seen Jake?"

Ray pointed to the side of the church. "I think Betty asked him to pull some chairs out from the other entrance."

"Thanks." Stan darted back inside the nearly empty meeting room and went to retrieve her bag from under the table where she'd stashed it. Instead of leaving through the main exit, she went to the side door in hopes of tracking Jake down. But when she shoved the door open, she nearly hit a tiny woman on the other side. Tinier than Betty Meany, even. She had tight, silver curls and wore a long red coat that probably weighed more than she did. She was engaged in what looked to be a serious conversation with Carla Miller, who was leaning against the building. Neither of them looked happy.

"Oh, my goodness, I'm so sorry!" Stan peered around the door. "I didn't mean to interrupt. I was looking for Jake."

The tiny woman glared at her, causing Stan to freeze in her tracks. *Whoa. Not so friendly.*

Carla shook her head. "It's fine. I haven't seen Jake out here."

Stan mumbled another apology and a thanks. As she shut the door, she heard Carla say, "You could try to be nicer to people, Maeve."

She didn't wait to hear Maeve's reply. Instead, she hurried back through the basement and out the main door. Helga still wasn't in sight when Stan stepped outside. Neither was Jake. Instead, she ran into the new mayor, Tony Falco. And her mother, who was always on Falco's arm these days. Here in Frog Ledge, instead of her home in Narragansett, Rhode Island. Falco, a newcomer to town, had usurped the incumbent mayor last November. And captured her mother's normally blasé heart at the same time.

Stan stifled a sigh. "Hello," she said, pasting on her best blankly pleasant face, a holdover from her corporate days, and trying not to wince as Falco pumped her hand a bit more enthusiastically than necessary.

"Kristan!" Patricia Connor bussed her cheek with a

kiss. "Hello, dear. How exciting to have my daughter as the gift-giver!"

That was a switch. When Stan had first started her business, her mother had brushed it off as nonsense and tried to encourage her right back into the dysfunction of corporate America. When she'd resisted, citing a much-needed rest from the cutthroat corporate world, Patricia had shifted gears and tried to push her into politics. Because *that* wasn't cutthroat at all.

"Yes, it's cool. I have to run, Mom. They're about to get started. I'll talk to you later," she promised, and hurried off, relieved to see Jake up ahead. He stood with Frank Pappas, the builder working on Jake's newest renovation project in town. Frank was doing most of the talking, and his hands moved in short, curt gestures in time with his lips. Jake listened, but he didn't say a word. Stan hesitated for a second, then figured she had every reason in the world to interrupt. She was the groundhog gift-giver, for goodness' sake.

She walked up and tapped Jake on the shoulder. "This event is getting wacky," she said. She smiled at Frank. "Hi."

Frank grunted.

"There you are." Jake twined her fingers with his. "Frank, I'll talk to you later."

Frank shrugged and walked away.

"What was that about?" Stan asked.

"Nothing. We'd better hurry—you need a spot right near the guest of honor and the head groundhog." Jake tugged her toward the crowd, in the opposite direction of where Frank had gone.

"Head groundhog?" Stan repeated.

He grinned. "You haven't met the head ground-hog?" He swung her hand as they walked. It fit nicely in his, she noticed, then felt like a silly sixteen-year-old again.

"I haven't. Do I know him?"

He maneuvered her into the crowd so she had a front-row view of the outside podium, which had been set up on a platform at the southernmost edge of the library parking lot. He stood behind her, hands resting lightly on her shoulders. Stan leaned back against him, content. Despite the chill of the day, she already felt warmer. Jake pointed to where a tall groundhog was rounding up all the child-sized groundhogs. "There he is. It's Michael Figaro. The undertaker."

The undertaker was dressed up as head ground-hog? Stan covered up her giggle with a cough. "Did they find Helga?"

Jake frowned. "Find her? Is she missing?"

A shrill whistle pierced the air. All heads turned to the podium. Betty removed her fingers from her lips. "We'll be starting momentarily. Please welcome Lilypad! And, Mrs. Abernathy." She did a Vanna White wave in the direction of a woman who, from a distance, looked like the star of *Mrs. Doubtfire*. Mrs. Abernathy bowed to the crowd and set the pink carrier with its precious cargo next to the podium.

"Perhaps Mr. Figaro will lead the groundhog children's choir through a couple of songs, while we wait," Betty suggested, then hurried from the podium before Mr. Figaro could protest. Stan watched as she made her way over to Char and Ray, spoke briefly to them, then continued walking. Sarah

Oliver intercepted her en route. The two exchanged words; then Betty marched in the opposite direction toward the street. Sarah waited a moment, then ran after her. They crossed the street, disappearing inside the Frog Ledge Historical Museum.

Jake followed her gaze. "What's going on?" he asked.

Stan repeated what she'd told Ray a few minutes ago.

Jake glanced back across the street. "I don't like this," he said. "I'm going over."

"I'll come with you," she said. She scanned the faces directly around her. Her mother was a few feet away, standing with a woman Stan had never seen. "Hang on," she said to Jake.

She hurried over. "Mom. Sorry to interrupt. Can you hold the gift for me for a few? I'll be right back." She shoved the bag at her mother.

Patricia accepted it. "Of course, Kristan. Where are you going?"

But Stan had already waved her thanks and weaved her way back to Jake. They headed for the street. After their conversation with Betty, Ray and Char were a few steps ahead of them. Before any of them could get to the sidewalk, Betty emerged from the museum and crumpled to the ground.

Stan gasped. She and Jake bolted across the street, Jake pulling his phone from his pocket as he ran to call 911. Char had already reached Betty—how, wearing heels that high, Stan couldn't figure out. Sarah was nowhere in sight.

Jake raced up the steps, knelt, and said something to Char, then disappeared inside. Behind them, the crowd had started to notice something wasn't right, and little by little people were turning in their direction. Some had already started over. Ray waited in front of the museum to try to hold them off.

"Stay back! Give her air," Ray called, motioning concerned friends away from the steps. "Give her some room."

Stan knelt next to Char, who leaned over Betty. The musical notes faded as the rest of the crowd caught on to the drama unfolding nearby. People lined up on the sidewalk, watching apprehensively.

"What happened?" Stan stared at Betty's white face. She felt sick, remembering Sarah Oliver's words. *Something's wrong.*

Betty stirred and opened her eyes. Stan and Char exchanged a look of relief. When Betty's eyes landed on Char, she burst into tears.

"Now, Betty, don't be upset." Char leaned over her friend as approaching sirens grew louder and an ambulance careened into sight. "The ambulance is here. You're going to be fine."

"It's not me," Betty whispered, struggling to sit up. Stan grabbed one arm and Char took the other, and they helped her to a sitting position. "It's Helga!"

Char looked around. "I don't see Helga anywhere."

"Inside," Betty whispered. Her next words were so soft Stan strained to hear them. "I think . . . I think she's dead."

Chapter 3

Dead? The hair rose on the back of Stan's neck. How? Where was Sarah? Before she or Char could ask Betty any of these burning questions, the ambulance arrived. Two EMTs spilled out onto the sidewalk. They grabbed their stretcher and converged on Betty, taking her pulse, shining a light in her eyes, asking her name. Finally, one of them gave a nod, and they hauled her up and on to the stretcher.

"Excuse me?" Char hovered next to the female EMT.

"Yes, you can ride in the ambulance," the EMT said, barely glancing at Char as she adjusted the stretcher to prepare for the trip down the sidewalk.

"No, no! That's not what I want. There might be an injured woman inside," Char said. "Betty went inside looking for a friend. When she came out she said Helga had fallen."

That wasn't what Betty had said, but Stan stayed silent. She certainly didn't want to repeat Betty's words—*I think she's dead*—for fear they might come true. Out of the corner of her eye, Stan saw Cyril casually snapping pictures, moving closer through the crowd. Always looking for the story.

The EMT paused. She held up a hand to halt her partner, then turned to Char. "Did she say where in the building?"

Char shook her head.

The EMT moved over to confer with her partner, a tall, thin man with carefully styled hair who looked like the senior of the two. After a whispered conversation, she pulled out her radio and called in a possible second ambulance needed. Her partner began wheeling Betty's stretcher away. Cyril edged closer, now jotting things down in his notebook.

Ray left his sidewalk duty and came over to take his wife's hand. "Is she okay?" he asked, looking from Stan to Char. "What happened?"

Stan opened her mouth, closed it again. She looked helplessly at Char.

Char pressed Ray's hand to her cheek. "We don't know if she was hallucinating or what, but she told us . . ." She dropped her voice and turned away from Cyril so he couldn't read her lips. "She told us . . . something happened to Helga. Inside. I don't know. We were just going to go in."

"Why don't you go with Betty in the ambulance, dear," Ray said, shooting a worried glance at Stan. "She probably needs a friend."

"Yes, yes, I think you're right," Char murmured with one last nervous glance at the EMT, who had just returned. "I'll go do that." She hurried after Betty's stretcher.

"I'm going in to take a look," the EMT said. But before she could head inside, the door opened and Jake emerged.

A shot of panic pierced Stan's chest and left her cold—her own sixth sense that things were about to go very wrong. Like when she was speeding down the highway and blew right past a cop. Only today there was a lot more at stake than a speeding ticket. Jake's face was pale and if she didn't know better, she'd swear his eyes were wet. He met her eyes briefly, then motioned to the EMT.

"You should come in here," he said.

"You're confirming an injury?" The EMT pulled her radio back out.

"Just come in," Jake said, urgency creeping into his voice.

The EMT obliged. Stan followed them, dread seeping through her body like a slow IV drip. She had no desire to see what Betty thought she'd seen, but Jake shouldn't have to go in there with only a complete stranger.

The heavy wooden door slammed behind them. Stan paused inside the doorway to look around. She'd never been in the museum before. At first glance, it wasn't what she'd expected. She supposed her definition of "museum" was geared toward a fancy art museum. This was small, about the size of her dining room and living room combined, and much less sophisticated. Preserved documents and historical artifacts made up the decor instead of gold-framed oil paintings or modern glass sculptures.

She didn't have time to take it all in. Jake moved through the main room purposefully, leading them past exhibits of old farming tools, collections of photographs, what looked like an old library card catalogue. Past a desk in a small alcove in the back of the room. A red purse—Helga's purse, probably—hung neatly on a hook on the wall next to the glittery purple cane Stan recognized as Helga's constant companion, next to Gerry. A black cape was draped over the back of the chair. She saw Jake's gaze linger on it; then he moved on, around a corner to another door.

This one led to a stairwell. The EMT coughed, the noise amplified in the small, quiet space. Stan jumped. Then, very faintly, Stan heard someone crying.

Jake pointed, his face grim. "Down there." He let the EMT pass. He'd already seen.

The EMT took the stairs carefully. Stan peered down and saw Sarah bending over a small, still form clad in pink at the bottom of the stairs. Stan couldn't see the entire scene, but what she could see looked . . . wrong. The pink-clad legs were splayed in an odd manner. She turned away, feeling light-headed and sick all at the same time. She hardly ever prayed, but found herself doing it now for Helga, the poor woman, and her daughter. And, of course, Jake. She thought about Sarah's insistence that something was wrong with her mother. Ray hadn't seemed confident in her medium abilities, yet she'd clearly been right.

"Is she . . ." Stan didn't want to say the words.

"I don't know," Jake said, but he didn't sound hopeful.

"Oh, Jake." She hugged him. "I'm so sorry."

He hugged her back. Held on until the crackle of static and disjointed voices floated up as the EMT radioed something. She moved away from the top of the stairs and sank into a chair. A minute later, the

EMT appeared, supporting Sarah as they climbed. Helga's daughter sobbed, her face in her hands.

"Can you . . ." The EMT motioned to Sarah. Jake slipped an arm around the distraught woman.

"Come on, Sarah," he said, his voice hoarse. "We should go outside. Let them . . . do what they need to do."

Stan followed them out the door, blinking against the light after being inside the dark museum. A small crowd had gathered around Ray at the foot of the museum steps. In the front was Don Miller, Helga's son. His wife, Carla, stood next to him, holding two small boys' hands, her face pale. When Miller saw Jake and Sarah, he pushed past Ray.

"What's going on here?" he demanded.

Jake pulled him aside and spoke in low tones. Miller's face paled, then just as quickly turned stone-like. Carla tugged her boys away so they couldn't hear the conversation. Sarah made no move to hug her brother or even speak to him. She kept her face pressed against Jake's shoulder until Jake gently handed her over to Don. Don took her arm rather roughly and led her away without another word, over to where his family stood. He motioned to Carla, and she and the two little boys followed them across the street.

Jake returned to Stan's side, looking exhausted. "How do you break this kind of news?" he asked quietly, looking at the people waiting for a party. Stan didn't think he expected an answer, so she didn't try to give him one. Instead, she followed his gaze.

The crowd hadn't thinned at all. If anything, more people had arrived. News spread quickly in Frog Ledge under normal circumstances, and half the town seemed to be waiting for an update. When things happened, it was like an electronic news feed beamed directly into each person's home. Everyone knew everything, immediately. And bad news seemed to travel even faster.

Most folks remained across the street on the green, where Mayor Falco tried to take control of the situation and keep people from descending on the museum. The group that had migrated across the street to the sidewalk kept a respectful distance from the museum steps, where Ray kept up a casual guard. The first ambulance was gone, having whisked Betty, accompanied by Char, away to the community hospital.

Ray left his post to join them. He looked just as distraught as Jake. His eyes searched their faces. "What . . . ?"

Jake shook his head. Stan stared at the sidewalk.

The second ambulance pulled up to the curb with flashing lights—no sirens. A bad sign. Another EMT jumped out. He unloaded a stretcher and hurried inside just as a state police car pulled up to the curb. Jake's sister, Frog Ledge Resident State Trooper Jessie Pasquale, climbed out.

Why is she here? Stan felt Jake brace himself next to her. Jessie wasn't always the easiest person to deal with. As the news rippled through the crowd that she was on scene, voices quieted as if they were going to be able to hear what would happen next all the way across the green.

Jessie walked through the crowd on the sidewalk, which parted for her like the Red Sea, until she reached them. Instead of her usual cop face, she wore the same sorrow as her brother. Jake looked like he wanted to hug her but didn't know how she would react, so he did nothing.

"I heard there was a possible unattended death," she said. Her voice sounded like sandpaper on wood, gravelly with grief. The official word—*death*—made Stan wince. Betty had been right, even though everyone had hoped she was wrong.

"Death?" Ray repeated, too loudly. A low buzz began circulating through the crowd.

Jake nodded, his face carefully blank. "Not confirmed."

Jessie looked away. Stan watched her eyes blinking furiously and realized she was trying to avoid crying.

"I'm going inside," she said.

Jake looked like he wanted to stop her, but then caught himself and nodded. "Okay," he said simply, and watched her disappear through the door, his sadness so palpable Stan felt it vibrating off his body.

She couldn't remember the last time she'd felt this helpless. Useless, really. Jake's own grandmother had been gone for years, and she knew what Helga meant to him. The loss of her own grandmother still nestled in her bones, resurfacing often and without warning, and she had passed away nearly a decade ago. Knowing Jake would experience that made her ache for him.

It was disorienting to see him so vulnerable. In such a short time he'd become her rock. It wasn't just her, either—most of the town relied on him for one thing or another. He was one of the strongest foundations this community was built on. It could be for something as small as setting up equipment for an event on the green, or as big as rehabbing a historic building, and anything in between. Jake had grown up in Frog Ledge and made a conscious choice years ago to return there, start a business there, be with his family, and nurture the town he loved. He always had a smile and a kind word, and always knew the right thing to do.

Today he looked nothing like that Jake. He looked lost. Adrift. Heartbroken. He paced around their little spot of sidewalk and kept glancing across the street at the crowd still gathered, waiting to hear what had happened.

"I'm going to go to the hospital," he said. "I feel like . . . she shouldn't have to go alone. And I don't know if Sarah or Don . . ."

"Do you want me to go with you?" She hated hospitals ever since her father's illness, but she knew Jake needed support. "Or would I be intruding?"

Jake looked at her like she was nuts. "Intruding? I would love if you came with me." He squeezed her hand gratefully, then held it tighter as the EMTs brought the stretcher out. They did a good job of navigating the people deftly and quickly so no one could get a good look at Helga. Jessie did not appear behind them.

"Let's go," he said.

Stan started to follow him, then saw Jessie come out of the building. She hesitated, then said to Jake, "Go grab the truck. I'll be right there."

Jake nodded, too distracted to ask why, and headed for the street. Stan approached Jessie, who looked at her warily.

"Are you okay?" Stan asked.

"Fine. Thank you." Jessie started to brush by her, but Stan persisted.

"I know your family was close to Helga. I'm really sorry," she said, then turned to walk away. But Jessie stopped her.

"My brother's going to have a hard time with this."

"I'll help him as much as I can," Stan said.

Pasquale nodded. She walked briskly back to her police car, got in, and drove away.

Stan watched her go, then hurried to join Jake, waiting in his truck behind the ambulance.

Chapter 4

The first time Stan met Helga Oliver, the older woman had been part of a reenactment event hosted by the local War Office volunteers. Char had coaxed Stan into going, convincing her that to fully appreciate living in Frog Ledge, one had to understand how important the town's role had been in shaping New England history. Beginning with the unassuming, two-story building that housed the Revolutionary War operations back in the 1700s.

The small red colonial on the green known as the War Office served as the area's "command center" during the war. Today it was a historical building that drew local visitors and tourists more often than one would expect in such a small town. Volunteers manned the office and offered tours three days a week from May through October and on special occasions. Most days during those months, if you drove by the green, you'd see two of the volunteers sitting in rocking chairs in the driveway, dressed in their period costumes and waving to people. They were the heart of the War Office—the ones who kept it running and made sure no one ever forgot an important date in town. The volunteers organized activities and made sure the costumes were up to snuff. They coerced enough people to be in each show they put on. Helga Oliver was instrumental in these activities.

Stan remembered Helga's role vividly in that first reenactment she'd attended. Dressed in a man's costume, a general's hat pressed tightly over her white hair, she stood out more than any other actor or actress. The suit worn to battle had been way too big on her five foot two frame, but she rocked it. Stan remembered Helga clumping around in heavy boots, leaning on her glittery purple cane as she made her way around the green barking orders at the "troops" like a real general. Stan thought Helga was probably the most noticeable character on the battlefield, mainly because of her sass. For an eighty-seven-year-old, she'd led the way and stolen the show.

Today, the memory made her sad. Even from that one day on the "battlefield," Helga's feisty personality and energy had shone through. Like Stan's own grandmother. Stan had so many memories of her dad's mother. Frannie Connor taught her to cook "real" food for animals. Her favorite was of Gram serving dishes of turkey on her front porch to stray cats, ignoring and inevitably laughing off her neighbors' scorn. A free spirit. Helga had the same vibe.

Stan perched on the edge of an uncomfortable chair in the hospital waiting room, watching Jake and Helga's boyfriend, Gerry, speak with the doctor who confirmed Helga's death. Gerry had arrived right after they did. No sign of Don or Sarah. Would they bother to come, knowing she was already gone?

She felt incredibly out of place. Not having known Helga well or her family at all, she didn't want to overstep. So she sat and watched, trying to pretend she wasn't. Jake looked terrible, but he was too much of a gentleman to be selfish about his own grief. He was going to have his hands full for a while. Stan's phone beeped. She fished it out of her jacket pocket to see a text from Char: I'm at hospital with Betty. Where are u?

Stan texted back: Here too w Jake. U in ER? What room? I'll come over.

Char returned: 202.

Stan rose and caught Jake's eye, signaled that she'd be back in a few minutes, then ducked into the hallway. She paused, taking a few deep breaths, trying to bring her own Zen back. This was certainly not how she—or anyone else—had expected this day to turn out. She thought briefly of Lilypad, her abandoned gift. It should've been a day filled with fun, community, and a glimpse of spring. Instead, it had turned darker than any winter's day.

Scanning the corridors for directions to the emergency room, she followed a maze of lefts and rights, past the chapel, the cafeteria, and three different elevator banks until she landed in front of the check-in desk.

"Betty Meany, room 202," she said through the glass.

The nurse buzzed her in and immediately went back to her phone call, not bothering to offer directions. Stan entered the U-shaped wing, averting her eyes from the rooms with open curtains where people were sick or injured. She hoped she was heading in the right direction. She felt like she'd been wandering for hours when she heard Char's voice. Relieved, she hurried toward it just as Char stepped out of the room and yanked the curtain behind her.

"Of course you should come! I'm happy to bring her home, but I think she'd like to see her husband, don't you?" She saw Stan and rolled her eyes, shaking her fist at the phone. "Why don't y'all go on in and see her while I finish arguing with her good-for-nothing husband," she said to Stan, not even bothering to cover the mouthpiece. At an indignant response from the other end of the line, she turned her attention back to the phone. "Well, I don't care, Burt. That's how y'all are acting!"

Stan slipped into Betty's room and pulled the curtain shut behind her. Betty lifted a hand in greeting. An IV was taped to the back of it. She looked pale, but alert.

"How're you doing?" Stan leaned over and brushed Betty's cheek with her lips.

"Oh, fine. I didn't mean to cause such a commotion. I got a little unsteady on my feet after . . ." She trailed off and blinked. Swiped at her eyes and sighed. "I take it Burt doesn't want to come down."

Lord. What was she supposed to say to that? "Char's talking to him. She didn't mention that."

Betty smiled. "Honey, these aren't soundproof doors. I can hear Char yelling at him. As I'm sure the rest of the unit can, too. It's okay. Burt is who he is. I'm not ready to see him anyway." She patted the edge of the bed, inviting Stan to sit. "Tell me what's going on. Was I right? Is Helga gone?"

Stan nodded and squeezed Betty's hand. "I'm so sorry."

Betty's eyes misted over. "I am, too." She motioned Stan to lean in closer. When she did, she whispered, "But it wasn't an accident."

Stan's eyes widened. She sat back. "What are you talking about, Betty? Of course it was. She was eighty-seven, for goodness' sake! I imagine it's very easy to fall at that age. Especially when you're going down stairs as steep as the ones going into that basement."

Betty grimaced and shook her head. Her hair had lost its sassy spikes and drooped into her eyes. She impatiently shoved it away with the hand not hooked up to a machine and struggled to sit up. Stan reached out and pulled her up higher on her pillows.

"That's the thing," Betty said urgently. "She never would've been going down those stairs. She didn't go into the basement. It was a rule, for precisely that reason. She had a bad hip already and didn't want to injure it further. She said that was the way to die a slow and painful death—break a hip first and everything else goes downhill."

Stan glanced at the bottle dripping into the IV. What were they giving her? Was she on some medication that was making her loopy? This was crazy talk. Helga had been alone in the museum . . . at least until Betty and Sarah had gone to look for her. Hadn't she?

Betty followed her gaze. "I'm not crazy. And I'm telling you the truth. I have proof!" She sounded immensely proud of herself.

Char chose that moment to burst back into the room, a fiery ball of red dress and matching hair. "They made me leave the area because I was too loud. But I couldn't help it. He is so infuriating. I'm sorry. I know y'all are married to him. But man oh man, if that was my husband—" She shook her fist. "He's on his way. I guilted him into it."

Betty didn't look thrilled, and she refused to meet Stan's eye. Clearly she didn't want to continue her conversation in front of Char. "You didn't need to do that, Char. I'm happy having you or Stan take me home."

"I know that, honey, but I wanted him to take some responsibility. He doesn't need to sit on his behind watching more sports. He wasn't even going to be at your event. *Our* event! Despicable." She spat the words, then satisfied she'd gotten her point across, turned to Stan. "Is it true? Did we lose Helga?"

Stan nodded.

Char pressed her hands against her cheeks and shook her head. "How devastating. How could this happen? Her poor children. And how is Jake? That poor boy." She clucked sympathetically. "He and his sisters loved that woman, let me tell you. And his mother, well, I'm sure she's going to be devastated. The whole town, really. What a tragedy. And on what was supposed to be such a wonderful day."

"Heartbreaking," Betty said. "Char, would you ask the nurse to come in here? I want to know when they're going to discharge me."

"Of course." Char thundered out of the room toward the nurse's station. Stan could hear her calling one of the nurses: "Ex*cuse* me! Mrs. Meany needs some help!"

Betty furiously beckoned Stan to come closer. Stan leaned back down so she could hear. "Like I said—I have proof. Her cane. She didn't have it with her. Did you see?"

Stan remembered when she walked into the museum with Jake, the cold, empty feeling she'd gotten, the forlorn cape and purple cane waiting neatly behind Helga's desk. "I did see it hanging up," she said slowly.

Betty nodded triumphantly. "She never went anywhere—not even ten feet—without her cane. Helga didn't fall down those stairs. Someone pushed her."

Chapter 5

Jake was quiet on the drive home from the hospital. Which was fine with Stan. If they were talking, he might bring up Helga or Betty, which would inevitably make her spill Betty's theory about Helga's death. Betty had sworn Stan to secrecy before she'd left her hospital room. With all the commotion of the ER and people coming and going, she wasn't going to be able to pry anything else out of her. Like who she thought might have pushed an eighty-seven-year-old town legend to her death, and why. She'd never finished her thought with those details.

Stan didn't want to accidentally mention any of that to Jake right now. Or perhaps ever, given the heartbreak he was already facing. She was hard-pressed to believe it anyway. Betty had to be feeling the effects of some pretty strong medication, combined with her own grief. Tomorrow she'd wake up and have no memory of this.

Stan hoped.

Jake pulled into her driveway. Her house was

well-positioned at the south end of the town green, a perfect spot for keeping an eye on all the important goings-on. From here, they could see that any trace of a crowd had dispersed up ahead where the ceremony was supposed to occur earlier. The area looked barren and empty. Sad.

"You're not going to the bar tonight, are you?" Stan asked.

He shook his head. "I talked to my mother while you were with Betty. I'm going to take her to the funeral home. Don and Carla asked her for help with the arrangements. Sarah's not in any shape to take it on. My mother will make sure it's done right. And she'll need support."

"That's sweet of you."

He looked surprised. "Sweet? That's what anyone would do for their family."

Stan focused her gaze on her pretty mint green Victorian house with the wraparound front porch. It looked so empty without her hanging plants or even the holiday decorations that she'd finally packed back in the garage until next Christmas. Hopefully spring would come soon—even though Lilypad hadn't had the opportunity to make her proclamation. "Sure they would," she said noncommittally. Truth was, she had no idea. Her own family, when she interacted with them, operated with a level of dysfunction that made the McGees look like the Brady Bunch. Supportive wasn't the first word that jumped to her mind, with the exception of her dad and her gram. But they were both gone.

Jake didn't need her to dive into a pool of self-pity right now, though. She turned back and laced her fingers into his, squeezed his hand. "I'll let you go get your mum. Call me later if you want. And again, I'm so sorry."

She got out and watched him back out of the driveway; then she trudged up the front steps. What a day. She was looking forward to spending some relaxing time with her dogs and cat tonight, and—

Her front door flew open. She gasped, jumping back, hand flying to her mouth.

Brenna McGee pushed the storm door open and held it for her. "Shoot, sorry. Didn't mean to scare you," she said. "I heard the truck and figured I'd save you the hassle of trying to unlock the door."

Stan had given Jake's little sister a key when she'd hired her permanently as her assistant baker. That way, Brenna had access to the kitchen and could come in to bake treats when Stan was tied up with other things. The system worked well. Until Stan forgot she could be inside and got the bejesus scared out of her, which happened occasionally. Like today.

"No problem," Stan said, stepping inside. Her schnoodle, Scruffy, immediately accosted her, *woo-wooing* pathetically. She stood on her hind legs and dropped her front paws on Stan's thigh. Henry, her pit bull, sat obediently and waited for a pet, tail wagging. It felt good—really good—to be home.

"I'm glad you're here. The dogs would've been lonely by now. Hey, guys. Hey, Nutty!" She brightened at the sight of her Maine coon cat, who perched on the windowsill, regal tail fluffed out behind him.

When she first moved to Frog Ledge last year, it had been just her and Nutty. He'd come into her life years ago as an injured stray in her old condo complex. She'd taken him to the vet and nursed him back to health. They both decided the investment was worth their time. Nutty adjusted to his new home quite well, especially when she began cooking him homemade meals to combat his irritable bowel disease. They'd been together ever since. And even though he considered himself superior to any canine, Stan could tell he liked having the two new family members around. Most of the time.

Right now, the newer family members, both rescues who had found her after she moved to town, were barking up a storm. "I know! I missed you guys, too." She shrugged off her coat. "Let's go get ready for dinner."

At the magic word, the dogs raced down the hall and into the kitchen to take their places. The one word that did not require repetitive training exercises to sink in: *Dinner.*

Stan turned to Brenna and gave her a hug, then stepped back and observed her friend. She didn't need to ask if Brenna had heard. By now, the whole town probably had. "I didn't even see you on the green earlier. Are you okay?"

Silly question. Brenna didn't look okay. She looked as sad as her big brother. Her eyes were puffy and she'd clearly been crying. She had one of Stan's fleecy blankets from the back of the couch wrapped around her shoulders. Her long brown hair was piled on her head in a messy ponytail.

Brenna lifted one shoulder in a halfhearted shrug. "I got there late. Just as . . . everything started going wrong." Her eyes welled with tears again and she furiously blinked them away, much like her sister, Jessie, had earlier. "I'm sad. I know she was old, but I wasn't ready for her to go. There's no way she should've died right now. She was so healthy and she . . . she . . . did so much around town. She was, like, everywhere. I can't believe she's really gone." Grabbing a tissue from her pocket, she blew her nose. "Anyway," she continued in a shaky voice, "I went back to the church and got all your stuff. And I hope it's okay—your mother saw me and gave me the gift back, so I gave it to Lilypad. I thought you'd want her to have it. Mrs. Abernathy was h-h-happy." She dissolved into tears.

Stan took her arm and led her down the hallway. The animals followed, Nutty leading the charge. "Come on. Let's have some tea," she said. "Unless you want to go be with your family. I can give you a ride, if you do."

Brenna shook her head. "No, I don't feel like it. Can I just hang here?"

"Of course!" Stan tossed her purse and jacket on the back of a chair—her favorite dumping ground—and pulled out the lavender tea Izzy Sweet had given her. Izzy was a good friend to have. She owned the gourmet chocolate and coffee shop, Izzy Sweet's Sweets, down on Main Street, and loved to give samples of her new inventory.

"I don't think it's a coffee day. I think we need tea, some cookies, maybe a fire and a funny movie. What do you think?"

Brenna's sad eyes brightened a bit. "Yeah, that sounds nice. And maybe we can bake?"

"I think I've created a monster. But sure. We have plenty of treat orders to fill." It still thrilled her to say those words: *Orders to fill*. It sounded so official. She, the diehard corporate girl who thought she couldn't live without fancy suits and an expense account, was making a go of her own business. An organic pet food business, no less, and one she often conducted in her pajamas. Some days she had to pinch herself to believe it. Her former cronies at Warner Insurance, the financial company where she'd led the public relations and media team, wouldn't believe it either. It was so un-Stan-like that it was funny. But really, it had been in her blood all along. For the umpteenth time since last summer, she sent a silent thank you to her old employer for firing her. Shedding her corporate identity had been one of the best things that ever happened to her.

She just wished her grandmother was around to see her make a go of her new business. And give her some recipes. "How're you doing with the meals for the new clinic?" Brenna asked, throwing her tissues in the trash.

Stan's neighbor, homeopathic veterinarian Amara Leonard, and her fiancé, traditional vet Vincent DiMauro, had teamed up to open a new practice in town. Their clinic, opening by the end of the month, would offer both types of veterinary care, as well as a small area for animal sheltering, thanks to their partnership with the town animal control officer. They'd commissioned Stan to provide a freezer full of healthy, organic pet meals with "real" food— meats, veggies and the like. And, of course, her signature treats. It was the first time she'd been asked to provide prepared meals on a regular basis. Right now, she did them for a select group of customers, including Char and Ray Mackey's dog, Savannah.

"Good," she said in answer to Brenna's question. "I have a few already done and frozen. Another that

I'm trying tonight on these guys." She smiled at her dogs, who waited statue-like in their usual dinner places. Nutty perched on the counter giving her the stink-eye. If he had one of those cartoon bubbles over his head, it would definitely say, *Less talk, more food preparation.*

She pulled a list off the fridge. "I have two meals of grass-fed beef with barley, carrots, spinach, and white rice; two turkey dinners with cranberries, potatoes, broccoli, and green beans; and a farm-raised, hormone-free chicken dinner with pan-seared salmon, squash, red potatoes, cheddar cheese, and spinach."

"Wow. Those sound yummy."

"If you eat meat." Stan wrinkled her nose. "Or if you're a dog. And hopefully a cat. So next, I have a pork-based meal, a venison meal, and a salmon one I'm going to package for the cats. That should give me enough for the grand opening. And I'm making one of the pork ones tonight. I thought about trying some kidney beans or chick peas, but that's an experiment."

The doorbell rang. Maybe Jake was back? Scruffy bolted toward the front door, always eager to be the welcoming committee. "Want to brew some hot water for the tea?" she asked Brenna. "I'll get the door."

Henry trotted behind her down the hall. It wasn't Jake. Stan pulled open the door. "Mom. Hi."

Patricia was alone at least. That was a plus. But she didn't look happy. She frowned at Stan. "I need to talk to you."

Chapter 6

Patricia Connor swept into the hallway the way only a woman of her social status could sweep, but her practiced movement stumbled when Scruffy bounced up and pawed her knee. Stan immediately pulled the dog back—it wouldn't do to get dog hairs on her mother's outfit. Patricia wore a long, impeccably cut black wool coat and matching hat. She looked like she was about to go out on the town. Manhattan, not Frog Ledge.

Stan *so* needed to get used to this. Before a few months ago, she saw her mother maybe twice a year, even though she lived only an hour away. Frog Ledge was not a place her mother, a Rhode Island socialite of the highest order, would have touched with a ten-foot pole in other circumstances. Now, thanks to her new love, she practically lived here. Stan had been trying extremely hard to look at her mother differently and improve their relationship. Her low opinion of Mayor Falco didn't help.

"Sure." Stan stifled a sigh. She nudged the dogs

back and closed the door behind her mother. "Come on in. I was just making tea."

Patricia eyed Henry with suspicion. Henry lumbered over and sniffed her, his tail wagging hopefully.

"Quit giving Henry that look, Mom. You know the drill. He's the nicest dog you'll ever meet." She hated when people—especially her own mother—showed bias to her dog because of his breed. Henry was a sweetie.

"I know you tell me that, sweetheart. It's just that you read so many terrible things about pit bulls—I know, I know." Patricia held up a hand as Stan opened her mouth. "You're going to be angry at me."

"Not angry, just disappointed. Nikki would give you an earful if she was here. I've told you a million times, Henry's an awesome dog. Think of his breed as 'rescue' instead of pit bull. That goes for both the dogs." Stan's best friend, Nikki Manning, ran a dog transport group that saved animals from death row down South. She was also the fiercest animal advocate Stan knew—and she wasn't afraid to get into fistfights if that's what it took. Defending pit bulls was one of her favorite pastimes. Nikki was responsible for both Stan's dogs, and Stan wouldn't trade them for anything.

"Yes, I know. Fine, you're right, I'm sorry." Patricia took her coat off and held it high in the air as Nutty appeared, twining his way around her heels. Stan bit her lip to keep a giggle back. Her animals had an innate ability to aggravate her mother. She loved it.

"I'll take your coat," she offered.

Patricia hesitated. Stan rolled her eyes. "I'll put it somewhere it won't get furry."

"Thank you." She handed it over after tucking her hat into the sleeve, then smoothed her sleek, silvery blond hair back into place. "Now. Shall we?"

Stan led the way down the hall, feeling like the Pied Piper—the pets followed single file and her mother brought up the rear. She paused to tuck her mother's coat safely into the coat closet she hardly ever bothered to use, then continued into the kitchen. Brenna glanced up from the recipe cards spread out on the table in front of her. "Hey, so—oh, hi, Mrs. Connor."

"Hello, Brenna."

"Tea?" Stan grabbed mugs out of the cabinet as the kettle whistled, signaling boiling water. "Or if you want coffee, I can make that, too."

"Tea would be lovely. I hope I'm not intruding." Patricia sat.

"Not at all." Brenna glanced at Stan, then self-consciously adjusted her ponytail. "Did you want me to go?"

"Oh, no, dear!" Patricia exclaimed. "I don't want to interrupt. I won't take much of my daughter's time. I just need her advice."

"*My* advice?" Stan turned, unable to conceal her surprise. That was a new one.

"Yes, this is your town, after all. My intuition tells me we might have a touchy situation on our hands." Patricia accepted the mug of tea and waited for Stan to sit. When she did, Patricia continued. "You know it was a terrible morning, with the circumstances at the celebration. Tony was so upset about that poor woman. She was a legend in the community, I understand. Did you know her well, dear?"

Stan resisted the urge to point out that Tony Falco knew Helga probably as well as she did. Not very. "I was lucky enough to meet her a few times," she said instead. "But, yes, it was very sad. Brenna and her family were extremely close to Helga."

"Oh, no." Patricia looked genuinely distressed. "I'm so sorry."

"Thank you," Brenna mumbled, shuffling her recipe cards together.

"Maybe you can give me some insight, then." Patricia leaned forward. "Tony and I were redirecting people at the celebration after we received the news. Offering condolences, of course. We were approached by a man who offered—actually, he was quite insistent—that he step into Helga's duties immediately."

Brenna's mouth dropped. *"What?"*

"I know," Patricia said. "Unseemly. Tony was instantly uncomfortable, of course, given the circumstance, but he did let the man speak."

"Was it Dale Hatmaker?" Brenna asked through clenched teeth. "Never mind—stupid question. Of course it was Hatmaker. Slimy piece of—"

"So what did Tony say, Mom?" Stan interrupted, shooting a warning look at Brenna.

"He did introduce himself as Dale, yes," Patricia said, answering Brenna's question. "But the point is, I'm concerned."

"Concerned about what?" Stan asked, but her mind had already divided itself between the part still listening to her mother and the part off and running on its own. Dale Hatmaker. The man who'd appeared out of nowhere this morning and offered himself up to "help" by filling in for Helga, suggesting she was shirking her duties before anyone knew what had happened. Then he'd panhandled for her job before she was officially pronounced dead? What kind of man did that? The kind of man who pushed an eighty-seven-year-old to her death? Crazy thoughts, but what if Betty's suspicions were true and Helga hadn't fallen on her own?

"Quite frankly, I'm concerned about Tony making a bad decision and letting this man have the job," her mother said. "I get the sense Mrs. Oliver was much loved in the community. Tony told Dale the museum would be closed for the next little while, while Mrs. Oliver was laid to rest and everything was sorted out; but once that's done, he'll have to address it. And he can be . . . easily led by outside influences. Especially given his somewhat rocky relationship with the council."

"Would he really be that stupid?" Brenna asked. "Because there'd be a lotta people here running him out of town. Helga's own son is on the council. And he knows karate."

Patricia raised an eyebrow at Brenna. Stan covered her eyes. She didn't want to watch. Then she heard her mother say, "I really can't say if he'd be that stupid. The running out of town is exactly what I'm trying to prevent."

Stan peeked through her fingers. "Did I just hear you right?"

"Of course you did. It's true."

"You must have magical powers," Stan said to Brenna. "No way would I have gotten away with saying that."

"Oh, Kristan, hush. This is no time to be fresh," Patricia said. "I need to help Tony."

"He didn't make any promises, did he?" Stan asked.

"No, but this Dale was quite pushy. I overheard one of the other council members giving Tony you-know-what about the whole thing a while later. Tony didn't appreciate it. Which makes me think he would be contrary just to prove a point."

"So what do you need from me, Mom?"

Her mother hesitated. "You're so good at public relations, dear. Tony could use some . . . executive coaching. From a professional."

At Stan's blank look, Patricia sighed impatiently and rapped her knuckles on the table. The sound sent Scruffy into a barking frenzy, thinking someone was at the door. "You, dear. You're a professional. Could you help him?"

Stan burst out laughing. "Me? You want me to coach the mayor? I'm not a leadership coach. Or a political advisor."

"No, but this will certainly make the newspaper if he makes a rash decision. He doesn't need negative publicity. He needs training. What do you people call it? Media training!" Patricia smiled triumphantly, like she'd just solved a particularly difficult *New York Times* crossword puzzle. "He needs some help. Please, Kristan? So he doesn't get off on the wrong foot?"

Stan resisted her natural urge to correct her mother. Falco had already gotten off on the wrong foot, at least with her. Instead, she considered her options. Running out the back door wouldn't help. She still lived here. Denying her mother would only serve to deteriorate the relationship even more, and most likely prove the bittersweet point that this town was too small for both of them. But saying yes would be a strike against her with all the people who hated Falco. There were a lot of them. And many had pets.

Both sets of eyes were on her, waiting for a reply. And her own pets were still waiting for dinner.

"He might not even be willing," she began, but her mother cut her off.

"I'm sure he will, dear. As a matter of fact, I'm going to ask him right now." She jumped up, leaving her tea barely touched. "Thank you! I'll call you with the verdict. Now, where's my coat?"

Chapter 7

The *Frog Ledge Holler* sat on the front porch when Stan got up at six the next morning. An early edition. She waited until her coffee brewed to read it, but it still didn't make the story easier to swallow.

Town Historian's Death Shuts down Groundhog Day Festivities

Tragedy Discovered as Ceremony Kicks Off

By Cyril Pierce

Helga Oliver, beloved town historian and founder and executive director of the Frog Ledge Historical Museum, died Sunday after a tragic fall.

According to witnesses at the scene, Oliver, 87, was working at the museum before the town's annual Groundhog Day ceremony, at which she was scheduled to speak. When she failed to arrive on time for her speaking engagement, friends and organizers expressed concern. Her body was discovered shortly after at the bottom of the museum's basement stairs.

Oliver was pronounced dead on arrival at Thornwood Memorial Hospital.

Oliver was a lifelong Frog Ledge resident and devoted her life to perpetuating the town's history. She is the author of *Frog Ledge: Connecticut's Revolutionary Headquarters*, a book detailing the town's historical highlights. In addition to her position as executive director of the museum, Oliver worked at the Frog Ledge Historical Society two days per week, and was champion of the town's efforts to digitize all paper records. She was also a long-time volunteer at the town's historical War Office.

She is predeceased by her first husband, state Senator Benjamin Miller, and her second husband, Henry Oliver. Oliver leaves behind two children: daughter Sarah Oliver and son Frog Ledge Town Councilman Donald Miller; daughter-in-law Carla Miller; two grandchildren, Donald Junior and Derek; longtime companion Gerry Ricci, also of Frog Ledge; and countless friends and extended family who will greatly miss her.

Arrangements have not yet been made public. A celebration of Oliver's life is being planned on and around the town green within the week.

Cyril Pierce didn't disappoint. The story offered everything there was to know about Helga's death.

Everything except Betty's theories about a murder, thank goodness.

Reading about Helga's accomplishments made Stan feel melancholy. This woman had contributed so much to the town, and now she was gone. Just like that. Even at her well-lived age, Stan still found it immensely sad. The only condolence was that her work would live on.

Stan flipped the *Holler* over to read below the fold. The story was about the postponement of an upcoming historical walking tour Helga was supposed to host. She wondered if Dale Hatmaker would try to worm his way into the job. She tossed the paper on her kitchen table.

The dogs were barking outside, and she needed to get moving. Lots to do today. She and Amara were walking up to Izzy's for their weekly planning meeting. Somehow, Stan had been "voluntold" into helping Amara with her grand opening well past preparing treats and meals. She didn't mind, really. The new clinic and shelter would be a huge advantage for the town, and it would promote healthier pets than practices that only catered to traditional medicine. The time commitment was worth it.

She went to the back door to check on the dogs. Henry and Scruffy were standing at the fence, probably waiting for a glimpse of their cow friends from the Happy Cow Dairy Farm farther down the street. They loved to watch the cows, although they mostly stayed in their enclosure this time of year.

"I think it's too cold for the cows!" she called, opening the door a crack. "Want to come in?"

Both dogs' heads swiveled to look at her, then

went back to watching through the fence. "I guess not," Stan said, and closed the door.

Nutty jumped up on the windowsill next to her and watched the dogs, wistfully, it seemed. He still had a touch of that stray cat blood in him.

"You don't want to go back outside," she told him. "Remember all the bad things that happened out there?"

Nutty swished his tail, leaving it standing in a tall plume. He didn't look at her.

"Besides, you wouldn't get any home-cooked meals out there. Or homemade treats. And I'm sure that wouldn't work for you."

That got his attention. He fixed his blankest stare on her. The one he gave her when he thought she was being extra stupid.

"Fine. You know the truth. I'd miss you." She leaned over and kissed his head. He gave in and nuzzled against her. "We have to cook up the venison today. You'll get to try some. That's the benefit of living in the pet food chef's house."

That perked him up. He hopped off the windowsill and headed for the kitchen, as if to say, *Well, come on then, what are you waiting for, lady?*

She followed him into the kitchen, letting the dogs stay outside a few minutes longer for some exercise and fresh, albeit cold, air. She wouldn't be able to bring them with her to Izzy's this morning. It became too distracting when they were trying to work. And this afternoon she hoped to stop by Betty's house with some homemade soup. She didn't normally cook for anyone other than herself and sometimes Jake—her cooking was usually reserved for dogs and cats—but figured a traumatic event like

Betty had endured yesterday called for some soup. She could also bring some of her new Strawberry Bites for Betty's cat, Houdini, to sample. And she wanted to press Betty about her allegation that Helga had been pushed. If it had been the medicine talking and she wasn't singing the same song today, Stan could forget about it, as well as Dale Hatmaker's potentially incriminating request for Helga's job. If Helga hadn't been murdered, she could chalk that up to bad taste. If Betty stuck to her guns, well, that was another story.

She pulled out her large slow cooker. She wanted to get the soup, a hearty harvest vegetable, simmering while she was out so the veggies had plenty of time to soften and release all their yummy flavors into the broth. She'd picked up fresh kale, carrots, chick peas, and a bevy of other veggies from the winter farmers' market she'd visited on Saturday in the town hall. Her mouth watered just thinking about it. She planned to make a double batch for herself. She had plenty of veggies. What better meal for an end-of-winter week?

Especially considering how frigid it was outside. A lot colder than yesterday, as if the Groundhog, Interrupted act had ensured winter would return in full force. She longed for spring and a run at the green with warm sun shining down and people doing yoga on the grass as she passed. The spring, summer, and fall seasons were so beautiful here it almost made her forget about the winter. But every year, January through March seemed like the longest months. She might have to consider that vacation house in Florida once the business really took off.

She gave Nutty a sampling of the venison before

putting it in another pan to sauté and letting the
dogs back inside. They bounded in happily. Their
fur was cold and a little wet. "Is it snowing, guys?"
She peered out and noticed it was, indeed, flurrying.
Maybe she and Amara would drive to the sweet shop.

Once the soup was cooking in the slow cooker
and everyone had eaten their breakfast, Stan show-
ered and bundled up in case they walked, and
headed next door to Amara's. The snow still swirled,
but it didn't seem to be accumulating. Despite the
long, cold winter, Stan had to admit it made a beautiful picture—the quaint New England town, the
historical green with the church steeple in the distance blurred by white flakes.

Amara greeted her at the door with car keys. "Did
you have your heart set on walking?"

"Nope, I was hoping we'd drive."

Amara breathed a sigh of relief. "Thank goodness.
I'm so sick of being cold." She jammed a knitted
hat over her chin-length brown hair, adjusted her
glasses, and picked up her coat. "Let's go."

Stan hopped in the passenger seat of Amara's
little Prius. "Can you believe how yesterday turned
out?" she asked.

"*So* sad." Amara backed out of the driveway and
turned the car toward Main Street. "She was a nice
lady. A little abrupt, but she was old enough that she
was entitled, you know?"

"Did you know her well?"

"I was getting to. She was actually working on
some genealogy research for me."

"Really? She's a genealogist, too?" Jake had never
mentioned that.

"She dabbles. Dabbled. I met her right after I

moved to town." Amara had moved to Frog Ledge about two years ago. She'd told Stan once that she'd felt a connection to the little town when she'd visited as a child, and eventually kept her promise to herself to move there. Stan had felt the same way last year when she'd stumbled upon Frog Ledge and the house that she would buy only weeks later. Until then she'd never known Frog Ledge existed, but it immediately felt like home.

"I went to the historical society after I moved in to look around, learn about the town's history," Amara continued. "Helga was there and we got to talking. She eventually convinced me to let her look into my mother's side of the family, since I don't know much about them." She pulled into Izzy's lot and parked.

Stan remembered Amara telling her that her mother had died when she was only seven. She hadn't been in contact with her family for many years before she died. Amara's father had remarried within a year and he hadn't known her mother's family anyway, so she had no information on them. "Did she make any progress?" Stan asked, climbing out of the car.

"She was getting there," Amara said, beeping her car locked. "She actually had just done a DNA test."

"A DNA test? Really? How does that work?"

"I gave a sample and she sent it off for testing with another sample, I think. Said she'd found a possible connection to my family. Of course, I agreed." Amara sighed. "I don't know if she ever got the results back. So I'm sad that she's gone because I genuinely liked her, but also for my own selfish reasons. I really wanted to know about my mom's family."

Chapter 8

Stan stepped inside Izzy Sweet's Sweets behind Amara and inhaled. The scents of cinnamon and chocolate mixed with bold coffee enveloped her like a warm hug. Behind the counter, Izzy Sweet loaded freshly baked pastries into one side of the pastry case that zigzagged through the middle of the café while keeping up an animated conversation with a woman waiting for her coffee. The other two-thirds of the case was loaded with spectacular handmade chocolates Izzy purchased and had shipped in from all over the world. Stan tried to avoid looking at them. She was a sucker for truffles.

The café was packed. Most mornings it was packed. Despite some locals' opposition to having a fancy café in town rather than a greasy spoon diner, Izzy's place attracted visitors from all the surrounding towns—especially college students from the two nearby schools. And she had her share of Frog Ledgers who wouldn't dream of getting coffee anywhere else, Stan and Amara being two of them. Izzy saw them and held up two fingers in the universal peace sign.

Meaning, she'd be right over. Stan snagged the corner table as two wholesome-looking housewife types vacated it.

"Will you try to find a new genealogy person? I'm sure there are tons of them these days." Stan picked up the thread of the conversation from the drive over as she hung her coat on the back of her chair.

Amara wrinkled her nose. "I don't know yet. I liked Helga's style. And she was a perfectionist. So I felt confident with her. I guess we'll see."

"What's cookin', kids?" Izzy appeared at their table, tossing her long braids over her shoulder. As usual, her caramel-colored skin was flawless without a touch of makeup, save for some eyeliner. With her exotic looks, she could more easily pass for a runway model than a small-town café owner. Even dressed in leggings and fuzzy boots, Izzy had *presence.* Like Stan and Amara, she was a transplant to Frog Ledge, though she'd been here for a few years now. Which made her the first of the three to own a successful business. Despite a rough start, her café had come a long way. "Here to work or play?"

"Work," Amara said. "But if play means we can have one each of whatever smells so good, we're playing, too. Right, Stan?"

"You don't even have to ask," Stan said. She'd given up worrying about her workouts. The cold weather killed her motivation. Now she just wanted to sit at Izzy's, drink strong coffee, and eat delicious pastry.

"Two mini chocolate Bundt cakes with caramel filling. You got it," Izzy said. "And I have two special drinks on the menu for the next two weeks. For Valentine's Day. An amazing Swedish drinking chocolate—way better than regular hot chocolate—and a chocolate coffee peppermint kiss latte."

"I want the drinking chocolate," Amara said immediately. "I might even want two."

"I'll try the latte," Stan said. "With soy."

"You got it. When I come back, I'll tell you the latest on the building." With an eye roll, she headed back to get the food and drinks.

"Uh-oh." Amara looked at Stan. "What's going on with the building? I bet Jake is wishing he never got involved."

With the success of the café, Izzy had ventured into business number two—a project that had gotten off to an even rockier start. She'd chosen one of the town's oldest, unused building a few doors down from the café as the perfect location for a bookstore, a resource the town was sorely lacking. The building needed extensive renovations, however, and had been a financial burden on Izzy right from the get-go. Jake had recently stepped in with financial backing, so she was back on track. Renovations were under way, but they weren't going as smoothly as everyone had hoped. Stan had heard more than her share of stories from Izzy about Frank Pappas, the general contractor running the project. Who also happened to be Jake's buddy, although they hadn't looked too enthralled with each other when she'd seen them talking at the Groundhog Day event.

"I don't know. I think he hoped he could just hire Frank and be done with it, since he knows him. It hasn't worked out that way." Jake didn't go into great detail about it, but Stan knew there'd been challenges. And he already had enough on his plate with McSwigg's. Plus, he and Izzy didn't have the smoothest partnership in history, even before this venture. "Problems over there will be the last thing he wants to deal with this week, given everything else."

Izzy returned with a tray full of goodies. The smells alone made Stan feel like she'd died and gone to heaven. Izzy unloaded everything, then pulled a chair over. "Mya's covering the counter for a few minutes. So get this. Last week I get a letter delivered asking me to halt work on the building."

"Get out." Amara sipped her drinking chocolate. "Oh. My. God. Izzy. This is . . . there are no words for this drink."

"Right?" Izzy grinned. "Delish. Anyway. Did Jake already tell you this?" she asked Stan.

Stan shook her head.

"Figures." Izzy pursed her lips.

"Who was the letter from?" Stan asked, sipping her own drink. It was delicious, too.

"Some state committee on historical buildings."

"The State Historic Preservation Office?" Stan asked.

"Yeah, something like that," Izzy said with a dismissing wave of her hand.

"But your building isn't technically deemed historical, right?" Amara asked, starting on her Bundt cake.

"That's the point. They're now saying they want to try to get it designated as a historical building, which would totally mess up my plans. And take *forever*."

"So what'd you do?" Stan broke a piece of her cake off and nibbled. Still warm. She forced herself to eat one tiny bite at a time—otherwise, she'd be in danger of inhaling the whole thing within minutes.

"I brought it to Jake and Frank. Frank threw a hissy, like he does pretty much every day, about everything. Typical contractor."

"What did Jake say?"

"He suggested we call them. Actually, he suggested I call them." She frowned. "Like I'm not trying to run a business, too."

"So did you?" Stan sipped her latte.

"Not yet. It's on my list for today."

"But they aren't halting the work," Stan said.

"No, the letter didn't *tell* me to stop, it *asked*. So until further notice, I'm keeping it moving." Izzy sighed. "Crazy stuff, right? So, that's all. I better get back to the lattes. Mya can't make them as fast as I can. Enjoy, girls." She winked, picked up her tray, and hurried away.

Amara raised an eyebrow behind her red glasses. "Again, poor Jake."

"Seriously. I wonder why he didn't mention all that."

"Probably to keep you out of it, since he knows you're friends with Izzy."

"True."

Amara finished the last of her cake and sighed contentedly. "Now I'm ready for our meeting."

Stan took her iPad out of her purse and pulled up the document where she kept track of each meal she had on the list for the grand opening, which was now less than three weeks away. They spent the next hour poring over display setups, recipes, and meal planning for the next few months until Stan noticed an older woman with impeccably-styled frosted blond hair wearing a velour running suit hovering nearby. She stared hopefully at Stan, trying to catch her eye.

"Hold on one sec," she said to Amara, and smiled at the lady. "Do you need one of us?"

The woman moved closer, her hands fluttering anxiously. "Oh, I'm so sorry to interrupt. I just had to come over and see if it was really you!"

Stan glanced at Amara. "Me?"

"Yes, you are Stan Connor, right?"

"I am," Stan said cautiously. Was this someone her mother had sent to talk her into something?

"I'm so thrilled to meet you. My name is Dianne Richardson. But everyone calls me Dede." She offered a cold, dry hand to Stan. "I live here in town and I'm a huge fan of yours."

Stan rose and shook her hand. "Lovely to meet you, Dede. This is Amara Leonard. She's the veterinary homeopath in town." Amara waved. "Would you care to join us?" She pulled over the chair Izzy had vacated. Dede sat gratefully.

"What can I do for you?" Stan asked, sitting, too.

"Well." Dede clasped her hands together and stared adoringly at Stan. "I've been hoping to run into you because I felt funny calling, even though my friend—I think you know her, Millie Abernathy?— told me to."

"Mrs. Abernathy with the groundhog?" Stan asked.

"Exactly!" Dede nearly dropped her purse in the excitement. "She was so pleased with the treat for Lilypad. Even with the unfortunate circumstances of the day. Anyway, I've been following your Pawsitively Organic business. My dogs and cats love your treats. I'd like to hire you."

"You mean you want to order some treats?" Stan asked.

"Well, no. I mean I want to hire you. For an event."

"Oh, a party. Of course." She'd been getting requests for parties on and off since her first one last October, a birthday party for Benny, the fox terrier, had been so well received. Stan opened a new document on her iPad and prepared to take notes.

Dede smiled. "It's a bit more than a simple party, but I know you'll understand. Animal people always understand. I'd like to have a wedding ceremony for my rescue dogs. They love each other so much, and look out for each other all the time. I think it's only logical that they should be married. That way, if anything ever happened to me, there would be no question that they would stay together.

"I'd like them to have a beautiful doggie cake," she continued. "And all their friends as guests. I'd like it on the town green. On Valentine's Day." She sat back in her chair, hopeful eyes trained on Stan. "What do you think? Can you do it?"

A doggie wedding? Outside in the New England winter? Stan had heard of a lot of quirky things people did with their pets since starting this business, but this—well, it took the cake. Literally. But who was she to judge this sweet lady who loved her rescue dogs? At least Nikki would approve. And it would be something else to add to her repertoire— doggie wedding cakes. She sent up a silent prayer that the temperatures would begin rising.

"I'd love to," she said, smiling at Dede. "It sounds fabulous."

"Oh, thank you!" Dede clapped her hands. "They'll be so thrilled. I'm going to ask my daughter to help me with their outfits. She's a seamstress," she added. "I'm so excited. You've made my day, Ms. Connor. Here." She reached into her purse and pulled out two crisp, new hundred-dollar bills and handed them to Stan. "You'll need a deposit, I'm sure. Oh, and I nearly forgot. Can you have some nibbles for kitties, too? My two cats, Mittens and Diamond, will attend, of course."

"Thank you," Stan said, trying to hide her surprise at the deposit. "This is very helpful. And, of course we can accommodate Mittens and Diamond. We'll have to put some time on the calendar in the next few days to iron out details." She handed Dede her business card, a paw-print–shaped creation that Brenna had helped her design. "If you have time on Thursday, I can come by."

Dede assured her Thursday would be wonderful. After she went back to her own table amid a flurry of hugs and thanks, Stan turned to Amara, who watched the entire proceedings with an amused smile.

"What do you think?" Stan asked her.

"I think," Amara said, "that you're definitely going to make a name for yourself around here. One way or another."

Chapter 9

"You'll never believe what I got asked to do today." Stan said to Nikki when her best friend answered the phone. She'd just arrived home and checked on the soup, which had filled her house with the amazing aroma of garlic and veggies. Nutty dozed on the counter next to it, likely dreaming of his next meal.

Nikki sounded like she was hauling dog crates or performing some equally taxing task. She could even be on the road—Stan hadn't talked to her much lately. "Do I want to know, given your track record?" she said a bit breathlessly. "Does it have to do with cows?"

Nikki wouldn't let Stan live that one down. Stan decided to ignore the dig. "I got asked to cater a doggie wedding. On Valentine's Day."

The guffaw from the other end of the phone wasn't entirely unexpected. "I guess the better question would be, did you accept the offer?" Nikki asked when she could speak again.

"Of course. It's good for business," Stan said. "But I'm a little overwhelmed. There's a big guest list and

I have less than two weeks. And it's outside. It's still cold out. I need to make the perfect cake. Heart-shaped. Three layer. Something with strawberries."

"No offense, but your town is whack," Nikki said, her tone matter-of-fact. Nikki didn't mince words.

Stan couldn't completely disagree. "It's charming, though."

"Wait a second," Nikki said. "This person isn't doing this weirdo wedding thing because they're gonna breed the dogs, right? 'Cause I've seen that before and I would have to disown you if you contributed to that."

"Oh, no. They're two rescue dogs. Fixed. A Shih Tzu and an Irish setter. This lady adopted them separately and they're really bonded. She wants them to be married. It's cute, but I felt bad for her. She said if she dies, she doesn't want anyone to separate them."

That seemed to pacify Nikki. "At least they're rescue dogs. Where'd they come from?"

"Someplace up here, I think. Oh, that reminds me—I have to find cake toppers. I need to start making lists. You should come! We can find a way to promote Pets' Last Chance. You know, adopt a rescue dog, get them transported to you, then marry them off." She was only half kidding.

"It sounds wacky enough that I might. I'll be in town that week, I think. Who's performing the ceremony?"

"That's a good question." Did Dede think she was doing that as part of the package? She might have to draw the line at that one. "I'll have to find out."

"Are you going to have human cake, too?"

"Shoot. I probably should. Jeez. I better go, Nik. I have a lot to do."

"Keep me posted," Nikki said, and disconnected.

Scruffy and Henry were sprawled at her feet. They complemented each other, her silver and black schnoodle and her brown and white pit bull. Stan regarded them curiously. "You hear that, guys? Would you eventually want a wedding?"

Scruffy wagged. Henry dropped his face back onto the floor and closed his eyes.

"I guess he's not ready to commit yet," Stan said to Scruffy.

Later, after she had loaded Betty's portion of the harvest veggie soup into a smaller slow cooker for easy heating, Stan donned her favorite pair of Ugg boots, a fuzzy scarf, and warm parka, and set out to deliver her goodwill gesture.

The Meanys lived two streets behind Stan. It was how they'd met, actually—Houdini, Betty's cat, had slipped outside and turned up on Stan's porch her first week in town. He'd been one of the first to hear the rumor that Stan was a whiz with an oven. Luckily, he'd been wearing a collar with Betty's number, so Stan was able to help reunite them. Betty had been a fan of her treats ever since.

The trip was a three-minute drive through a tree-lined neighborhood filled with well-kept Cape-style homes and yards that were probably pretty in the spring. She parked in Betty's driveway next to a red Buick. She didn't see Betty's little Mazda 6 anywhere, but figured it must be in the garage. She climbed out and went around to the passenger side to grab the soup. Making her way carefully up the front steps around the still-remaining patches of ice, she rang the bell and waited. A few minutes later, a man—presumably the disagreeable husband—answered the door. She thought she remembered Char calling him Burt. He was shorter than Stan's five foot seven frame by about three inches, bald, and round. He didn't look incredibly friendly, which jived with the conversation Stan had overheard in the hospital.

"Yes?" he said, opening the door a crack.

Stan smiled her best smile. "Hi. I'm Stan, a friend of Betty's. I brought her some homemade soup."

Burt—if that was his name, since he didn't introduce himself—continued to regard her with a slight frown. "Do you want to come in?" he asked, finally.

That would be helpful if you want the soup. She forced her smile to widen. "Why, sure! That would be lovely. Thank you."

Without another word, he swung the door open and motioned her in. He walked through the kitchen and vanished, leaving Stan to figure out where to put the food and, more important, where to find Betty.

"Who was at the door?" she heard a familiar voice ask from a room to the right. A muffled response, then Betty came around the corner. She looked different today—tired, and not dressed to the nines, like Stan was used to seeing her. Her hair wasn't even spiky, and instead of one of her colorful dresses, she wore a pair of sweatpants and a Frog Ledge Community Theater T-shirt.

"Oh! Stan! What a love you are." Betty threw her arms around Stan, who had luckily already placed

the soup on the counter. "That smells delightful."
Betty took a deep breath. "What is it?"

"It's a harvest veggie soup. My own creation. It was
a good week at the farmers' market last week."

"How kind and sweet. I'm very sorry my husband
is such a sourpuss." She glanced behind her and
made a face. "I'll tell you, I don't know how I've
made it more than thirty years with that man. Must
be because he worked a lot when we were younger.
Oh, well. Come sit, please. Would you like some tea?"

When Stan declined, Betty ushered her into the
living room. With the exception of the paisley
couch, Stan immediately fell in love with the room.
It shouted *peaceful* and *cozy*. She was a sucker for fire-
places, anyway, but Betty's was gorgeous—the old-
fashioned kind, not gas, with a granite mantel.
Houdini, the original escape artist, dozed on the
back of the couch, curled up in a blanket. Comfy
pillows and throw blankets were strategically positioned on the couch and two chairs. The red
carpeting was soft, deep, and immaculate. In true
Betty-the-librarian fashion, the walls were nearly all
built-in bookshelves, except for the one wall on
which the TV was mounted. Stan caught sight of
some of the titles—*Jane Eyre, Moby Dick*. Classics, as
she would have expected. But on other shelves, she
could see fiction—from Lilian Jackson Braun to
Lee Child.

"I read everything," Betty said, noting Stan's interest in the books. "I can't leave my job at work."

"It's great," Stan said. "Somehow, I usually end up
too busy to read much, but I do love it. I thought
when I left my job I would read all the time, but then
I just got busy with other things."

"Since you have company I'm going out for a bit." Burt had materialized in the doorway, causing Stan to jump.

"Stan, this is my charming husband, Burt," Betty said in a voice dripping with sarcasm. "I'm sure he properly introduced himself to you, but I wanted to make sure."

Stan smiled weakly at Burt. He nodded at her, then turned and walked out of the room. A minute later, Stan heard the front door quietly close.

"Is he angry that I showed up unannounced?" She didn't want to cause Betty any problems, especially with everything else going on.

"Oh, heavens, no." Betty waved Stan's comment—and her husband's negative energy—away. "Don't give him another thought. He's going to go down to Jake's and watch sports and have a beer with his old fogey friends. It's much nicer when he's doing that, trust me. Sit, honey."

Stan sank into the comfy couch, thinking that was a crappy way to exist in a thirty-plus-year marriage, but what did she know? She'd never even been engaged. "How are you feeling?" she asked, instead of commenting on Burt's behavior.

Betty sat down heavily on the couch and tucked one of her blankets around her legs. "Physically, I feel fine. Mentally, well, that's another story." She fiddled with a loose thread on the blanket. "I just can't believe she's gone. Helga took my own mother's place—God rest her soul—in my life. She died young, my mother. And Helga—they were friends their whole lives. She stepped right in and treated me like one of her own. It's so overwhelming."

She sniffled and snagged a tissue from the box on the coffee table next to her.

"I'm sure it is," Stan said sympathetically. "It sounds like Helga had a lot of surrogate families. Jake and his family are going through the same thing."

"Oh, my goodness, of course they are." Betty shook her head. "We all knew she couldn't live forever, but there was so very little wrong with her that no one ever thought about her not being here. I'm devastated—and angry at the same time." She glanced at the doorway, as if making sure her husband wasn't standing there. "I don't know how the town will ever recover."

"Is there someone other than Dale Hatmaker who could keep up the work she was doing?"

"Oh, the work will be kept up, honey. It just won't be kept up the same way. And it won't be Dale Hatmaker, if I have any say over it. There was only one Helga. No one else will ever carry such a deep connection to this town."

That sounded a tad dramatic to Stan, but she let it go. And made a mental note to mention these types of concerns if her coaching job with Tony Falco came to fruition. "Will her boyfriend be okay? How's he doing?" she asked instead.

"Gerry? I honestly don't know. I lost track of him yesterday. I really should give him a call. But I don't feel like talking about her yet." She sighed. "The funeral and the celebration will be difficult enough."

Stan nodded sympathetically. "Who's putting the celebration together?"

"We all will have something to do with it. Mostly her fellow volunteers from the War Office, I suspect, but all the historical buildings and, of course, the library will participate. I have a lovely collection of work Helga was part of, including her own book, over at the library that we can put on display." Talking about it had some of the color returning to Betty's face, and she reached for a notepad on the table next to her. "I need to get back to work tomorrow. There's so much to do!"

"Will her family help?" Stan asked.

Betty's pencil stilled. "Meaning who?"

"Like, her kids. Why, did she have other family?"

"Well, the McGees of course. Gerry's family. Her own?" She snorted. "I doubt it. Sarah's just a kook, and Don and Carla are too busy thinking they're related to the Kennedys or something. Politics have really gone to their heads."

It was enough of a segue. Stan took the cue. "So, is Sarah a real medium?"

Betty snorted. "Oh, dear Lord. She may as well be one of those TV mediums, from what I can gather. The ones on late-night commercials for all the depressed people to call and find out about their sorry love life and give up their life savings. If she's a medium, then I'm the Queen of England."

Stan raised an eyebrow. "So what do you make of her gut feeling, then? Before anyone knew something was wrong with Helga?"

Betty glared at her. "That's a pile of pure horse pucky."

"Well, then, she's a good guesser," Stan said. "Because something was wrong."

Betty said nothing.

"Didn't they get along?" Stan pressed.

Betty sighed. "Not well. Helga often wondered

where that girl came from. Crazy as a loon. I shouldn't be saying that out loud, but it's true. She wasn't very good to her mother, and Helga tried so hard for her. It's just like Sarah to show up and try to capitalize on her mother's death. Now Don, well, I know how proud she was of him. Her first husband was into politics, you know. She always had a hearty respect for people who give so much back to their town or their state. I shouldn't be so harsh on him. I'm sure he's beside himself, too. Don is much more reserved with his emotions. Usually his wife is the one making their feelings known." She made a face.

Interesting. But family dynamics usually were. Stan finally got to her burning question. "Do you still think someone pushed Helga?"

Betty pulled off her glasses, which were attached to a beaded chain, and let them fall against her chest. She looked around again, as if someone might have materialized out of nowhere to hear her answer. "I do. And remember I said that to you in confidence. It wouldn't do to have that rumor all over town. At least not before there's anything to it."

"I understand it was in confidence," Stan said. "But if it's true, you'll have to talk about it, Betty. Are you going to tell anyone? Jessie can help. She would want to help. She loved Helga, too."

"I know that," Betty said. "But it's not wise to go to Jessie right now."

"Why not, though? I don't understand."

"Because I don't have any evidence. Just my hunch."

"So what are you going to do about it?" Stan asked. "You can't take it upon yourself to solve the crime, if it was a crime."

Betty didn't answer.

Stan sighed. "So who do you think did it?"

"I don't know."

"You have to have someone in mind," Stan said. "Otherwise, why would you think she was pushed at all? Did she have a lot of enemies?"

"Of course not. She was lovely."

"Did you see someone around the museum that morning? Someone who shouldn't have been there?"

"No, I wasn't even at the museum. I was tied up with event details at the church until right before ten, when we started the slide show. We were missing tablecloths, and the microphone at the podium outside wasn't working. So many logistics to handle." Betty worked harder at the loose thread .

"Do you think Dale Hatmaker had something to do with her death?" Stan asked. "Would he . . . really kill a person because he wanted her job? That sounds a little extreme, but I guess you just never know."

Betty was quiet for a long time. Stan decided to take the hint and leave, when Betty spoke. "Stan, you have to understand something about Frog Ledge. A lot of secrets live here. They've lived here for a lot of years. And Helga, well, Helga knew most of those secrets."

Stan felt a sudden chill. She rubbed her arms to get rid of the goose bumps. "What kind of secrets? The kind that could get her killed?"

Betty looked straight at her. "The kind that should be left alone."

Chapter 10

Betty knew more than she was telling about the Helga situation. Either that, or she'd gone completely off her rocker. Neither of those options sat well in Stan's gut.

She backed out of Betty's driveway as darkness slipped into Frog Ledge. A light snow had started to fall again. The flakes swirled through the wind and kissed her windshield before puddling into water. She flicked her windshield wipers on, pausing before she drove away. In an upstairs window, a light went on. Stan caught sight of Betty's face in the window before the room winked into darkness behind rapidly closing blinds.

She drove away quickly, the heebie-jeebies chasing her. All Betty's talk about murder and secrets seemed extra eerie on this dark, winter night. On autopilot, Stan didn't realize she'd headed for the pub until she turned into the parking lot. Here, there was guaranteed warmth. She wanted to run in and tell Jake about Betty's claims, but she couldn't do that. She'd promised. Instead, she'd have to take comfort just in being here.

It was a light customer night judging by the cars in the lot, probably due to the weather. Unless a lot of locals were walking over, which wasn't uncommon. She parked next to Burt Meany's red Buick— Betty had been right about his destination—and went inside.

As soon as she stepped through the door, the feeling of "home" washed over her and she immediately felt better. She'd always been comfortable here. It wasn't like any other bar she'd ever been in. Probably Jake had a lot to do with that, but overall this place wasn't solely about having a drink—although there were plenty of opportunities for that. McSwigg's was about community. Family. The place, corny as it sounded, where everybody knew your name. Or mostly everybody, like when the place wasn't overrun with college kids.

But even filled to bursting, it was special. Ireland was still on her "to visit" bucket list, so she didn't have the real thing to compare it to, but if she had to bet, Jake's place rated pretty high on the authentic Irish pub experience list. He'd done most of the interior work himself, from the elaborate wooden doors with Celtic engraving, to the gleaming mahogany bar, to the homey feeling he'd cultivated with a fireplace and mix of high bar tables, couches, and comfy chairs scattered throughout. The mirrored shelves behind the bar displayed his impressive collection of alcohol with a 3D effect. The live band area in back was quiet tonight, but Stan had seen it rocking many times with everything from Irish step dancers to full-on rock bands—all Irish themed, of course. He also had started hosting poetry slams and open-mic nights in an effort to cater to the age-appropriate student population. So far, it had been very successful.

Irish flags, clovers, and various blessings, as well as photos of real Ireland castles and other scenery adorned the walls. And over the bar area, her favorite piece of McSwigg's—the hand-cut, engraved wooden blessing that read: AN ÁIT A BHFUIL DO CHROÍ IS ANN A THABHARFAS DO CHOSA THÚ. *Your feet will bring you to where your heart is.*

Hers certainly had.

She scanned the room. Jake stood behind the bar, but not in his usual mode of pouring drinks and chatting with people. Instead, he was in the far corner having what looked to be a heated discussion with Izzy Sweet. Stan hesitated, thinking maybe she shouldn't go in after all, but it was too late. Brenna had already spotted her from her position behind the bar. She waved. Stan threaded her way over, noticing Burt Meany planted in front of one of the big-screen TVs. He sat with a couple of other guys, drinking Bud Light from a can.

She felt bad for Betty.

"Hey, Bren." She finally got to the bar and dropped her purse in the chair while she unzipped her coat and unwound her scarf. "Slow night?"

"Really slow. I heard it's snowing again." Brenna wiped the counter in front of Stan and pulled out a wineglass. "Merlot?"

Stan resisted the urge to swoon. "Yes, please."

"French fries?"

Stan hesitated. She loved Jake's homemade fries. Especially the Cajun ones. But she had her good-for-you soup at home for dinner. Although she could use something to tide her over until she actually went home.

Brenna watched her inner struggle and laughed. "I'll bring you fries."

Stan smiled sheepishly. "I'm that easy to read?"

"Nah, I just know you by now. And how much you love fries." Brenna grabbed a glass and selected the wine.

Stan glanced over at Jake and Izzy in the corner. Izzy's long braids obscured her face, but Stan could tell from her body language—long nails drumming on the bar, body angled away from Jake—that she was not happy with the conversation. She wondered if it had to do with the letter Izzy had told her about that morning. "What's going on over there?"

Brenna rolled her eyes. "Typical. All those two ever do is fight. It's all they ever did, right?" She poured a generous sampling of the red wine into the glass and presented it with a flourish. "Enjoy. I'll be back in a few and we can talk about our plan for tomorrow. We're still baking, right?"

"We are. I came by to tell you about the new job we have." She hadn't, really, but it was as good a reason as any. And she did need Brenna to get on the wedding planning quickly.

"A new job? For Pawsitively Organic?" Brenna clapped her hands together in excitement. "What is it?"

"You're not gonna believe it. It's cool. Quirky, but cool." Stan sipped her wine and tried not to look over at Jake. He hadn't seen her yet, which meant it was a serious conversation. He was usually on top of everything that happened in the bar—sometimes before it happened. And he always was the first to greet her when she showed up.

"Excuse me. Can I get my wine?" A woman with six-inch stilettos, a too-short-for-winter dress, and a foul-looking face leaned in next to Stan. "I've been waiting."

"I'm so sorry. That was a Chardonnay, right?" Brenna hurried off to fill the order. The woman looked Stan up and down, clearly rating her outfit. She appeared to find it lacking, which didn't bother Stan one bit if the alternative was looking like her.

Brenna returned with the glass and Stan's fries. She took the woman's money. The woman didn't leave her a tip and flounced away. Brenna frowned after her. "Jerk." She put Stan's plate of fries in front of her.

"I hope that doesn't happen often." Stan popped a fry in her mouth. Heaven. "So, anyway, this new job—"

Izzy appeared at her side. Irritation set her jaw and made her eyes flash, but to her credit, she tried to mask it with a smile. At the same time, two guys approached the bar.

Brenna sighed. "I'll be back." With a curious look at Izzy, she headed for the new customers.

"Hi," Izzy said.

"Hey," Stan said. "Everything okay?"

"Yeah, fine. Listen, I gotta get going, but you should stop by tomorrow."

"I'll try. I have to figure out tomorrow's schedule. Lots of baking to do and I got a new job today." She saw Jake hanging back, waiting until Izzy was finished before he came over.

Izzy saw him, too. "Well, try," she said. "New coffee shipment coming in. And you can tell me about the new job. I heard some gossip about it today." With a wink, she hurried away.

Jake finished straightening the bottles on one of the shelves behind the bar, then came over. "What are you drinking?"

"My usual." Stan observed him, saw the fatigue in his eyes, the pale of his face behind his usual one-day stubble. "What are you drinking?"

He half-smiled. "Nothing. Yet." He tipped his Red Sox hat back, rubbed his forehead. "Long day. But it's all good. How are you? Wasn't sure I'd see you tonight."

"I wasn't sure either. Fry?"

"No, thanks. I already ate."

"Did you guys, uh, get the funeral planned?" She hated to bring it up, but didn't want him to think she was rude if she didn't ask.

Jake's face clouded over again. "We did. It'll be private. Don wants to focus on their immediate family, the boys, you know. The town-wide celebration will be for everyone else. I think that's the right thing to do. It's supposed to be Sunday."

Stan nodded. "Sounds appropriate. The celebration sounds like it will be a lot of work to pull together in such a short period of time, though."

"Yeah." He grimaced. "It will be a busy week. So, will you go with me? To the funeral? It's Thursday at eleven."

"Me?" She tried to hide her surprise. "If you're sure no one will mind, of course I'll go. But I thought it was private."

"Why would anyone mind? You're with me."

The statement, even delivered so casually, flooded her body with warmth. Too bad she was so relationship challenged that she had no good response. "Great," was the best she could come up with. "So you're officially working tonight?"

He shrugged. Either he didn't notice her awkwardness or he was too polite to call attention to it. "Gotta jump back in sometime, right? Can't sit around and mope." He held up a finger to someone across the room. "Gonna hang for a bit?"

"Sure," she said.

He paused and scanned her face. "Everything okay?"

She hesitated. She really wanted to tell him about Betty's crazy theories and her own bad feeling about Dale Hatmaker. But she also didn't want to cause him more heartache. Or break Betty's trust. She would wait another day, see if anything came of it. "Of course. Everything's fine."

He gave her the not-sure-I-believe-you look, but went to talk to whoever was beckoning. Stan sipped her wine. If she told him and he confronted Betty, which wasn't unrealistic considering his proximity to the situation, that could be problematic. Betty would never forgive her. And if Jake told Jessie, that would be a whole other can of worms. No, silence was probably the best option in this situation.

"Is this seat taken?"

Stan swiveled on her stool to find her mother standing next to her wearing her best practiced smile and a thousand-dollar suit that didn't fit in with the denim and flannel set. Which meant—yup, there he was. Stan wanted to crawl under the bar as

Tony Falco finished clapping somebody on the back and joined them.

"We meet again. Hello, Kristan."

"It's Stan," she said through gritted teeth.

"My grandfather's name was Stan," Falco said. "It doesn't feel right to call you by the same name. Please forgive me." He smiled charmingly at her. Behind them, Brenna pretended to stick her finger down her throat and throw up.

"May we sit?" her mother asked again. The smile had faded a bit at this point.

"Of course, help yourself." Stan waved at the seats and swallowed more wine. "I can't stay much longer anyway." She'd lost her appetite for her fries. Which was infuriating.

"But we just got here. This is perfect timing for you and Tony to have a conversation, right, dear?"

Stan recognized the tone and the accompanying look, mostly from her teenaged years. It meant, *Do what I tell you and love it like it is your idea.*

She had hated the look then, and she hated it now. The french fries weren't even worth sticking around for.

But Falco leaned over. "Yes, I heard you were interested in talking to me about coaching opportunities. I'll be honest, I don't think I need that much coaching, but I'm happy to take any tips you'd like to provide. And of course, if you're looking for a longer-term paid arrangement, we can certainly discuss that." He flashed straight white teeth at her.

Theme song for this guy: "Big Shot." She could picture Billy Joel making fun of Falco as he sang. She drained her wineglass and set it on the bar, then stood. "The only tip I really have right now is pretty simple." She leaned closer, past her mother, so Falco could hear her. "Don't dishonor a woman who meant so much to everyone in town by appointing someone to her job who just wants a title and his name in the newspaper." She straightened, shrugged her coat on, and picked up her bag. "If you need any other tips, please feel free to call me." She flashed them a dazzling smile, then headed out the door, waving to Jake on the way. He'd certainly forgive her for leaving once he saw Falco. He probably wished he could walk out, too.

Chapter 11

Stan woke at the crack of dawn Tuesday with her mind on weddings. Her upcoming meeting with Dede Richardson later this week would help her get to know the dogs and get a feel for their "party style." But that was only a formality. With the exception of the dress and tux, which Dede's daughter was handling, Dede had not-so-subtly conveyed the message that she expected Stan to plan the entire party, from the fabulous gourmet cake right down to wedding "rings." *Oy*.

She couldn't help but feel like she was the wrong person for all of it except the cake. She had zero experience with weddings. She hadn't even been to one in about ten years. And now she was being trusted to send a couple of dogs on their happy ever after? She hoped the bride wasn't a bridezilla. At least Dede was securing the "wedding official." She had no idea how to go about finding a doggie minister.

Stan rolled out of bed and checked out her window to see what was happening on the green. It was the first thing she did every morning, especially when spring was on the horizon. Not today, though. It was gray again. The town green was hidden behind a cloud of foggy drizzle. On the bright side, maybe it would melt the snow. It seemed like spring wasn't planning to make an early appearance in New England this year. It had been a long winter. With a groan, she dropped back on the bed and crawled under the covers. She didn't have to get up yet. The dogs hadn't even stirred—Scruffy was still sacked out at the foot of the bed, curled up with Nutty, and Henry hadn't even opened his eyes to peek at her from his bed across the room.

But it was too late for more sleep. Her mind had already kicked into high gear. She sat back up and grabbed her iPad. Opening the preliminary wedding list she'd made yesterday, she scanned it for priorities.

1. Figure out/buy ingredients for cake—strawberry flavored
2. Ingredients for secondary dessert—variety of flavors
3. Wedding "tags" for collars (in place of rings)
4. "Bow vows"
5. Flavored doggie water in a fountain

The bow vows made her smile. She'd found the term online when she Googled "doggie weddings" in a frantic attempt to assure herself this could actually be done. And had found mention of a number of other ceremonies, one on a beach with bow vows.

Doggie wedding vows? Whoever would think of such a thing?

She had forgotten to add setting up the green and figuring out if they could use the gazebo to the list. Whom was she supposed to ask about that? Jake would probably know. She should call him. Who had time to sleep? She needed to get to work. She got up, found her slippers, and went into the bathroom to brush her teeth. Nutty and the dogs still hadn't budged—they must've still been too full from sampling the treats she and Brenna had power-baked yesterday—so she headed downstairs alone to make her coffee.

It just started to spew into the pot when her phone dinged, signaling a text message. Now, if only she knew what she'd done with it. After riffling through pockets and her pile of stuff on the table, she finally located the phone in the bottom of her purse. She had to get better about keeping track of the silly thing.

The text was from Jake. **Want to take the dogs for a walk? Wondering what happened with Mum.**

He was up early. Was that good or bad? She texted back. **Sure, can you give me an hour?** Not that she really wanted to recap the discussion with her mother, but she did have to tell him about the doggie wedding. She hadn't even gotten to tell Brenna.

He responded: **Meet me at eight, the new building.**

The *clackety-clack* of nails on the floor signaled the arrival of the pups—they had a sixth sense for when she was in the kitchen.

"Morning, guys." She bent down for kisses, then let them outside just as Nutty chose to make his appearance. He eyed her hopefully and wound around her legs.

"Hi, handsome." She scooped him up and nuzzled his nose. "Turkey potpie this morning."

Nutty purred. Stan set him down and went to let the dogs in. Once the three were gathered, she fed them her new turkey potpie-style dish she was testing for the clinic's display, then filled her Vitamix with fruits and veggies for a smoothie. Drink in hand, she turned to find the dogs eagerly watching her. They always seemed to know when a walk or car ride was in their future.

"You guys want to go for your walk?" She smiled at Scruffy's excited squeals and Henry's tail thumping. "I'll go shower. Go wait by the door," she instructed.

Of course they didn't listen, and followed her upstairs. Having multiple pets meant she never got to do certain things alone anymore. Like shower or use the bathroom.

Oh, well. Good thing they were cute.

The building Jake and Izzy co-owned had, among other uses, been the former site of the Frog Ledge Library. In the late 1980s, the town had received a state grant to build a new library building adjacent to the town green, which allowed for more accessibility during events and such. Betty had told the story of the relocation at an event last year. She'd been librarian back then, too, and she talked about how excited she was at the prospect of setting up a brand-new building and how the entire town had pitched in to help.

Betty had championed Jake and Izzy's plans to

build a bookstore. Frog Ledge didn't have one, and Betty was such a staunch supporter of reading and literacy programs that it was a no-brainer. Stan wondered if she ever had a bit of nostalgia, though, for her old library. Sometimes when people were attached to things or traditions, even the most positive change seemed like a negative. Especially during the remodeling process.

The block was hopping with activity this morning when she, Scruffy, and Henry walked up. Trucks were parked all over the street, and workers hauled supplies inside. They looked cold, wearing heavy gloves and hooded sweatshirts. The building must not be much warmer inside. Sure, they had electric heaters and other equipment, but it was drafty and old, and they probably hadn't reached the insulation point yet. Stan shivered thinking about being in there five days a week, eight hours a day in this weather.

Seeing new development in town was exciting, though. While still small and rural, Frog Ledge was getting a reputation as the new mecca on the eastern side of the Connecticut River—a small, farming town cast in a different light. After years of being known for agriculture and history, its reputation was changing. New businesses were springing up all the time, from the flower shop on the other side of the vet clinic to a new Thai restaurant down by Izzy's place. The locals were split between loving it and hating it. There were some who flocked to the new establishments, loving the idea that they didn't have to go all the way to West Hartford or east to the casinos for some culture. Then there were others who were outraged at the thought of Thai food and gourmet coffee—and all the yuppies who went with it—taking over Frog Ledge, a simple farming town where the cows and goats and other farm friends could easily outnumber the people.

Betty and her feelings about reading aside, there had been some upheaval in town when Jake and Izzy announced their plans for the building. Izzy was one of those "troublesome newcomers," a nickname coined at a public hearing about the project, but most likely earned during her first go-round when she opened the café. Her partnership with Jake quelled a lot of the voices, but there were people who didn't want their Main Street winning any awards in *Connecticut* magazine for "best of" something or "unique places to see." The less strangers, the better, in some folks' opinion. Stan couldn't see the sense in letting Main Street fester with falling down properties, either, but there was no reasoning with some of these people. That nostalgia thing again.

Stan knew Izzy would put her heart and soul into the new store, as she did every day at Izzy Sweet's Sweets. She couldn't wait to spend a Saturday afternoon there. But first the darn thing had to get built, and it seemed to be slow going.

"I don't get the holdup, Frank," she heard Jake say as she walked up, Scruffy leading the way and almost yanking her arm out of the socket when she saw Duncan, Jake's Weimaraner, who barked furiously when he saw them. "You had to expect some of this. It's an old building."

Frank Pappas looked frustrated. And angry. Unless it was simply the way the majority of construction workers and contractors looked. Frank could've passed for a bouncer at the rowdiest nightclub, especially with his perpetual scowl. He had a lot of hair. Unkempt, long, curly hair on his head and an overgrown beard on his face. That much hair had to translate to the rest of his body. Stan was a little grossed out just thinking about it and quickly pushed the thought away. Frank's jeans were weighed down by a huge tool belt, and his work boots were covered in some kind of dust. A cigarette hung out of his mouth, and he puffed furiously on it when he wasn't speaking. In this case, speaking was mostly in the form of indignant grunts.

"I told you. We're running into a lot of unexpected problems," Frank said, shooting a dirty look at Duncan, whose barks were escalating in volume. He pulled a pack of cigarettes out of his sweatshirt pocket and slammed it against the palm of his other hand. "The wiring is garbage. I had to call the electrician back two days in a row just so we could use our equipment."

"Sounds like you need a new electrician," Jake said. "Dunc. Easy, boy." He met Stan's eyes and motioned to her, then dropped the leash and let him go. Stan sighed. She'd been trying to get Jake to stop doing that. It was dangerous. Luckily, Dunc ran right toward her, almost bowling her over giving her kisses.

"Then find one," Frank said, his gravelly voice rising a notch. "It took me a week to get this guy out here. Not to mention the days we lost talking about putting the job on hold." He took another cigarette out of his pack and shoved the box back into his coat pocket.

Stan's ears perked up. This is what Izzy had been

talking about yesterday morning. Jake apparently didn't like Frank's response. Or maybe his tone. He turned slightly so Stan couldn't hear him, but she could tell from his gestures the conversation had gone south.

It didn't look like she was about to hear anything else interesting, and she didn't feel like sitting here watching a testosterone battle today. She pulled her plastic baggie filled with treats out of her jacket pocket. Duncan, Henry, and Scruffy gathered around her like worshippers at a church seeing their favorite priest. She passed out banana oatmeal treats to each of them and couldn't help but smile watching them wolf them down.

"Another?" she asked when Henry came up and nudged her hand with his nose. She fished second helpings out of her bag. "I'm glad you like these. I think I'll make this kind and maybe a batch with apple, too, for the bakery case at that new store Auntie Nikki sold my treats to." She looked up and realized both Jake and Frank were watching her. Jake grinned. Frank looked at her like she had three heads.

"What?" she asked, reddening.

"Nothing," Jake said. "I like how you talk your orders out with the dogs."

"Duncan appreciates the recipes, too."

"You don't have to tell me that."

Frank rolled his eyes, not bothering to hide it. "Anyway, the electrician's gonna be an added charge. Should I put it in a change order?"

"Yeah, of course we'll need a change order," Jake said. He sounded annoyed with the question.

"I told Izzy about it," Frank said defensively. "She already okayed it."

"That's great. Izzy's a whiz at running a business. But I have a stake in this, too, so I'd appreciate you running that sort of thing by me, also."

"You think I'm screwing you? After all these years?" Frank's voice rose, attracting the attention of a young couple walking by. He stared right back at them until they moved on.

Jake fixed him with a withering stare. "Calm down, Frank. I'm doing what any responsible owner would do and asking that you get approval on certain things first. That's all. Send the paperwork and I'll take care of it. Ready, Stan?"

Stan pushed herself to her feet and pocketed her treats. "I'm ready."

Jake took Duncan's leash back and they started down the street. Stan looked over her shoulder. Frank hadn't gone inside yet. She turned back. "I know he's supposed to be your friend, but he's kind of creepy," Stan said. "Why is he so angry?"

Jake brushed it off. "No big deal. Frank's Italian. He's never been the calmest person I know. And when he's on a big job he tends to get a little nuts. He's had a lot of extra expenses, and I'm trying to make sure I'm tracking them well."

"So are you mad at Izzy?"

"Not at all. She just wants the building done as fast as possible. I get it." He hit the button for the walk signal. "Frank's a good guy. This is a complicated building. It'll all work out."

Stan glanced behind them again. Frank watched them go, his stare unnerving. He met Stan's eyes, threw his cigarette down and ground it out slowly with his heel, then turned and went inside. She shivered. "I hope so. Do you think the push to stop the construction will happen?"

He glanced at her. "You knew about that?"

Stan shrugged. "As of yesterday. Izzy mentioned it."

"Not gonna happen. I told her she shouldn't worry about it. So tell me what that thing was about with your mother last night." His way of brushing her question off. Before she could circle back to it, a black van turned down the street, slowed, then pulled over behind Frank's van. A guy leaned out of the passenger window and called out to one of Frank's crew, who'd taken the spot Frank had vacated and was having his own smoke. "Hey. Okay to park here?"

Jake followed Stan's gaze. The worker stepped over and said something to the guy in the van. He motioned for the guy to get out. The passenger door opened and he hopped out, followed the other guy around the side of the building.

Jake frowned. "That doesn't look like Frank's typical supply van," he muttered. "Hang on, I want to check this out," he said to Stan, and started back down the block with Duncan. Stan followed. Something about the van was familiar to her, though she couldn't quite place what.

The van's engine shut off and two other people climbed out. They walked over in the same direction their friend had gone, though one of them lingered in the front of the building, looking up.

Jake reached the lingerer first. "Can I help you with something?"

Stan reached the van. New York plates. She circled

it, noted the discreet logo with no accompanying words.

Holy crap.

"I'm one of the owners," she heard Jake say. "And I wasn't expecting anyone."

Stan walked over to them, Scruffy straining at the leash to meet the new person. Stan kind of felt the same way, but had to hold on to some level of decorum. As she got closer and saw his face up close, her heart pounded with excitement. She was totally right. She couldn't help the smile that escaped onto her lips.

"Hi, Stan Connor," she broke in. "And you're . . ."

"Adrian Fox. Pleased to meet you," he said, offering his hand.

Stan shook it, trying to contain her excitement. He bent to pet Scruffy, who preened at him. Henry sniffed his hand, then sat down, disinterested. Fox gave the dogs just enough attention to make Stan swoon, then turned to Jake and held out his hand.

"Adrian Fox," he said, in case Jake hadn't heard the first time

Jake looked from Stan to Adrian, eyes narrowing. "Jake McGee. Co-owner. Sorry—do you know each other?"

Fox chuckled. Stan reddened. "We don't *know* each other, but I watch the show. I love it," she said to Fox before she could stop herself.

"Thank you. I love to hear feedback."

"Wait. Show? What show?" Jake interrupted.

"Sorry." Fox turned back to Jake. His shockingly white teeth gleamed when he smiled. "I'm a paranormal expert. Stan is referring to my show, *Ghosts in Your Neighborhood.* My team investigates sites around the country with known or suspected paranormal experiences."

"Okay," Jake said, looking thoroughly unimpressed. "I don't watch. Why are you looking for me?"

"We came to check out this site." Fox turned, motioned to Jake and Izzy's building. "Someone sent in a tip that this building might be experiencing some paranormal activity."

Chapter 12

Despite Jake's obvious and immediate cynicism about the subject matter, Stan's primary thought was that Adrian Fox looked exactly like he did on TV every week. Tall, dark, and bad. Bad in a good way. Like a man who could take a poltergeist and chase it out of your house with a combination of ghostbusting tools and pure physical force. Stan had harbored a secret addiction to his show—and him—for years. It was her one true guilty pleasure, unless you counted coffee and sweets. She'd always been a fan of anything scary. Sometimes living alone with no security system made it hard for the post-scare enjoyment to linger, but it had to be pretty hardcore to cause her a real sleepless night. Fox and his ghost-hunting compadres were the only ones who'd really come close, unless you counted the old *Halloween* movies. One of their recent episodes, about a haunted, abandoned asylum in New York, had sent Stan scurrying to turn on every light in the house. Fox definitely knew how to turn up the creep factor.

Now here he was in all his tattooed, black-garbed glory. In Frog Ledge. At Jake's building.

Jake wasn't as easily impressed. "Activity?" he asked at the same time Stan breathed, "Here? Wow. That is *so* cool." He raised an eyebrow at her.

She shrugged. "It is." She wondered why Izzy hadn't mentioned this to her.

He ignored her and focused on Fox. "What exactly do you mean by 'activity'?"

"Great question," Fox said, like he was encouraging a new student. "Activity can mean a number of things, like unexplained happenings. Voices, or footsteps. Missing or relocated objects. In some cases, the activity is destructive. But there was no record of blatantly destructive activity in this report." He pulled out a notebook and flipped through it to confirm.

Inside Stan's pocket, her phone rang. She ignored it and listened to Fox finish his explanation of paranormal activity, her mind racing the entire time. Who phoned in the tip about this building? What kind of ghosts were in there? Didn't Stevie Nicks have a song called "Ghosts"? Her brain searched for the lyrics as all the thoughts tumbled together. She tried to focus, hoping this wasn't bad news for Jake and Izzy's plans—and their construction schedule. From her pocket, chimes sounded. Voice mail.

Jake's skepticism was written all over his face. "Voices and footsteps, huh? I get lots of tips, too, but I only pay attention to the cash ones. How do you weed out the real possibilities from the nuts? And what report are you talking about?"

It was Stan's turn to frown. Jake usually wasn't

rude, but he didn't seem enthralled by Fox at all. Maybe he, like Frank, was worried about construction delays. Or ghost enthusiasts breaking in. That happened sometimes after a place was featured on these shows. Especially at the old asylum sites—people seemed fascinated with those places.

Still, he could at least pretend to be excited. Stan had always dreamt of being part of a ghost hunt, and one had just potentially walked into town. If the place was featured and they exorcised a ghost, it would be a total tourist attraction. Which would make Izzy the happiest girl on the planet once the store was open. It might also make a lot of people in town angry.

But Jake shouldn't be one of them.

Fox must've been accustomed to attitude in this line of work. His easygoing, conversational demeanor didn't change. "Another great question," he said. "Of course we get a lot of fake tips, or what I like to call 'hopefuls.' But when we think a place really has potential, we make a trip out to get a feel for what may be happening. We do an investigation to determine if there is activity, what kind, and what to do about it, depending on the type of spirit. If we feel we have a strong presence, we've got ourselves a show—if the folks want to sign on.

"Our whole fall lineup this year is going to be New England sites, from October through December. Perfect to kick off the Halloween season. New England is prime for ghosts, if you didn't know. We're in the process of selecting the sites right now, so this was perfect timing."

Stan's phone rang again. She grabbed it out of her pocket, glanced at the caller ID. Char. Well, she'd have to wait. She switched the phone to silent and shoved it back in her pocket.

"I'm still missing how you have a report. Since this is the first I'm hearing about any of it," Jake said, crossing his arms.

"We came in and spoke with the workers," Fox said. "We got to town yesterday and caught up with a few members of the crew. They took us around, told us about tools going missing, lightbulbs blowing out. Typical stuff we see during rehabs. Great place, by the way. Must've been amazing in its heyday. What are you doing with it?"

Uh-oh. Stan recognized the darkening of Jake's eyes, the tightening of his jaw. Little clues to anger she didn't see often in him, but when they appeared, it was for good reason.

"First of all, no one should set foot in here without permission from the owners. There are liability issues. If one of your people got hurt here, we'd be in big—"

"Mr. McGee," Fox interrupted. "I completely understand all that. We did get permission."

"From who?" Jake asked; then it dawned on him at the same moment Izzy walked up.

"From me, of course." Izzy winked at him. "I love me a good ghost story." She turned to Fox. "Good morning, Adrian. So, what's the verdict?"

"We definitely heard enough from the crew to support conducting an investigation. There's a great possibility, my friends, that you have bought yourself a building with some unsettled spirits. This could do wonders for your future prospects." Fox grinned.

Jake didn't. "Izzy, we need to talk about this," he

said through gritted teeth. "Why didn't you mention it last night?"

"Don't be a hater." Izzy flung her scarf over her shoulder, dismissing his words. "I knew you wouldn't want to hear about it. We might have ghosts. Frank's been trying to tell you about the setbacks the workers encountered. Although I'm sure ghosts aren't gonna be easy for Frank to swallow. But the evidence is real. All those things Adrian mentioned, that's why we need some of these change orders. I didn't believe it at first either when Adrian tracked me down yesterday, but it makes total sense now. We need to deal with it."

I listened, fascinated. Izzy hadn't know either until yesterday. So who had reported ghostly activity?

"And Adrian's right," Izzy added. "Once a place is featured on this show, people are obsessed—they flock to it. We'll have so much traffic when we open you won't even remember there were ghost hunters here. Or you'll thank them."

"That's great, but this might not even be for real, Izzy. You're getting ahead of yourself."

"Hold on a second," Fox said, stepping forward. "My team doesn't *invent* paranormal activity for the sake of a TV show. We have a TV show because the work demands it. From what the workers are seeing, it sounds like you have some kind of activity you may want to be aware of." He looked at Stan, who hadn't said a word during the exchange. "Did you know about the murder that happened here back in the late forties?"

"Murder?" Stan looked at Jake. "In this building?"

"Crazy, right?" Izzy said. "I almost died when he told me. No pun intended."

Jake said nothing.

"Yes, you had a murder here. We researched it after the tip. Another piece of our due diligence," Fox said with a pointed look at Jake. "If we have a site to consider, we look to see what its past was like. That's usually another indication. And we found that this place had a real story behind it."

Most older buildings in town had some story or other behind it—after all, many had been here for hundreds of years and been through different iterations. Stan had heard about famous people passing through town who contributed to history books, but she hadn't heard about murder. "Who was killed?" she asked.

"It was a boxer named Felix Constantine." Fox referred back to his notes. "Back in 1949. He was supposed to fight one of the locals and vanished after a big bash in town the night before the match. His body was found a few days later. In the basement. No one was ever charged, according to my research. Lack of evidence, supposedly. But perhaps Felix thinks it's finally time to set himself free."

Stan hung on every word. She loved ghost stories. Out of the corner of her eye she saw Jake's face turning cloudier and decided to ignore it. She couldn't concentrate thinking about his anger.

"So what does that mean? This ghost wants to tell us who his killer was?" Izzy asked. "Is that . . . dangerous?"

Fox's face turned somber. "There's always the possibility a spirit is demonic. It's actually not common. Spirits like those in *The Amityville Horror* and *The Conjuring* aren't the norm. Sometimes the deceased doesn't actually realize he or she is dead, and they're just trying to get home. But we have to be prepared for anything, and that includes 'evil' spirits." He accented the word *evil* with air quotes. "Have you felt or experienced anything while you were in here?"

"I haven't," Izzy said. "But I'm not here that much. Jake, have you?"

Jake's face remained stony. "No."

Izzy frowned at him. "He wouldn't tell you anyway. We just started renovations about a month ago," she said, turning back to Fox. "The building has been vacant for a long time. I wonder if all the work stirred something up?"

Fox nodded. "Could very well be."

"Wow. This is bananas." Izzy looked like she wasn't sure if she should be excited, nervous, or both. "I wish we could ask Helga about the murder." The words left her mouth before she caught them, and she cast a guilty look at Jake. His face didn't change.

"You said someone called and told you about this place," Stan said. "Who was it?"

"It was an anonymous tip," Fox said.

Jake looked skeptical. "Shouldn't you be able to tell me who it was, since I'm the owner?"

Fox spread his hands wide and offered an apologetic smile. "I'm sorry. That's part of my protocol. If someone asks to remain anonymous, I respect that."

Stan thought about that. "Did they tell you about the old murder, or only about weird things happening today?" she asked slowly.

"The tip was about the activity," Fox said, but there was something in his tone—a tad less confidence? a change of voice inflection?—that told Stan there was more to the story.

"Don't people usually want to be involved in

tracking down the alleged ghost if they call in a tip?" Stan asked. "Or at least knowing for sure there was something weird going on?"

"It really depends on the motivation of the person making the call," Fox said. "No two tipsters are exactly the same."

No, they certainly weren't. If it had been simply a worker spooked about something, would they have gone to all the trouble of calling Fox and team? Perhaps, if they were big fans of the show. But if it was someone else—someone who knew something about the old murder—they might have a very different reason for calling. And for staying anonymous.

Chapter 13

"So." Fox rubbed his hands together. "What day should I plan on getting the crew in? We'll need some setup time. I'm open to any of you joining us, since you have a connection."

"Really?" Stan must've sounded a little too excited, because Jake shot her a look. She pretended not to notice. A real, live ghost hunt with Adrian Fox? No way was she passing it up. Maybe they could help solve a cold case. Fox could help Frog Ledge find fame and fortune.

"Absolutely." Fox turned his highest wattage smile on her.

"I'm in," Izzy said. "Long as the ghosts aren't gonna possess me or anything."

"I'm in, too," Stan said, deliberately avoiding the daggers Jake sent her way.

"Well, in all seriousness," Fox said, "we do like to get a sense on our own, first, about what kinds of spirits we're dealing with here, even with the worker reports. We'll want to spend some time investigating before we bring in a civilian. So two separate visits are in order."

"A civilian." Jake shook his head and looked at Izzy. "Are you sure we want to waste time on this? You know it means construction's stopping, most likely for some ridiculous amount of time."

"We don't like to upset people's livelihoods any longer than necessary," Fox said. "Trust me, I'm a businessman, too. I understand the pressures. If everyone is comfortable being in the building, I'm not suggesting work stops. We can certainly come in at night after the crew is finished."

Izzy crossed her arms. "See? It's not a waste of time, McGee. This isn't like the stall tactic that committee is trying to use to flat out stop the construction. The committee who doesn't ever answer the phone, by the way. Nope, if there's ghosts in this building, I wanna know about them. And if they're ghosts who need relocating, I want some help before we open. Plus, haven't you heard what we've been saying about publicity? It's a no-brainer."

"Not if this drags on forver," Jake said. "Fine, Izzy. Do what you want. I'll let Frank know. Stan? You coming?"

With an apologetic look at Fox, Stan nodded. "Yep. Izzy, I'll call you later."

"It was lovely to meet you," Fox said, taking her hand.

Stan blushed. "You too, Mr. Fox."

"Call me Adrian." He smiled and let her hand drop. Behind her, Jake's thinly disguised snort became a cough.

"Thanks, Adrian. Good luck in your investigation." She turned and followed Jake, certain she was going to get an earful as soon as they were far enough away.

But Jake said nothing as they walked the next block. He walked fast, the way he did when he was annoyed and trying not to say something to make matters worse.

"It could be interesting," Stan offered, grateful for the three dogs yanking on leashes in between them. She kept her gaze on the sidewalk ahead, not wanting to see the look on his face right now. Still, she felt his frown vibrating in the air between them.

"Have you lost your mind?" he asked.

Stan sighed. "Jake. These guys are pros. If they're here, there's a reason. And I'm sure it's not undercover research for a new reality show about historical renovations."

"Come on, Stan."

"Come on, what? You really don't believe in the paranormal?"

He didn't respond to that question. "Did you know Izzy had met with them already?" he asked.

She stopped walking. "No, I didn't. Last time I saw Izzy was yesterday morning. Sounds like Fox got to town yesterday afternoon. If you're going to accuse me of lying or withholding information because Izzy's my friend, that's not okay. Just because you guys can't stop bickering."

"I'm not accusing you of anything. Don't be so defensive."

Stan huffed out a breath. "Me? You're the one having issues right now, not me. Come on, dogs." She tugged them ahead. Henry tried to remain in the middle of her and Jake. Scruffy pranced ahead, and Duncan strained to keep up with her. Jake stayed by her side but remained silent. They stopped at the crosswalk heading to the library area and the green. Stan jabbed at the button and waited for the walk signal. Jake checked for cars and started walking, then backtracked when he realized she wasn't joining him.

"I forgot you don't jaywalk. Look, I'm sorry. It's just been a crappy week so far."

Her mind flashed to Helga at the bottom of the stairs, and she immediately felt bad. "I know. I'm sorry about that, but don't take it out on me."

"You're right. I just . . ." He blew out a frustrated breath. "Between Helga, and Frank, the regular stuff at the bar, and now this, I could use a vacation."

Stan brightened. "Somewhere warm? I could get on board with that." Then she remembered her new commitments. "But I can't. With the wedding and everything."

"Wedding?" He slowed and stared at her. "Is there something you need to tell me?"

She laughed. "No, my new job. I got sidetracked last night and didn't get to tell you about it."

"Whose wedding? You're doing human events now?"

"Nope, it's a doggie wedding." The light turned and Stan stepped off the sidewalk. Scruffy, recognizing the familiar town green ahead, wooed in delight and tried to run. Stan kept a firm hold on the leash.

Now Jake stopped dead in the crosswalk. "A what?"

"Lucky you're not jaywalking. You'll get hit just standing there. You heard me. Long story. But it might be fun. It's on Valentine's Day. Although it's outside. Which might not be fun if it snows or something."

"Whose dogs?" He jogged the rest of the way across the street to keep up with Duncan.

"Dede Richardson."

"Really? I know Dede. She's sweet. Her dogs are great. Well, the little one's kind of a yipper, but the setter is awesome. Okay, then I guess it will be cute."

"Gee, thanks." Stan frowned at him. "It would be cute anyway because I'm going to put on a rockin' wedding."

"Of course you are." But he'd shifted back to the problem at hand. "To go back to your earlier question, I wonder who the anonymous tipster is? If that's even true." He jammed the hand not holding Duncan's leash into his pocket. It was getting colder, and he wasn't wearing gloves.

Stan didn't want to bring up her conspiracy theory yet, especially given Jake's reaction to the whole situation. "Are you sure it isn't Frank?"

They jogged down the gravel path, lightly dusted with snow from last night's flurries, and hit the trail. The dogs immediately began their sniffing-everything-in-sight routines.

"Frank? Why would Frank do that?" Jake asked. "It just means he'll have to work at this job site longer. And it hurts me and Izzy, because if he gets another job, we're on the back burner. Plus, Frank isn't the type to believe in ghosts. Trust me."

"Does he want to hurt you? He didn't look all that happy back there."

"No way." Jake shook his head emphatically. "He's a friend. He's done a lot of work in town, and he's hoping for more. This could go either way on the popularity scale."

"I don't know. You sure there's nothing he'd get

out of this? Does he want fifteen minutes of fame? You know, he was the one who experienced the haunting, that sort of thing?" Maybe he wasn't making enough on the job after all and wanted to find a way to up his fee. She didn't say that to Jake, but it was possible.

"Frank's not one for the spotlight. No," he said. "It's not Frank. Although I'm clueless about who it could be."

"What about someone else in town who doesn't want the construction to move forward?" Stan asked. "What about that committee that's trying to shut it down?"

"I doubt a historical committee would resort to ghosts to plead their case. And I can't think of anyone else." He glanced at her again. "Unless it was Izzy."

"You think *Izzy* was the tipster? No, she would've said something if she thought there were ghosts in the building, for crying out loud."

"Not if she's the one with an ulterior motive."

"What motive? She wants a bookstore. Yesterday."

Jake shrugged. "Maybe she's looking for a guaranteed sales number when she opens. They were talking about all the publicity that comes from this stuff. She mentioned it three times during the conversation. Look, I don't care that she wants to buy me out. I support that wholeheartedly. But while we're co-owners, I don't need any nonsense."

"Buy you out? What are you talking about?"

"Well, yeah. As soon as she can get a handle on the finances, she's going to take it over. I was trying to help her out with the construction and all that. I didn't want it to be forever."

Izzy probably doesn't want it to be forever either. "No?" she asked, noncommittal.

"Nope, I've got enough on my plate with the bar. And you're going to need more cooking and baking space soon. We might have to expand the kitchen at McGee's so you have a place to work when you're really busy."

"Wait. What?" This was the first she'd heard of that plan.

"Yeah, Brenna's always talking about how busy you're getting and how long it takes to make all the batches of treats to fill orders. I figured at some point you could start using the oven in the bar's kitchen. Depending on how well it goes, we might need to expand."

"Oh." She didn't really know what to say to that. "That's really sweet of you."

He grinned. "You didn't think I was sweet a few minutes ago."

"You weren't being sweet a few minutes ago."

"Not when you were making google eyes at Adrian Fox or signing up for *Ghostbusters.*"

"Oh, *please!*" It was nice to be joking around again. "Did you know about the murder?" she asked as they started around the circle.

"I remember Helga talking about it once or twice, but didn't really pay much attention," he said. That dismissive tone again.

It struck Stan as odd that he wouldn't care about something as big as a murder on his property, but she didn't feel like getting into another spat about it. It was too cold to fight. For the second time that week, she wished she'd brought her hat. Her ears were starting to freeze. Jake either noticed or he was

just as cold. Maybe they had been a little too eager
for spring.

"Want to go halfway around?" he suggested.
"Then you can drive me back to the pub?"

"Sounds good to me." She glanced wistfully down
the green. Her house was a little green dot in the distance. "Maybe we can run?"

By the time they reached her driveway, even the
dogs were ready to go inside. Stan made them all a
bowl of her turkey, kale, and potato hash, and fed
Nutty some treats. While Jake made coffee, she
checked her phone. Char had tried to call her two
more times and sent three texts since her first attempt, all some variation of **Where are you?** And
Call me! There was also a voice mail from last night
that Stan hadn't noticed.

Stan slipped upstairs and called her back. "What's
up? Is everything okay?" she asked when her friend
answered.

"You'll never believe who's staying here," Char said.

But Stan had already been putting two and two together. Fox said he'd been in town since yesterday.
They had to stay somewhere, and Char's place was
the only B and B in town. Although, if they were looking for discretion, they'd gone to the wrong place.
Char would never make a good operative. She had
too big of a mouth.

"Adrian Fox?"

"You knew?" Char sounded deflated.

"I didn't until a few minutes ago. Fox came by
Jake and Izzy's place this morning. He mentioned
he'd been in town since yesterday."

"How's that going over?" Char asked. Always eager for the gossip.

"Izzy's all for it. Jake's not. I'll fill you in later," she said, and hung up despite Char's protests. Once she dropped Jake off, she'd call her back.

But Stan got sidetracked at the general store on the way back to her house. She needed ingredients for today's recipes. Abbie, the owner, was behind the register. She waved when Stan ran in.

"Hello there! Did you bring my order?"

Stan hadn't, but she had good reason. She'd run out of carob chips to make Abbie's requested carob chip and banana biscuits. Abbie would know if the ingredients weren't from her store.

"I didn't, but I'm going to bring it by later today. I ran out of carob chips, and you know I wouldn't buy them anywhere but here. Is that okay?" She flashed her brightest smile and held her breath. Abbie could get testy. She was very fickle—some days she loved you, but if you fell out of her good graces, watch out.

Abbie must've been in a good mood, though, because she only had to think about it for a second before she smiled back. "No worries, hon. Later today is fine. Or even tomorrow. I have to rearrange my display. I'm going to put them right there." She pointed to the handmade chest sitting next to her counter. Today, it featured a spread of homemade scones and muffins from a local bakery. "I can include a sign about how they're made from all local ingredients. Including mine."

"That's great. Thanks, Abbie." Stan hurried down

aisle three, grabbed two bags of carob chips and a jar of honey, and returned to pay for them.

Abbie took the purchases and punched keys on the computer, then leaned forward, her eyes gleaming. "So is it true Adrian Fox is in town?"

Char must have been in. "He is," she said cautiously.

"Did you meet him?"

"I did." Stan made a big show of pulling a twenty-dollar bill from her wallet. "Here you go."

Abbie went back to ringing up the order, but her mind was clearly elsewhere. "I figured you would. I heard he's been poking around Jake's building."

"He's looking at Jake and Izzy's building for a possible investigation." Stan took her change and waited for Abbie to bag the chips.

"It's the boxer, isn't it?" Abbie said triumphantly. "I knew that would come out someday."

"The boxer, yeah, he mentioned that. So . . . do a lot of people know that story?" Stan asked, tucking the small paper bag Abbie handed her into her over-sized tote.

Abbie shrugged. "Die-hard Frog Ledgers do. And it's become sort of a town legend, too. Like how Salem has the witches."

Slightly different, but Stan let it go.

"But let me tell you," Abbie continued, "a lot of people are going to object to that story leaving our boundaries. That ain't the kind of dirty laundry the people of this town are going to want aired out. Especially if these fancy TV people think they're gonna help solve it."

Chapter 14

Stan walked slowly back to her car. It had been cold when she went inside, but now everything about this day seemed downright frigid. Abbie's words bounced around in her brain. While her statement had sounded dramatic, Stan couldn't help but think there were kernels of truth inside it.

The boxer had been murdered. Adrian Fox's research had confirmed that. He'd also confirmed that no one had ever been arrested for the crime. Whether or not that meant a local person had been involved was anyone's guess—if they hadn't solved it in fifty or sixty years, what were the chances of solving it now? One of Stan's other favorite pastimes, in addition to *Ghosts in Your Neighborhood,* was watching *Cold Case* reruns. The team of detectives very rarely tackled cases that old, because the likelihood of solving them was low. And if the murder was that old, wouldn't that make any suspects really old? Would they even still be alive?

It occurred to her that Helga had been that old. And she wasn't alive. As of two days ago. She thought of Betty's words: "A lot of secrets live here. . . . Helga knew most of those secrets." A sinking feeling started in the pit of her stomach. It sounded crazy, even tumbling around in her own brain, but what if Betty's assessment of Helga's death was true? What if it wasn't an accident—and what if it had something to do with this cold case?

Oh, Stan, you're such a conspiracy theorist, her annoying inner critic chided her. *This is not the* X-Files. Why in the world would someone kill an old lady, even if she did know something about an old murder?

Because she knew who the killer was, maybe.

Stan cranked the heat on high and pulled away from the curb. She looped around the eastern tip of the green, cutting through the library parking lot and heading down the other side toward her house, past the historical society and the Frog Ledge Historical Museum.

The historical society. Stan slowed and impulsively swerved into the parking lot. She could stop in there and get some info on Felix Constantine's unfortunate demise. Maybe it would give her a clue about Helga's death. If nothing else, it would make the ghost hunt more exciting. Plus, she'd lived here seven months now and never yet visited. That was just wrong.

Before getting out of the car, Stan glanced at the clock on her dashboard. She had a little time before Brenna came over to bake. She'd just have to be quick. There were two cars in the parking lot behind the society. Probably the staff or volunteers on duty. There was also a car in the parking lot behind the museum, adjacent to the historical society. Odd. The museum was supposed to be closed in honor of Helga. Maybe someone had come to gather her things.

Stan hurried inside. The wind blew the door shut behind her. She took a moment to look around. It looked as though the historical society building had been upgraded, too, probably when the museum was done. The floors were all hardwood, with historical-themed throw rugs in front of the exhibit cases. An oversized easel stood right inside the front door with flyers announcing upcoming events: an antique show, a Civil War photography exhibit, a demo on raising show chickens. Show chickens—now that was something to put on the "not to miss" list. And something she could honestly say she'd never seen advertised before.

As she pulled her hat off, she noticed the woman sitting behind the large front desk. As she got closer, she recognized the tight, silver curls framing a face lined with wrinkles. It was the woman who'd been with Carla Miller outside the church the morning of the Groundhog Day celebration. The not-so-friendly one. Maeve. A large pin attached to her shirt read, VOLUNTEER. Stan sighed inwardly and braced herself.

Maeve didn't recognize her, or if she did, she didn't acknowledge it. "Welcome to the Frog Ledge Historical Society," she said in a raspy voice that suggested years of cigarette use. "How can I help you?"

"Hi. I'm Stan Connor. I live right down the green from here." She pointed in the general direction of her house.

Maeve didn't introduce herself. Or crack a smile.

Hello, Ms. Personality. "This looks like a great place,"
Stan said. "It's my first time in here, I'm embarrassed
to say."

That perked her host up slightly. "Then you have
some catching up to do. These are a sampling of our
latest exhibits." Maeve motioned at the cases lining
the room. "We have a lot of the town's genealogy
records, family histories, that sort of thing. The
museum has a larger sampling, but unfortunately it's
closed this week." She dropped her head, but not
before Stan saw a shadow cross her face.

Stan nodded. "I heard. Such a tragic thing."

"Did you know Helga?" Now the woman stood,
letting her clasped hands fall in front of her. Her
voice warmed just a notch.

"I did," Stan said. "Not well, but I know she was a
lovely person."

"I shouldn't be surprised. Everyone knew Helga."
She heaved out a big sigh. "I'm Maeve. Maeve Johnson."

"Nice to meet you, Maeve. I hear there's going to
be a celebration of Helga's life, since she was such a
large part of the town. Are you involved?"

Maeve nodded. "Of course. The War Office volunteers are doing most of the organizing. We're doing
some reenactments, showing some videos of her favorite events. People will read about some of the
town's most notable events from some of our history
books. Including her own book. Did you know Helga
wrote a book?" At Stan's nod, she went on. "We'll
have refreshments and games for the children. We
want her memory to be happy." She pulled a tissue
out of a box on her desk and dabbed her eyes.

"It sounds lovely," Stan said. "Do you have Helga's book here?"

Maeve nodded and blinked the rest of the tears away. "Yes, although I'll have to think of where." She looked puzzled.

"Don't worry. I'll take a look for it."

"Are you looking for something in particular?" Maeve asked.

"I am. I'm wondering if you could point me in the direction of records from 1949?"

"1949. Hmm." Maeve blew her nose. "What kind of records? Are you looking for a particular person, or an event? Or just general town information?"

"An event. The unsolved murder at the old library building."

Maeve's smile froze in place. "Murder? Why would you want to know about that? Who likes to read about murder?"

Taken aback by her response, Stan frowned. "I'm curious. I'm new to town and I've heard people talking about it."

Maeve frowned. "Carla!"

Carla Miller's head popped out from a door in the back. "Yes? Oh, hello. Stan, right?" She approached the desk. She wore the same large volunteer pin as Maeve.

Stan nodded. "Hi, Carla. I'm so sorry about your mother-in-law."

Carla smiled sadly. "Thank you. She was . . . a unique woman. So, what can we help you with?"

"She wants to read about that murder," Maeve said. Her tone dipped on the word *murder,* indicating how distasteful she found the whole conversation.

"Murder?" Carla repeated, just like Maeve. "Which murder?"

"The boxer. 1949," Stan said, feeling like a broken record. "Allegedly in the old library building?"

"Hmmm." Carla tapped a finger against her chin. "Our town has so many lovely things going for it, and you want to read about murder?" Her tone was light and teasing, but Stan caught the smallest hint of a hard edge.

What was up with these people? Murder happened all the time, unfortunately. It had even happened in Frog Ledge. Recently, not just sixty years ago—Hal Hoffman and Carole Morganwick both within the last year. And murder was in the paper or on the news on every channel, pretty much daily. Stan tried her brightest smile. "I've always been fascinated by crime," she confessed. "It's just a hobby of mine."

Both Carla and Maeve looked like they thought anyone with that kind of hobby wasn't fit for society, but Carla shrugged. "You can try the archives room. If we have anything, it would be in there. The filing cabinets have all the clippings that didn't have another place to be." She pointed to the left of the front door. A posse of bracelets winding its way up her arm jangled with the movement. Stan recognized the brand. Pricey.

But her info was not so helpful. Stan tried to conceal her disappointment. Abbie might have been a better source of information, after all. "Thanks," she said brightly, and followed Carla's direction.

Chapter 15

Stan opened the door marked *Archives* and slipped inside, breathing in the scent of musty paperwork and old, old books.

The room wasn't large to begin with, but it was crammed so full of stuff that it appeared even smaller. Wooden display cases encircled half the room, boasting books, pictures, and laminated documents propped on tabletop easels. A large, wooden table took up the center of the room, a place where people could remove books or papers and read or take notes. Glass cases were filled with photos and other artifacts. Shelves of binders lined one wall. The rest were adorned with historical weapons, soldier hats, quill pens, and other memorabilia.

She had no idea where to start. There was a filing cabinet and two bookshelves against the wall closest to her filled with books, their jackets crumpled and yellowing with age. She perused the titles: *Revolutionary War: A History of Connecticut. Bartleby's General Store. Around the Frog Ledge Green.* And a lot more of the like, plus a whole book devoted to the role of frogs in the revolution. Interesting stuff, certainly, but not what she was looking for. Unfortunately, nothing titled *Unsolved Murders in Frog Ledge*. That would've made her life much easier. She didn't even see Helga's book.

She checked the time on her phone again. Shoot, she'd forgotten to call Char back. She'd have to do that when she got home, too. Brenna was due around two o'clock. It was one-forty. She had time for a quick riffling through the file cabinet, maybe, and then she had to get going.

The top drawer in the file cabinet had files ranging from documentation on Revolutionary War soldiers to old land plans to the history of farms in Frog Ledge. The next drawer was all about agriculture. The third one down had old town council records. Then, in the bottom drawer, something interesting. The folder was titled, "Notorious Frog Ledge News," and contained a collection of old *Holler* articles about a scandal involving a local businessman and an alleged member of the Mafia, all carefully clipped together from earliest to latest; a collection of photos of women in a newfangled getup called a bikini, apparently considered risqué; and finally, the headline, "Still No Leads in Dead Boxer Case." Bingo. She unclipped the stack and flipped through it. Another headline read, "Boxer Found Dead, Foul Play Suspected." And there were a number of clippings in between, so hopefully she would find a coherent story.

She scanned the top clipping. Her eyes caught a familiar name in the byline. Arthur Pierce. Cyril's father. The guy with the nasty-smelling cigar who had showed up Sunday. Arthur Pierce had reported on this murder? She wondered if Cyril knew the facts passed down by his dad. Maybe he even had old research in his office. She should ask him. Maybe she could stop by the *Holler* under the guise of wanting to see the office. She skimmed the article, which detailed Constantine's scheduled fight, the party, the last time anyone saw him. It closed by asking for anyone with information on his whereabouts to call the local police. This was before his body was even found.

As much as she wanted to keep reading, she had to get home. Maybe the historical society volunteers would let her borrow the clippings pertaining to the case. She went outside to ask. But Maeve wasn't at the desk, and Carla was nowhere in sight. Stan glanced around. Perhaps they were in the break room. She flipped through the clips again while she waited, scanning the stories for the highlights. She wanted to sit and read them in order when she had time, so instead she wandered over to peruse the genealogy section, which was really a library of family names and any history associated with the family. She recognized a few names in there: Mackey, Ray's family; Hoffman, the dairy farm family; Morganwick, the former town veterinarian. She'd just located Oliver when the front door opened. She turned and saw Harry, the mailman.

"Hey, Stan. Anyone around?"

"Hi, Harry. Maeve and Carla were both here. I'm not sure where they went."

"Huh. Can you do me a huge favor and sign for this certified mail? I'm behind on my route and if I don't get home for my daughter's basketball game tonight, my wife is gonna kill me." He smiled apologetically and handed her an envelope.

"I guess, but—"

"It's no problem. Maeve won't care." His face clouded. "It's addressed to Helga anyway."

Stan took the envelope and signed where Harry indicated. With a thanks and a wave, he was gone. She glanced at the return address: *Family Tree DNA*. Something to do with Helga's genealogy practice, clearly.

Then her eyes widened. DNA. Hadn't Amara just told her Helga had done a DNA test for her? Maybe these were the results. She hesitated. She really shouldn't take the package, but if no one else had been working on this with Helga, it would just sit there for who-knew-how-long. Maybe even get tossed in the trash. If she took it, Amara could have an answer about her long-lost family. It would be a shame if the information got lost or filed away and Amara never got answers.

Sticking the envelope in her bag, Stan wandered to the window in the back of the room and peered out. Both cars were there. Stan frowned. Where on earth had they gone?

"Maeve? Carla?" she called. Waited. No answer. Well, she couldn't wait all day. She leaned over and grabbed a piece of scrap paper from the desk and scrawled a note that she'd borrowed a couple of newspaper articles, then headed to the door.

She pushed it open and stepped outside before her conscience got the better of her. What if Maeve had fallen or become ill and Carla was in a storage room or something, unable to hear? They didn't need another tragedy around here. She should look for them. With another peek at her watch, she saw she had five minutes to get home. At least Brenna had a key.

She went to the door in the back marked "Staff Only." Stan knocked. "Maeve? Carla? Hello?"

No answer. She opened the door. It was a break room. An empty one. Another door led to a bathroom, but it was open and also empty. Great. Now what? She went back into the main room and looked around. The only other area was the archive room, and she'd been the only one in there. She doubted they had vanished into thin air. Unless the historical society had its own demonic ghost.

Stan glanced around one last time. Her eyes fell on a white paper tacked to the wall in the back corner. The paper had two words typed in bold— TO MUSEUM—and an arrow pointing to a door.

There was a way to get to the museum from here? Stan tucked her papers into her oversized bag and tried the knob. The door opened into a hallway lined with windows on one side, facing the front of the building. The carpeting looked new. A connector. She'd had no idea. She stepped through, closing the door quietly behind her after testing it to make sure it didn't lock. It was about fifteen steps to the next door. That, too, was unlocked. She pushed it open, listened. Nothing. "Hello?" she called. "Maeve? Carla?"

She recognized where she was—in the back of the museum, behind Helga's desk. Not far from the staircase where the historian had fallen. Even though it had only been two days since Helga's death, the place already smelled musty and unused, as if her very presence had been the only thing keeping the town's history from fading away.

She proceeded toward the main room of the museum. She knew someone had to be there because of the cars in the back lot. She jumped when a figure appeared in the shadowy hallway in front of her. A man, talking to someone. She heard the tail end of the conversation: ". . . just give me a list of what pieces should be moved out," before he noticed her.

As he stepped into the light, she realized it was Dale Hatmaker.

"Hello there." Hatmaker waved, as if she were coming to join a party he'd been planning for weeks. "What can I do for you? We're technically closed this week. An unfortunate incident." He stepped forward, then recognized her. "Oh, hello. I believe we met on the green," he said, offering his hand. "Dale Hatmaker."

"We did." She didn't take his hand, but glanced around him and saw Carla. She was bent over the old library card catalogue, the kind with the narrow wooden drawers, that Stan had noticed the day she'd followed Jake inside. "I'm looking for Maeve. She's not at her desk and she doesn't seem to be anywhere over there. Have either of you seen her?"

Carla stood up, shoving the drawer shut behind her. "I think she did come over. Dale?"

"Why, yes, she did." He pointed. "Maeve is right up front. She came over to pick up a piece for an exhibit that we're done with. The connecting hall is so convenient that way. Quite useful for the colder months."

"That was so sweet of you to look," Carla said, hurrying over to her. "Especially given her age and the things that can happen, as we were reminded of this week. I'm sorry we left you alone over there. Were there any other customers? I'd better get back." Flashing a grateful smile at Stan, she hurried back into the connector hallway.

Hatmaker was still smiling that saccharine smile. "Did you need Maeve for something?"

"Yes, I'll go find her." She wanted to make sure Hatmaker was telling the truth and Maeve really was here. And okay. Even though Carla had been here, too, Betty's paranoia and her own active imagination were getting the better of her. But if Hatmaker had done something to Helga, he could certainly hurt someone else. She edged past him and almost ran right into Maeve, heading back her way carrying a flag in a glass case.

Maeve looked surprised to see Stan. "Did you find what you were looking for?"

"I did find a couple of things." Stan remembered the note she'd left. "I borrowed a couple of articles to make copies. I'll return them tomorrow if that's okay? I left you a note but wanted to make sure you were okay. I couldn't find you anywhere."

"Oh. Sorry. Yes, you're welcome to them." Maeve's gaze fluttered to Hatmaker, then away. "I should get back to the desk in case we get any more visitors." She walked past both of them to the connector hallway, closing the door firmly behind her.

Was it her imagination, or did Maeve look afraid

of Hatmaker? Anyone looking at him would agree
he appeared harmless enough. Even a bit spacy
behind those glasses. But something about him
made her uneasy.

He smiled at Stan. "See? She's safe and sound."
Stroking his ratty beard, he asked, "Is there anything
else?"

"Are you working on something for Helga's celebration?" Stan asked.

Hatmaker's smile faltered, but he caught it. "No,
I was stopping by on the mayor's request to ensure
the museum is ready to open next week without any,
er, dark clouds hanging over it."

"Don't you think that's a bit premature? I thought
they were keeping the museum as-is out of respect
for Helga."

Hatmaker narrowed his eyes. "As tragic as the
events of Sunday were, the museum must reopen.
My only concern is preserving the history of the
town," he said.

Tony Falco apparently hadn't taken her tip to
heart if he was putting Hatmaker in charge of re-
opening. "Oh," Stan said. "So what kinds of pieces
are you planning to move out?"

Hatmaker looked surprised that she had heard
that—or maybe that she'd had the gall to ask about
it. "Well, naturally things that have run their course,"
he said in that condescending tone that suggested
he thought she was overstepping, but since she had
a tenuous connection to the mayor he would humor
her. "Old items that may not have any place in the
exhibits anymore."

"Like what?"

Hatmaker's smile turned into a grimace. "Well,

my dear, let's just take a spin around the room and I can point out some examples." He motioned for her to follow him. "Now, see this?" He pointed to a cabinet full of really ugly quilts. "This is an exhibit of some of our founding mothers' quilting projects, done for the soldiers returning from the war. It's a perfect example of what we want to showcase. What our museum is really about. But this"—he pointed to another cabinet with a jumble of photographs— "this is a haphazard attempt to promote these pictures as historical photo documentaries, when really they're just a bunch of old photographs assembled with no rhyme or reason."

Stan stepped closer and examined the pictures. They were all old photos of the town, different buildings, even an old shot of the green. "Why aren't these a good example? They're all pictures of the town."

Hatmaker dismissed her with a flick of his wrist. Clearly she couldn't know anything about topics such as this one. "There are many things you wouldn't understand about historical collections," he said, his tone growing more pinched with each word.

"Really? Look." She pointed to one, leaning in closer to see the details. "That's the old library building. Jake and Izzy's new place." Chances are Hatmaker hadn't heard about Fox and friends' appearance in town yet, but it seemed like something that would garner a lot of attention once the story about the murder came out.

"I didn't say the photos weren't *relevant*. I simply said the *way* they're *displayed* needs some work. These dreadful cabinets need upgrading. And some of them can be displayed in a much more relevant way. Like this thing." He waved at the old library catalogue that Carla had been perusing when Stan walked in. "There is no need for this . . . monstrosity to be taking up so much space in the main room. This is a holdover from the library upgrade that, in my opinion, is here for more sentimental reasons than historical. And, of course, all these things get dumped in the museum with no particular regard for the objective of the exhibits. Those are some examples of what the mayor is sanctioning as acceptable changes."

"So where are you sending the pieces you're having removed?" Stan asked.

"Most likely to storage until we determine a better use." He glanced at his watch. "It's been lovely chatting. Now, my apologies, but I must get back."

In other words, get lost. Stan thought about calling Jessie to report him for trespassing. "Thanks for helping me find Maeve," she said, and retraced her steps back the way she'd come. On her way by Helga's old desk, she paused to look. Helga's glittery purple cane still hung on its hook, forlorn and alone.

Chapter 16

Brenna's car was already in her driveway when Stan pulled in at ten after two. She smiled. Her assistant was overly motivated, which meant she was super prompt. Stan loved it. Her business had taken off so quickly and the demand was so high, she'd be lost without Brenna. As an added bonus, her young assistant was a talented baker with a sixth sense for combining good nutrition with taste. And she loved animals.

When she let herself in, her dogs weren't even at the door. Maybe they couldn't hear over the music blasting from the kitchen. Usher. "DJ Got Us Fallin' in Love." Not her top choice of music. But when she entered the kitchen, she saw what was really distracting them. The two dogs and Nutty sat in a semicircle around Brenna, who stood at the stove. She had them all at attention, waiting for pieces of banana. Nutty most likely thought it was one of the freshly baked cookies, of which the aroma filled the room and tickled Stan's nostrils. Her stomach growled. Embarrassing, especially considering the food in question was technically for dogs and cats. Even though they were made of all human ingredients, she felt silly eating them. But she'd missed lunch again, with her detour to the historical society. Maybe she could make something yummy for her and Brenna to eat while they baked.

She leaned against the wall, watching with a smile as the dogs took their treat and Nutty, as expected, turned his nose up at it and meowed indignantly at Brenna.

"I just thought I'd give you something before the treats came out of the oven," Brenna defended herself, then noticed Stan at the same time the dogs did. They ran up, wagging and barking, pretending they'd been waiting for her all along. "Hey, Stan. I wanted to get started." She turned the radio down.

"You're the best. I'm sorry I'm late."

"No worries. I had nothing else on my schedule, and I know you had meals to work on today. Don't you need to bring Abbie's order over?"

"Shoot." She'd nearly forgotten her promise to get back to Abbie's this afternoon. "Yes, I do."

"They're in the oven. I stopped for carob chips on my way over. You'll be all set in a few." She pointed to the clock. "Plenty of time, too. She's open until eight."

"Thank you. So much. I don't know what I'd do without you," Stan said, shrugging off her coat. "I stopped for the carob chips, too, but got sidetracked." She noticed the shadow that crossed Brenna's face before the girl turned away. "What's wrong?"

"Nothing's wrong." Brenna checked the white board Stan had hung in the kitchen listing all her orders. It was a simple system, but it worked for them. When one of them finished something, they wiped it off the list. And if Stan wasn't home, Brenna would always know what she'd worked on. "Do you want me to work on the granola next?"

Stan could tell Brenna was lying. Something was wrong, but she didn't want to push her. It might be none of her business. Or it might be about Helga. She let it go for the time being and consulted the board. The granola was top of the list, but that was more of an experiment for the clinic opening. Something to serve for the pets who came to the party. She wanted to make it without using wheat, and she was still thinking about the best way to do that. She'd planned to work on some sample batches before declaring a final product. But she had six other treat orders to fill by Friday. She hadn't even filled Brenna in on the wedding planning yet.

"I'm going to have to work on the granola later in the week," she said. "I need to get the Cheesy Apple Nips to Nicola before her next training class, and the order for the co-op needs delivery tomorrow. What I really need is another oven. And a delivery person. Hey, Jake said something about letting me use the pub oven. Did he mention that to you?"

"He did." Brenna smiled. "It's what I was shooting for. I kept telling him how busy you're getting. We definitely need more room. Hey—you never finished telling me about the new job."

"Thanks for the oven push. That's an awesome idea. Yeah, I'm sorry about last night. My mother and the mayor sidetracked me." She shook her head. "Want to sit?"

"Sure. I made coffee." Brenna grabbed two mugs

and poured them each a cup. "What was that about with your mother? That whole coaching thing? Yes, I was eavesdropping." She smiled mischievously.

"You're a lifesaver." Stan took a grateful sip of her coffee and sat. "Yes, the coaching thing. It's hard, because it's my mother. But Falco's so arrogant. I can't coach someone I don't like. I don't know if I can coach anyone. Never done it before. But I'd had a long day and I just wasn't in the mood. Especially after he insinuated he was smarter than me a hundred times over, but he'd take my 'tips.' Jerk."

She didn't mention how she'd just come across Dale Hatmaker in Helga's museum, allegedly at Falco's request. Brenna was likely to march over there and punch him, then go hunt Falco down.

"What did you say?" Brenna asked.

"I told him my tip was to stop disrespecting Helga's memory by handing her job off before we'd even paid tribute to her."

"Oh, snap." Brenna grinned. "Good for you."

"Yeah, well." Stan shrugged. "I'm sure my mother is furious with me. Again. But that's the story of my life. You want to hear about the new job?"

"You bet." Brenna sat with her own mug while Stan filled her in on the doggie wedding and all the pieces they had to help coordinate, along with the super-cool cake.

"That's amazing," Brenna said, but she didn't look as excited as Stan hoped. Helga's death was still fresh, Stan reminded herself. There was no law saying the girl had to be over it two days later.

"We're ten days away," she said. "I think this

will take up most of our time. Are you available for extra hours?"

Brenna burst into tears.

Stunned, Stan reached for a tissue from the box she kept on the counter. "Bren! What's wrong? If you don't want to help with the wedding you totally don't have to."

"I do," Brenna sniffled. "I really do. I love working with you and cooking for animals. And that sounds like so much fun."

"Then what's wrong? Aside from being sad about Helga. I get that."

"It's not that. Well, of course I'm sad about that." Brenna accepted the tissue and blew her nose. "I got offered a job."

"You did?" Despite the sinking feeling in her stomach, Stan kept her face neutral. It was inevitable. Brenna was finishing up her graduate degree and she needed a steady gig. "What kind of job?"

"At the nutritionist's where I'm interning. It's full-time." Her focus was on health, which was why the job with Stan had been a good fit.

Unless Stan was mistaken. "That sounds like it's right up your alley," she said. "Isn't it? I mean, you eventually wanted to work with people, right?"

"I guess," Brenna said, and started to cry again.

"Or not. Don't you like the place? Is the boss mean?"

"The place is fine. The owner is fine. I just think . . . I don't want to do it." Brenna took a deep breath. "There. I said it. I don't want to do it."

"Okay, then, you shouldn't. Simple. Right?" Stan asked.

"Not really. My dad is giving me a hard time about my 'lack of direction.' And the fact that I'm crashing at Jake's."

Stan frowned. "I don't think you have a lack of direction. And I don't get the sense Jake feels like you're 'crashing.' What did he say about it?"

"I didn't talk to him about it. He's got so much on his plate right now. But he always says he wants me to do what I want to do, and he tells me he likes having me there. I think he really just likes to keep an eye on me. But it's okay, because he's not a jerk. And, of course, he doesn't see anything wrong with working at the bar."

"That would be silly of him. And of course he loves having you there." Stan drummed her fingers on the table and thought about this. It wouldn't do to tell Brenna how much she needed her, because then she'd feel like she was letting Stan down if she chose another direction. "What *do* you want to do, Bren? Like in the future?"

"I don't know." She looked miserable.

"Look. You're twenty-six, right?"

Brenna nodded.

"If I had it to do over, I'd live my twenties a lot differently." Stan got up and poured them each a glass of ice water. "I would definitely do more of what I wanted, rather than what people thought I should do. You're doing what you want, and I think it's great. Are you making enough money?"

"Yeah, I'm saving a lot, too. And I'm already working in nutrition. With you."

Phew.

"But," Brenna continued, "I don't have health insurance."

"That's important. But," Stan added, "it's not as scary as it used to be. There are a lot more options now, and inexpensive ones at that. I don't know, Bren. I can't give you the answer. You have to think about what's best for you. Just make sure whatever it is, it's what *you* want to do, not what anyone else wants you to do. Make sense?"

"Yeah." Brenna tossed her tissue into the trash can and rose as the oven timer went off. "I'll think about it. We better get moving, though. We have lots to bake." She smiled. "And a wedding to plan."

After the marathon bake session ended and Brenna left to drop off Abbie's cookies, Stan called Char back, knowing this would be a long conversation. Char didn't disappoint, regaling her with the tale of Adrian Fox and his crew's dramatic, last-minute appearance at the B and B and THANK GOD they had been able to accommodate them. The four-story inn had five really nice guest rooms, in addition to Char and Ray's room at the very top of the house. A couple of the crew had to double up since they had guests already, but in all it was pretty good for a five-person party showing up with no reservation. He'd even slipped Char some extra cash for accommodating them on the fly. And with their presence, she was in the best position to hear all about their ghostly findings.

Stan did almost none of the talking. When she was finally able to hang up, she dug the newspaper clippings she'd absconded with from the historical society out of her bag. When she pulled them out, the envelope from the DNA place she'd signed for came out with them.

"Shoot," she muttered. She'd forgotten to call Amara to tell her about it. She found her cell phone and dialed Amara's number. The phone rang three times and went to voice mail. She left her a message, then carried her clippings and a glass of wine to her den. She turned on her gas fireplace, pulled the blinds, and tugged her favorite fleecy blanket over her lap. Her animal companions followed her and settled in their usual spots: Nutty on the back of the couch by her head, Scruffy next to her snuggled in the blanket, and Henry at her feet. The four of them agreed this was their favorite room in the house. She'd painted it a deep cranberry red, selected black furniture and bold cityscapes for the walls, and added bookcases along one side of the room. She had lamps of varying sizes placed around the room with low lights for ambience. She'd mounted a TV on the wall but hardly ever watched it. She could stare for hours into the fire. Especially since the cleanup was so easy—nothing like fighting with a real fireplace.

Stan laid the clippings out on the coffee table in front of her and put them in order by date. Satisfied she had the flow right, she dug in. The first one detailed Constantine's disappearance:

Boxer Missing, Fight Forfeited
By Arthur Pierce, Frog Ledge

Felix Constantine's no-show to a fight with local Tommy Hendricks has cost him a win, but family members say Constantine would've been there if he'd been able.

"I'm concerned," said Lucas Klein, Constantine's manager. "I haven't heard a word from him, which is not like him."

Klein asked that anyone with information about Felix's whereabouts contact him.

Felix Constantine arrived in Frog Ledge on Thursday to prepare for a Saturday fight with Hendricks. He was last seen at a party on Friday evening.

Then, the following Monday morning:

Body of Boxer Found in Library Basement
By Arthur Pierce, Frog Ledge

The body of missing boxer Felix Constantine was discovered Monday by a library worker who'd gone into the seldom-used basement to retrieve a box of supplies.

The worker, who declined to be identified, noticed a shoe on the floor. After investigating, Constantine's body was discovered and police were called. The medical examiner hasn't revealed cause or time of death at press time.

"We're heartbroken," said a tearful Arlene Constantine, Felix's mother. "Our son was a good, kind boy and didn't deserve this."

The story was accompanied by grainy, black-and-white photos of the library basement, as well as some

outside shots of the front of the building and all the
activity as the medical examiner and police removed
the body. She flipped to the next story, filed a few
days later. The headline said it all:

Murder!
Boxer's Death Declared a Homicide

The article went on to recount the medical examiner's ruling that Constantine had suffered blunt
head trauma. Estimated time of death was late
Friday night—consistent with the height of the
party. The investigating police detective—a local
Frog Ledger, which meant they had their own police
force at the time—promised a speedy resolution to
the case. And a plea by Constantine's younger sister:

> "Whoever hurt my brother, please come
> forward," said Carmen Constantine, sister
> of the deceased. "Give his family the closure
> we deserve."

No one had. But plenty of people could've been
involved.

And that's where it got interesting. A local group
of young adults was questioned, largely due to the
fact that one of them had keys to the library building and there was no sign of forced entry into the
basement. A girl named Alice Donahue's mother
was co-librarian, and therefore Alice had access to
the keys. It was intimated that the kids used the basement for harmless partying quite a bit, with no terrible incidences or repercussions. Until now.

Some of them were named on the record, likely

based on their ages. The names Maeve Johnson and Helga Cross jumped out at Stan. She didn't recognize the last name, but how many Helgas could have lived in town then?

So Maeve *had* known about the murder. Her confusion at the historical society when Stan asked about it could have been age related. Or she could have deliberately pretended not to remember.

Stan flipped through the other articles. Coverage continued for a few days, then gradually trickled off as leads became scarce. And that was it for Felix Constantine. Until now. Maybe he felt it had been long enough.

Stan set the articles aside and picked up her iPad. She Googled Constantine's name and sifted through the more modern references to other Felix Constantines. She found a Wikipedia piece about her subject that described him as an up-and-coming boxing star. All the other information about his death was the same as Stan had just seen. Apparently news items from sixty-odd years ago weren't as easy to find on the Internet as she'd hoped.

Just for the heck of it, she Googled "Tommy Hendricks Frog Ledge." She'd never heard that name around town. One reference came up—ironically an ad for Hendricks's fight with Felix Constantine. She deleted the "Frog Ledge" and searched again. There seemed to be a lot of Tommy Hendricks in the world, because forty-eight pages came up. She scrolled through the first few and found nothing interesting. She tried the middle, in case there was an obituary that might match. Then she tried the very end, thinking maybe since he was old it might be one of the last hits. Nothing. Unless he was going by Thomas Hendricks, or Tom. Or maybe he had changed his name altogether after the stigma of the murder had touched him.

Maybe Betty was on to something. Maybe someone else—someone still alive—*didn't* want the story to come out, as Abbie had suggested, and thought silencing Helga would keep it hidden. But someone had tipped Fox off about the murder in the first place. Why? Maybe there really was ghostly activity. Or maybe Fox and team's presence was a convenient way to bring this story back to life. And then there was the Dale Hatmaker piece, which wasn't fitting anywhere.

She gathered the articles and clipped them carefully together to return to their rightful file at the historical society. Someone around here had to know how these pieces fit together. Perhaps it was the ghost of Felix Constantine. But she had a hunch there were some living, breathing people who also may know more than they were telling.

Chapter 17

There was absolutely no reason why Stan had to be awake at five-thirty on Wednesday morning, but she was. Years of waking up early for jobs with traditional hours had rewired her brain so it fought sleeping past seven a.m., and usually woke her up a lot earlier. She didn't mind, usually. It gave her some good kitchen time, and she needed that this week with all her deadlines. Plus, cooking and baking was therapeutic for her. Some people found peace and meditation in their garden, or in a yoga center. Stan had her kitchen. She hoped the rituals would help her sort all the information in her brain.

She made coffee, let the dogs out, and sketched out a few recipes for secondary wedding desserts while she waited for them to do their thing. She was thinking peanut butter—that was always a hit—and perhaps something with oatmeal for the pupcakes. Then she'd have some regular treats, maybe broccoli and cheese and cinnamon apple, with some fancy decorations on top. Perhaps a batch with an English setter cookie decoration and another batch with a Shih Tzu? That could be fun. And something pumpkin flavored. She could hardly wait to get started.

After she let the dogs in and fed them and Nutty, she focused her attention on cooking while the pets camped out in their usual kitchen spots, awaiting samples.

First on the list today were the next few meals for the clinic opening. She had a few more batches of salmon and chicken for both dog and cat meals that she was going to customize with different veggies. She'd tested broccoli, zucchini, and squash so far on Nutty and the couple of neighborhood cats who loitered on her porch all the time. Nutty was the pickiest, and didn't care for zucchini. The other cats ate it, but loved the squash best. And all of them liked broccoli. She needed more cats to test her recipes on. Maybe Dede Richardson's cats. She made a mental note to ask her tomorrow when they got together.

As she cooked and assembled meats and fish with their vegetable counterparts and froze them, she contemplated the state of Frog Ledge. It certainly wasn't the calm before the spring season. She felt like the whole town was unsettled right now, between the tragedy of Helga's death, the ghost hunters, and now the dredging up of Felix Constantine's murder. Not to mention her personal problem with her mother, which she still hadn't figured out how to solve. She hadn't laid eyes on her mother since their encounter Monday night at McSwigg's, and knowing Patricia, she wouldn't. Her mother was the queen of the silent treatment. Stan wouldn't see her until she either sought Patricia out to apologize, or they came face to face at a public place.

Since she didn't feel she had anything to apologize for, Stan figured she'd see her at Helga's tribute on Sunday.

She wondered if Betty had gone back to work yet. Stan hadn't heard a peep from her since their strange conversation on Monday. Was she still operating under the assumption that Helga had been murdered? It bothered Stan that she had been so adamant but hadn't offered a reason or a suspect. Now, if she'd said Dale Hatmaker had threatened Helga recently or tried to bully her into handing over some duties, she might be more inclined to believe her. There was something about Hatmaker that Stan didn't like. But without anything to back it up, it seemed like a stretch. The timing of the ghost hunters and the rekindling of a sixty-year-old unsolved murder bothered her, too. It was enough to keep her cooking for days.

She called it quits around noon. Today's additions meant she was up to nine different dishes, and she had at least three servings of each. Time for a break. She needed a second freezer, at this point, as well as another oven. She'd already brought a bunch of meals to Amara's, who did have an extra freezer.

Stan made herself a smoothie and drank it while she thought about the strawberry wedding cake. She had to start testing the recipe for that. She also needed to find a heart-shaped cake pan, stat. Somehow that had escaped her list. With a mental smack to the head, she grabbed her iPad and searched for one online. How could she have forgotten that? It was the most important piece of the wedding. From her perspective, anyway. Now she'd have to shell out the cash for two-day shipping. She couldn't risk the pan not showing up on time.

Once she'd solved that problem by purchasing three sizes of heart-shaped cake pans—the different sizes would make gorgeous layers—she changed into jeans and a long-sleeved T-shirt, grabbed her coat, and headed out the door. She had a date with Cyril Pierce to talk about his dad's take on the Felix Constantine story. Although he didn't know it yet.

Stan knew from Char that the *Frog Ledge Holler* office was a one-room operation on the top floor of the local flower shop. She wondered if it had always been in the same location, even back in the time of Felix Constantine's death. She imagined Arthur as a young man—it wasn't hard, she just pictured Cyril with a cigar—hunched over an old typewriter, pounding out the details of Felix Constantine's tragic demise, a cloud of foul-smelling smoke enveloping him as he raced against his printing press deadline, those clunky glasses drifting down the bridge of his nose and his impatient nudges to get them back into place.

She parked on the street in front, squeezing in between leftover mounds of snow, and hurried upstairs. The door had a small but official-looking sign nailed to it with the paper's name. A business card holder on a tiny table held Cyril's card with his cell phone number. Stan tried the knob. Locked. She rapped on the door, listened. No sounds from inside.

Frustrated, she rapped one more time, just in case he was in the bathroom or something. Still nothing. Disappointed, she turned away, wondering if she should wait. But maybe there was breaking news to cover somewhere in town. She grabbed one of his cards and pocketed it, then headed back down the stairs. Shoving the front door open, she almost knocked over Jessie Pasquale. In official cop gear.

"Oh. Hi," she said, holding the door open awkwardly.

Pasquale stepped in with barely a nod, as if Stan wasn't dating her brother and turning up at family events regularly these days, including Christmas. With a gift. She didn't return Stan's greeting. Typical. Pasquale glanced up the stairs. "Coming from the *Holler*?" she asked.

Stan hesitated, though she wasn't sure why. "There's no one up there," she said, finally.

"What are you doing? Reporting breaking news?" Pasquale's voice had that slightest twinge of sarcasm—so slight it could be easily denied.

Well, Stan could be sarcastic, too. "I was looking for a bouquet of flowers," she said, nodding at the flower shop door. "Have a nice afternoon." She stepped out, letting the door bang shut behind her. Pasquale was always so abrupt. And sarcastic. Why did she care even if Stan had been at the *Holler*? And what did she want with Cyril? Usually the reporters chased the cops, not the other way around. Maybe she'd heard about the ghost hunters and wanted information.

Oh well, not her problem. She got back in her car. Before she pulled away from the curb, she fished Cyril's card out of her pocket and dialed the number. Voice mail. She left him a message asking him to call her, and headed home.

Chapter 18

Stan had barely let herself in the front door when Char pulled into the driveway behind her car. Extracting herself from her yellow Volkswagen Beetle, she waved. "I brought us lunch! Well, a late lunch," she amended. "Or an early dinner. Whichever you prefer."

Stan went over to help. "This can only mean you've been on a cooking spree. Impressing the paranormal guys, eh?"

Char smiled and tugged the bust of her green dress back up to a respectable level. "They love my cooking. Max especially. Max is his second in command. He does some technical thing, too. Do you know Max from the show?" Without waiting for Stan's answer, she continued. "He's originally from Mississippi, you know. He appreciates the taste of home. Here, honey. Take this." She thrust a shopping bag at Stan. "I'll grab the slow cooker. Shrimp étouffée. The fried catfish is in your bag. I had a huge shipment delivered. Don't smash the bag, there's a bottle in there." She winked.

Of course there was. Char never went anywhere without a drink at the ready. Stan worried about her friend's liver, but she knew Char would scoff at her concern and call her an uptight Yankee. Which she probably was. Char's New Orleans roots ran deep even after twenty-odd years in New England. Stan thought she still expected to see her beloved drive-through daiquiri shops on every corner and offer her guests a swamp tour with the B and B stay. She often wondered how much her friend missed her home. Especially in the dead of a New England winter.

"Come on in. I just got home," she said, holding the front door wide so Char and her slow cooker could fit through. The dogs immediately pounced on her, noses going a mile a minute.

"I brought you something, too, pooches!" Char followed her to the kitchen and set the food on the counter. She bustled about, turning on the oven, plugging in the slow cooker. "I made this today, so it's fresh. I want to keep it warm," she explained. "So, where've you been?"

"Sweet. I'm starving. I went to Cyril's office, but he wasn't there."

"Oh?" Char raised an eyebrow. "News to report?"

Everyone was so . . . curious around here. Actually, that was an understatement. They were down-right nosy. But she'd always found Char's nosiness charming. "No, a question for him. I stopped by the historical society yesterday to read up on the murder from 1949. The one Adrian mentioned. I found a couple of newspaper articles about it written by Arthur Pierce. I wanted to see if he had more information on it, or some old reports or something."

"Yes, Adrian mentioned that murder." Char shivered. "Such a terrible story."

"It is. But with the ghost hunters looking into it, I thought it might be interesting to see if Cyril had some insight, or maybe even his father. Do you think he still remembers that far back?"

Char laughed. "You mean, does he have Alzheimer's? You Yanks are much too polite. No, he doesn't have Alzheimer's. Cancer, yes, sadly, but brain problems, no. Where's the butter?"

Stan grabbed it from the fridge and handed it to her. "I figure, it's Jake and Izzy's building, I'd like to know what's going on. Adrian said I could go on the investigation."

"He *did*? Bless your heart." Char's eyes widened as she ladled étouffée into bowls over rice. Like clockwork, Nutty chose that moment to rise from his nap and leap onto the counter. Stan plucked him off into her arms. "That stuff makes me have anxiety attacks." Char fanned herself. "I can barely watch. But I force myself, because he's such a doll. I just hide when they do the scary things."

Stan laughed. She nuzzled her face into Nutty's fur. He purred, but sniffed the air. He wanted shrimp.

"You're really going to go?" Char handed her a bowl.

"Heck yeah," Stan said. "I can't wait. Not sure when they're doing it yet." She let Nutty down and accepted the food. Sniffed. "Yum. What's he like? Adrian?"

"He's a lovely guest. Very quiet. He and Max joined us for dinner last night. The rest of his guys went out looking for some action. I told him, honey, y'all are in the wrong place." She laughed out loud at her own joke and slipped the catfish into the oven to warm it up. "But he said that was okay, it would keep them busy and hopefully out of trouble."

They sat. Stan tasted her food. "This is amazing. Not that I expected anything different."

"Well, thank you, honey. I love when people enjoy my food. I made Adrian some catfish last night. He told me it was the best meal he'd had in a long time. I darn near swooned." She sat and picked up her spoon. "Raymond didn't say much. He doesn't like celebrities much. But that's okay. I like them enough for both of us. Anyway, Adrian did tell me there's a town meeting tonight. Unofficial, but he was asked to be available."

"Town meeting for what?" Stan had almost devoured the entire bowl.

"To discuss the investigation and its potential repercussions." Char rolled her eyes.

"It's private property," Stan pointed out.

"I know. The whole thing is absurd." Char slurped her food. "You're right, this is excellent. Anyway, I wanted to ask if you'd go with me. I thought we could show our support."

"Absolutely. You didn't have to bring all this food to get me to go with you, silly," she said.

Char waved her off. "I wanted to have lunch with you. And ask your advice."

"My advice?" Lots of people seemed to need her advice lately. She hoped it was an easier question than her mother's had been.

"Yes." Char pushed her plate away without finishing it. Totally unlike her. Stan noticed she hadn't mixed herself a drink with the bottle of vodka she'd brought either. "Something's wrong with Betty. She hasn't been herself since Helga died."

"That's to be expected. It's only been a couple of days." Trying to keep her tone nonchalant, Stan rose when the oven timer dinged and she went to take the catfish out of the oven.

"I know, but . . ." Char shook her head. "It's so unlike her. I've been trying to call her, and she's never got time to talk. She was supposed to go back to work yesterday, but she called in sick. She wasn't home when I stopped by. I'm worried about her."

Stan kept her back to Char while she served the fish. No sense telling her she'd been wondering the same thing just a few hours ago. Then she'd have to explain why.

"There's a piece of fish for Nutty and the dogs. With no breading," Char added.

Stan served the fish and put the animals' portion to the side to cool. "Have you talked to her at all?"

"Once."

"Did you ask her?"

"I did," Char said. "She got very defensive and said she was handling things the best she could. I told her she could come stay at the inn for as long as she wanted so she had company, since Burt is useless, but she declined. Do you think . . . do you think she's suicidal? Should I do something?"

"Suicidal? Betty? I don't think so." Stan felt guilty letting her friend worry like this, but Betty had sworn her to secrecy. Although aside from telling her Betty's theory about Helga, Stan wouldn't be able to offer any insights into her strange behavior either.

"I hope not. I researched the signs, and some of them are there. Not showing up for work, withdrawing from friends." Char ticked them off on her fingers. "She's supposed to be helping plan Helga's celebration, and I don't know if she's even doing that." She sighed. "She's just been . . . silent."

"Let's give it another day or so before you jump to that kind of conclusion," Stan said. "This was definitely a blow for Betty. Helga was like a mother to her. At least that's what she told me."

"She was, of course. But really . . ." Char's voice trailed off and she looked troubled.

"What?" Stan asked.

"I know Betty loved her like a mother. But the truth was, Helga wasn't always that nice to Betty."

"No?" Betty hadn't mentioned *that*.

"No, she was very critical of Betty. Even tore apart one of her historical displays at the library a month or two ago. Right in front of a roomful, too. They had a bit of a dysfunctional relationship, if you ask me." Char shook her head. "Honestly, Helga was like that with Sarah, too. Donald, never. But her daughter, and her 'adopted' girls? Very tough. I never understood mothers who acted that way. I don't have any babies, but if I did, that wouldn't be the way I helped them through life."

"So Betty and Helga didn't get along?" Stan asked slowly.

"Not all the time. It had its ups and downs. But recently they weren't doing so well. I think there was even a period last month where they weren't talking at all. I hope they made up before she passed. Who knows, maybe that's Betty's problem. She regrets the fighting." Char stood. "Thank you for letting me talk that out. I have to get back and get working on my dinner menu. You have a little extra fish and étouffée for the next few days. Keep the cooker until you're done."

"Thank you so much. This was awesome," Stan said.

"I'll pick you up for the meeting? Around six-thirty? We want to get a good seat."

"I'll be ready." Stan walked her to the door and watched her drive away as she worked this new piece of information into the puzzle. To hear Betty tell it, she and Helga couldn't have been closer. But they had their problems, too.

She'd no sooner shut the door when the bell rang again. Char must've forgotten something. But when she opened the door, Cyril Pierce stood there.

"Oh," she said, surprised. "You could've just called."

Cyril gave her a funny look, like he wasn't sure what she was talking about. "I need your help," he said.

Chapter 19

What could Cyril Pierce need her help with? And why was she suddenly everyone's Dear Abby? This was happening entirely too often.

"Come on in," she said, swinging the door wider. Cyril looked troubled. And he wasn't dressed in his reporter clothes. Meaning, he wasn't wearing his trench coat, which Stan didn't think she'd ever seen the man without, even in the dead of summer. Instead, he wore a regular winter parka. Stan could see frays in the fabric of the shoulders. He also wasn't carrying a notebook. She shushed the dogs, who had raced down the hall barking excitedly. Lots of company to entertain them today. Stan knew they were thinking, *Did this guy bring us food, too?*

"I left you a voice mail. That's why I thought you were here," Stan said, closing the door behind him. "I stopped by your office earlier."

"I haven't checked my phone." Cyril awkwardly wiped his big boots on her tiny welcome mat. "Is this, uh, a bad time?" Cyril waited while Henry and

Scruffy sniffed every inch of him they could reach. Then Scruffy sat down and *woo-wooed* at him.

Cyril looked at Stan warily.

She smiled. "She's friendly. The most she'll do is lick you to death. And, no, it's not a bad time. Would you like some shrimp étouffée? Or catfish? Char just came by with a feast."

"I saw her. I waited until she left. I'm not hungry, thanks."

He saw Char but waited until she left? That was weird. Should she worry about this guy? She didn't know Cyril well. Like most other people in town, she kind of took him for granted. She got annoyed with him at times, but that was a hazard of his profession. Used to seeing him at public events, she still didn't particularly enjoy when he approached her with a notebook and pen. Aside from that, mostly she didn't think much about him. And here she was, letting him into her house. The dogs weren't freaking out, though, which made her feel better. Besides, he looked depressed, not crazy as he followed her to the kitchen.

"Sit," Stan said, waving at the table. "Want coffee?"

That seemed to perk him up. "Sure." He hung his coat over one of the chairs and sat. He hesitated, then said, "I didn't mean to intrude. I just needed to talk to you alone."

"Okay," she said. "I'm listening." She set up the coffee maker and turned it on. He watched, tapping his fingers on the table incessantly. She tried to ignore the repetitive noise.

They both watched the coffee drip into the pot. Painfully slow, it seemed to Stan. She grabbed two mugs from the cabinet. "How do you take it?"

"Cream and sugar, please."

Stan drank hers black, but kept a small carton of cream on hand for occasions such as this. She got his mug ready. Finally, the coffee beeped. She filled both mugs and carried them to the table and decided to jump right in. Otherwise, this conversation would continue in its current black hole of nothingness. "So what do you need my help with?"

"Don't worry." He finally cracked a smile. "I don't need a quote."

"Well, hallelujah. Because I probably have no comment."

"I need a favor." He sipped. "This is really good coffee."

"Thanks. It's from Izzy's shop. I would think as a journalist you'd be all over good coffee."

He shook his head. "Too expensive."

"You have to treat yourself once in a while. Especially with coffee, being a newspaper guy. So, a favor? From me? What kind of favor?" Maybe he'd gotten a dog or cat and needed some food.

Cyril took a deep breath and adjusted his shirt. It was buttoned incorrectly, leaving one side hanging lower than the other at the bottom. "I need a reporter."

Stan frowned. "Okay. So what does that have to do with me?"

"The only person I know of who would know how to be a reporter is you."

"Me?" Stan stared at him, setting her mug down before even taking a sip. What the heck was going on around here? From her mother's ridiculous coaching request this week to last year's stint at the Happy Cow Dairy Farm, people seemed to think she was in need of a new profession. Or three. Did this whole town think she needed things to do because she "only" cooked dog biscuits for a living? "Cyril. What in the world are you talking about?"

He stopped fidgeting and leaned forward. "Maybe I'm not being clear. I need someone to write a story for the paper."

"Okay. I'm sure we could find you a reporter somewhere. You must know people from being in the business. Are you using your website to advertise? Social media? With the colleges around here, I'm sure you could find someone. Maybe an intern?"

He sighed. When he spoke again frustration tinged his voice. "No, you don't understand. I don't need a full-time reporter. I need someone to write a story. One. Tomorrow."

"Why? Are you going on vacation or something?"

"No, I don't take vacations. As a matter of fact, it's been about five years since I've left Frog Ledge. The paper has kept me busy." He frowned. "I really should do something about that."

"Yeah, you should," Stan said. "So, if you're not going on vacation, why can't you write your story?"

"I'll help with all the background stuff," he said, ignoring her question. "I promise I won't make it hard for you. I just need someone to do the interviews and carry the byline."

"Wait." Stan held up a hand. "I'm confused. Let's start over." This conversation required more coffee than she had in the house. And Cyril really needed a lesson in effective communication skills. But she wasn't about to say that, or next thing she knew she'd be coaching him, too.

Cyril sighed. He toyed with the handle of his mug, spinning it around and around on the table. "Sorry. I know I'm all over the place. The story is breaking news. Someone has been questioned in the death of Helga Oliver. The state police have reason to believe they're looking at a murder."

Stan's mouth dropped open, her mind racing. Had Betty finally come to her senses and gone to Pasquale? "What? Why?" she managed finally.

"The why is what we'll—you'll—have to find out. You're the best person in town to do it. Don't worry, I'll pay you. I can give you fifty dollars."

Thankfully she hadn't gone to journalism school. *Then* she'd be poor on top of everything else. "I still don't understand why you need me. Why aren't you doing it?"

"Because I can't. It's a conflict of interest." He looked her straight in the eye. "I'm the person of interest Pasquale questioned earlier today."

Chapter 20

"This is so silly. It's not like they can vote against the ghost hunt." Char leaned forward, her bulk dangerously straining the small folding chair in the meeting room at town hall. She'd dressed for the impromptu town meeting as only Char could—a black dress, red platform heels, and a scarf with skulls. Her bright orange hair had been tamed, if you could call it that, by a headband sporting voodoo dolls in various stages of being jabbed with pins. A treat from her hometown of New Orleans, Stan figured. Where else could you get authentic voodoo paraphernalia?

"Closest thing I had to something ghostly," she said with a shrug when she noticed Stan admiring it. "I wanted to show my support for Adrian."

The hastily convened meeting had drawn a crowd. After Fox and his team arrived in town, word spread fast. It spread even faster when the location of the investigation was confirmed.

Char had gotten most of the scoop. Dissenters—she couldn't confirm who but had her suspicions—had arranged the meeting, likely as a way to get names on a petition they could give to the mayor. Supporters heard about it and had worked virtually overnight to get the word out for their side. Both efforts were rewarded with a jam-packed meeting room in the basement of the town hall. Stan figured the meetings held there in the past had been of a different nature, perhaps town committees discussing their party's nominee, or a group exploring a new rule or regulation. She felt fairly certain this was the first time folks had gathered to discuss ghosts. Or at least the possibility of a ghost hunter coming to town to tell old secrets.

"A meeting like this seems typical around here," Stan said in response to Char's earlier comment. "Part of the reality that everyone is involved in everyone else's business. Speaking of that, I didn't get to tell you about bumping into Dale Hatmaker." She filled Char in on her visit to the historical society and subsequently the museum, and Dale Hatmaker's project to remove certain items.

"I don't trust that rat," Char said. "Who's directing him?"

Stan shrugged. "The mayor, sounds like."

"Can you mention it to your mother?"

"Ugh." She hadn't told Char about that debacle. "Actually, I'm not sure I can do that right now." She filled Char in.

"Good heavens," Char said. "Maybe I'll try to talk to her. Speaking of the rat Hatmaker, he's already here and in the front row." She pointed.

Stan spotted him through a gap in the growing crowd. He sat alone, on the opposite side of the room near the side exit, consulting a leather-bound notebook on his lap. She checked other faces to see who she knew. Cyril was there, notebook in hand. He didn't glance her way. They had agreed to keep her "freelancing" on the down low until the murder story was done. At least he was still free to cover this story. Pasquale hadn't thrown him in the slammer yet. Though he'd evaded her question on why Pasquale had pegged him as a suspect, other than citing his proximity to the museum early on Sunday morning. And, given the immediacy of this new development, she'd never even gotten to ask Cyril about his father, and Arthur's coverage of the Felix Constantine murder.

It had taken her a while to get on board with his harebrained scheme to hire her, but she'd finally agreed to help him with the story. Part of it was that small-town sense of duty. If someone had killed Helga—and it wasn't Cyril, which she certainly hoped it wasn't since she'd let him in her house and had agreed to work with him—then someone needed to follow the story. The other part was just plain self-serving. She wanted to know what was going on. The small-town mentality was contagious.

She didn't think Cyril was a killer. So that begged the question of who killed Helga, if indeed this was a murder. Same question she'd been asking Betty, to no avail.

She continued scanning the room. Don and Carla Miller sat a few rows in front of Stan and Char, all the way to the left, as far from the crowd as they could get. They looked like they were arguing, too. Carla's heated voice rose and fell, sending a few words back to Stan: ". . . should really put out a plea to stop this nonsense . . . enough going on around

here . . . detracting from your mother's memory . . ."
Miller angled himself away from his wife and didn't
look like he had a response.

Betty Meany was up front, next to Burt. At least
she'd made an appearance. Stan was surprised Burt
had come, given the level of engagement he seemed
to have in his wife's life. Betty, meanwhile, looked
stressed and agitated. Because of Burt maybe. Or
Helga and the ghost hunt. Maybe she'd tipped off
Pasquale and now she was worried about what she'd
started. Had she been the one to plant Cyril's name
as killer? Betty had been around the general vicinity
of the museum and the green early on Sunday
morning, too, setting up for the Groundhog Day celebration. If Cyril was there, of course she would've
seen him. But he couldn't have been the only one
there at that time.

The town cranks also joined the meeting. That
was Char's name for the regulars who showed up
to council meetings to complain—like Sam Oster-
ling and Mickey Cronin. Other attendees included
farmers and shop owners, soccer moms and teenagers. The teenagers were interesting. Either their
parents had dragged them, or they'd caught wind
of Adrian Fox's presence in town. And though it
was an unofficial meeting, Char had heard Tony
Falco planned to attend just to hear people's
thoughts on the subject.

Stan didn't see Amara anywhere. She'd tried calling her again about the DNA report still sitting on
her counter, but they hadn't connected. Amara was
crazed with getting the clinic ready to open.

Char riffled through her enormous bag and
pulled out her lipstick. "I still think it's a waste of

time. This has Edgar Fenwick written all over it," she said. "He's one of those change-haters. But he's a people-hater, really."

"A people-hater?" Stan chuckled. "Doesn't he volunteer at the War Office? He has to sort of like people."

Char scoffed. "He's afraid of anything new or different. Although around here it's the typical New England attitude—'Stay out of my business, but I want to know your business.' Do you agree?"

"I guess you're right," Stan said. "But really, this shouldn't be a big deal. It's not like Adrian and his team are going to go into every house in town, find some ghosts, and do a reality show."

"Ha! Now that would be hilarious. And devastating for half these folks." Char finished layering her lipstick and tossed the tube back in her bag.

Voices quieted as Adrian Fox, accompanied by Max from Mississippi, walked in. Haters could say what they wanted—Fox had presence. Stan swooned, just a bit, before snapping herself back to reality.

Char, on the other hand, fanned herself. "My, my, my," she murmured. "I love my Raymond, but I'll tell you what . . ."

Stan laughed. "It's worth it to have a few ghosts in town." She dropped her voice as the woman sitting in front of her turned to glare.

"You can poke fun all you want, but they'll turn our town into a circus! This should not be allowed." The woman looked like she was about to cry.

Next to her, a man rolled his eyes. "Lena, get a grip. It's a TV show. They'll be here for a few more days, do their thing, and it's over. We'll get new people coming to leave money in our town."

"We don't want new people!" Lena burst into tears. Char looked like she was about to offer her own opinion, but was interrupted by Tony Falco, who strode in and headed to the front of the room. Her mother, to Stan's surprise, was nowhere in sight.

"Folks, thanks for coming," Falco said, holding up his hands for quiet. "This isn't a town meeting, but the gentlemen who organized it asked if I would come and say a few unbiased words to all of you." He observed the audience, perhaps waiting to see if anyone would challenge him. An older gentleman Stan didn't recognize took out a handkerchief and blew his nose loudly. Falco waited a few seconds for the noise to cease, then continued. "We have some visitors in Frog Ledge, which is presumably why you're all here. First and foremost, they are guests in our town, and I would ask that you welcome them as you would anyone new who came to visit."

A couple of snickers, but mostly everyone behaved.

"Our town, as you all know, has a long and rich history. Our dear friend Helga, who left us this week, would tell you that any opportunities to learn about our past are important and should not be squandered. So whatever Mr. Fox and his team's investigation brings, please use this experience to learn. Get involved. Stop by the museum and read about the historical places in our town. See what secrets some of our buildings hold. There are stories here that have yet to be told.

"Now, I promise you that we, and Mr. Fox, are taking any concerns quite seriously. We have no interest in attracting unsavory people to Frog Ledge, or capitalizing on this opportunity. We don't want people to feel like their privacy is being invaded, although this is private property and we can't legally prevent them from doing this investigation, as long as the owners agree. Once again, Mr. Fox and his team have years of experience, and they have assured us they will do everything in their power to protect the people of Frog Ledge."

A smattering of applause went through the seats.

Falco nodded. "I'd like to thank Edgar Fenwick and Jeremiah Dunlap, who were kind enough to organize this meeting, and turn the floor to them. Thank you."

Char rolled her eyes. "Told you," she whispered loudly.

Falco took a seat in the first row as Edgar and Jeremiah rose and made their way to the front of the room. Edgar looked like he'd just rolled off a tractor at one of the local farms. He hadn't bothered to dress at all. His jeans had stains on one knee, and his shirt looked like it had been washed upward of a hundred times. The buttons strained against his portly frame.

The other man, Jeremiah, wore a suit that could have graced a red carpet somewhere. Even from the back of the room Stan could see the quality. She couldn't help but admire it. It was a bad habit she'd picked up from her days in corporate America. Spending so much time in conference rooms around the country, she'd learned to assess and identify fabrics and cuts, and still enjoyed a good suit. It had been a good way to stave off boredom during meetings.

As Edgar began to speak, the door flew open in

the back of the room. Izzy and Jake hurried in and took the seats behind Stan and Char. Jake looked like Izzy had forcibly dragged him there. Their entrance wasn't quiet—Izzy attracted attention wherever she went simply by virtue of who she was. Tonight with her jeans she wore high-heeled boots that clacked loudly, the noise accented by the chains dangling down the sides. She oozed confidence, knowing everyone in the room would turn to look. Izzy loved attention. Jake, on the other hand, looked like he was being dragged to the gallows, though he did flash Stan a smile as he sat down.

Izzy ignored the stares as she settled herself, then leaned forward. "What'd we miss?" she asked in a stage whisper.

"A whole lotta nothing, yet," Char whispered back, a tad too loudly. The two men at the front of the room fixed icy stares on them.

Stan reddened. "They're just getting started," she said in low tones to Izzy.

Izzy nodded and settled back in her seat.

Edgar Fenwick cleared his throat. "As I was saying. Thank you, Mayor. And thank you to all the concerned citizens who turned out here tonight. We wanted to give folks a chance to voice their opinions about the proposed ghost hunt. I'll stress that this isn't an official town meeting, but we thought it was important to have a forum available for people to talk this through. And we are"—he paused and cleared his throat—"fortunate to have Mr. Fox, the ghost hunter himself, in attendance." Edgar glared at Adrian Fox, who lifted his hand in a wave for the benefit of the audience. One of the teenagers sitting near Stan uttered a short, shrill screech. Stan could sympathize. Char fanned herself again.

Jeremiah Dunlap cut in. "Before we get started with comments, I'd like to provide context for everyone. The building on Main Street that housed the old Frog Ledge Library is the building in question. That building has been purchased by two of our locals, Jake McGee and Isabella Sweet." He waved his hand in their direction, maybe hoping they would stand. They didn't.

"That's *Izzy* Sweet, mister," Izzy said, not quite under her breath.

But Jeremiah heard her. He bowed slightly. "My mistake. *Izzy* Sweet. I don't want to speak for them, but it's my belief that she and Mr. McGee are committed to this building and want only good things for it and the town. They have employed a local contracting firm to take care of the cleanup and interior renovations, in accordance with town guidelines. This is no small job. In the midst of the construction, Mr. Fox and team received a tip that this property might be experiencing paranormal activity—"

"Where'd the tip come from?" a man from the front row interrupted.

Edgar opened his mouth, but Jeremiah jumped in first. "That's not a matter that we would be privy to. If Mr. Fox wants to address the question, he's welcome to, but his firm is not required to disclose where they get their information."

Fox stood up. "Thank you, Mr. Dunlap," he said. "The tip was provided anonymously. Regardless of the tip and who made or didn't make it, my team does extensive research on any property we're called to investigate, as I've explained to some of you already. We take our work very seriously. As many of you know, New England is a hotbed of paranormal activity, by virtue of its age and its past. So immediately I knew it wasn't far-fetched to believe something was here. And on a property like this with a recorded history, we were able to validate the potential for spirit activity. So we came out to explore it further."

He went to sit again, but someone else called out a question. "What kind of information did you find?"

"Mr. Fox, perhaps it would be easier if you came up front," Jeremiah said.

Edgar glared at his co-presenter. Jeremiah ignored him.

"I'd be happy to." Fox rose and walked to the front of the room, dazzling the teenagers in his path with his pearly white smile. He stood between the two men. Edgar Fenwick immediately moved away, as if Fox had the plague.

"The first thing we do when we get a tip is exactly what you might do if you wanted to get quick background on something—we Google it," Fox began. "We had the address and the background story, so we simply did a search on those keywords." He paused. "And what came back was an unsolved murder. That's really what brought us to town."

Chapter 21

A buzz made its way through the crowd, escalating to a higher pitch as comments and questions traveled. Stan leaned forward in her chair so she wouldn't miss a word.

"Is this the old story about the boxer?" "Does that mean the spirit is angry?" "Is it trying to hurt people?" "Do we need an exorcist?" Voices grew louder.

Fox held up a hand, asking for silence. The noise level immediately dropped. "First, just because someone was murdered, it doesn't mean they are angry or trying to retaliate. In many cases, the death happened so quickly and unexpectedly that the spirit might not know he or she is really dead. Usually when that happens, they stay in a place that's familiar to them, like their home. Or the person may simply be stuck.

"I had the pleasure of speaking with your town historian before her tragic death, and she had an enormous amount of knowledge about this particular event. She shared with me the pieces that were

written on the murder, from the time it happened to entries in local history books."

Fox spoke with Helga? Stan and Char exchanged glances. That was interesting. Stan was dying to get Jake's reaction, but she didn't want to turn around.

"Luckily, there's a wealth of information available here, through all the people so dedicated to the town's history," Fox continued. "People like Betty Meany, your librarian. I'm sure she'd be happy to help anyone interested to find out more about this story." He looked at Betty. She remained frozen to her seat.

Char looked at Stan. "See what I mean about Betty? She certainly looks like she doesn't want to be here." Char frowned. "She usually doesn't miss a chance to direct people to the library or tell them stories. And you know she loves murder stories." In her free time, Betty'd been known to watch marathons of *Murder, She Wrote* and all the *CSI*'s ever made.

Maybe she is too worried about real-life murder stories. Stan kept her face neutral.

From a seat on the side of the room, Dale Hatmaker bristled. "I'm the historian-elect," he said, rising to his feet. "I can certainly share the story of the murdered boxer."

"Boxer? That's mad cool." This from a teenaged boy who had been slumped so far down in his chair he'd practically been on the floor.

"How dare you!"

The voice came from the front of the room. Stan caught a glimpse of Helga's boyfriend, Gerry

Ricci. He shook his fist at Hatmaker. "You're not an elected anything, you old—"

Betty cut in gracefully, glaring at Hatmaker. "Helga was the expert. And since there's no voting process for town historian, I'm not sure how you can be the historian-elect."

Fox looked amused by the exchange, but Hatmaker was getting hot. "It's an appointed position, and the mayor—" Hatmaker began, but Falco, whether to try and smooth things over or to save his own face, had the wherewithal to jump in. He didn't look at Don Miller, who sat stone quiet as the argument flew around him.

"Dale, no one's disputing your ability. I think Mr. Fox was put in touch with Helga and found her expertise valuable, that's all. We should let Mr. Fox continue."

"That's *all*?" Betty turned on him, too, looking murderous.

Behind her, Izzy laughed. "This is getting good. Who's gonna throw the first chair?"

"Folks," Fox interrupted. "I'm sure there are many, many people in town who could offer perspective and history on so many things, it would take me months to talk with them all. Everyone's perspective and offering is valuable.

"Now, as far as the investigation goes, I've been working closely with Izzy Sweet." His eyes scanned the crowd for Izzy. The rest of the room turned to look, too.

"Guess I'll make it easy on him." Izzy rose and squeezed past a stone-faced Jake. She sauntered to the front of the room to join Fox and flashed a smile at the audience. "I'm behind this all the way," she

said. "I'm totally committed to Frog Ledge, and I can't wait for the bookstore to open. I think it's best to clear up any mysteries first, that's all."

"Are you going to move the café into the bookstore?" a lady from the third row called anxiously.

"I don't have any plans for that right now," Izzy said. "But let's keep the conversation to ghosts for now, shall we?"

"I'll betcha Jake doesn't agree with this nonsense." A man sitting up front whom Stan didn't recognize called out that comment. A challenge. "Jake knows this'll bring the wrong kind to our town. We'll have worse troubles than a ghost."

"Amen," a woman with hair wrapped in a severely tight bun and an even more severe face, chimed in. "Once those gangs come in, there's no getting them out. It doesn't take much."

Stan stifled a giggle. Gangs? These guys gave "uptight New Englander" a whole new meaning.

Behind her, Jake muttered something that sounded like a curse. She turned and caught his eye, sending him telepathic instructions on solidarity and united fronts. He stood up. He didn't look at Izzy or Fox. "I'm satisfied with Mr. Fox's proposal, and if the workers on the site feel this is warranted, then I have no objections." He sat back down. The guy in the front had no further comment.

Stan turned and smiled at him. "Nice job," she whispered.

"Yeah, I'm a stand-up kinda guy," he said. "I have to get back to the bar. Can you stop by later?"

"I'll try," she promised.

He looked puzzled, like he wanted to ask why she had to try, but the meeting was ramping up again.

Edgar Fenwick, who'd been brooding behind Fox the entire time, stepped back into the spotlight. "Can we get back to the issue at hand?" he demanded. "We need to talk about how the town feels about allowing this circus."

"Amen!" Lena from the next row agreed.

Fox smiled, but Stan could see a glimmer of annoyance. "My team doesn't run a circus, we run a ghost hunt," he said, while Cyril scribbled furiously in his pad.

"When is the investigation?" someone called out.

"Friday evening," Fox answered. "It is not open to the public."

From the corner of her eye, Stan saw Jake slip out. She wanted to get up and follow. Take him aside, tell him everything from Betty's crazy talk to Cyril's crazy favor. Maybe they could take that vacation until this was all over. But that was a fantasy. He needed to attend the funeral, help plan the celebration, and run his bar. And she needed to write a story about a murdered woman. And plan a doggie wedding. She remained seated and watched her opportunity slip away.

"Does anyone have any other questions for me? Concerns?" Fox asked.

"No, but I'd like to offer my help."

All heads turned to the back of the room as Sarah Oliver walked in. She wore a flowing navy blue skirt with little silver moons on it. A matching scarf contained her wild hair. Dozens of silver chains, all in varying lengths, were draped around her neck. Like clockwork, "Gold Dust Woman" took over Stan's brain.

Sarah moved to the front of the room and bowed slightly to Adrian. "My name is Sarah Oliver."

Stan held her breath. What was Sarah going to do now? Her eyes automatically traveled to the front of the room where Don and Carla Miller sat with a couple of other council members. Carla had one hand partially shielding her face, most likely in embarrassment. Don had no expression whatsoever. The guy was a master.

Adrian Fox regarded Sarah with open curiosity. "Ms. Oliver, a pleasure to meet you. What help would you be interested in offering?"

Sarah reached the front of the room and offered a stiff curtsy to Fox. "Mr. Fox, I'm a medium."

That sent Don's non-expression right out the window. He rose, murder written all over his face, his bald head shiny with sweat. "Sarah, what do you think you're doing?"

Sarah ignored him. "Helga Oliver was my mother," she explained to Fox. "I feel she'd like to finish telling her story, and your investigation will be important to that." She smiled at him. "I think we can make a great team."

Stan sat back in her chair as the buzz picked up again within the room. Izzy leaned forward. "What the heck is she talking about?" she muttered. "What story does Helga need to tell?"

"I have no idea," Stan said. And she didn't—there were too many missing pieces. But the pieces she had so far did not paint a sunny picture. Especially with the new revelation that the police were actively pursuing Helga's death as a murder. The story could be how Helga was killed because of what she knew about Felix's death.

Chapter 22

In her dream, two dogs Stan didn't recognize dressed in wedding garb pranced around the town green. There were no humans in sight, but there were hundreds of dogs and only one cake, which the wedding couple didn't seem to like. The pup-cake desserts were missing, and she ran frantically around the green looking for them. Instead, she found a groundhog behind a tree eating a cookie, but it wasn't hers.

"Why aren't you eating my cookie?" she asked the groundhog (probably Lilypad, since that was the only groundhog she knew of that ate cookies), but got no answer. When she ran back to the crowd of dogs, Sarah Oliver stood in the middle of the pack, holding a crystal ball. "My mother's dead," she kept saying, and the dogs were barking like crazy and wouldn't stop. . . .

Stan's eyes flew open. It was her own dogs barking, not the dogs in her crazy dream. Which she hoped wasn't a premonition of how the real "wedding" would go. But before she could worry about the wedding, she had to get through today's funeral. After Sarah Oliver's hijacking of last night's town meeting, the funeral was sure to be a happening event. She'd certainly thrown the remainder of the meeting into an uproar.

After her offer to help Adrian Fox, the whole room had erupted into pure mayhem. Stan imagined there were a few different things going on—the camp who thought Sarah was nuts, the camp who thought the whole thing was nuts, and the camp who now wanted to go on a ghost hunt and be part of a seance. Edgar Fenwick's friends had finally escorted him out of town hall before he had a heart attack. Betty had vanished, too. Don Miller had refrained from physically dragging his eccentric sister from the building, but Stan figured the after-conversation had not been pleasant. Char had soaked up the whole scene to discuss at the inn, and Izzy sat back and watched it all with the same amusement one would watch a particularly bad reality show—a train wreck you couldn't help but remain glued to, glad it wasn't your life.

But if Sarah really was on to something—if Helga did need to tell her story, and it was related to this ghost hunt—things could get interesting.

The dogs were still barking up a storm downstairs. Stan looked at the clock. Six-ten. A ruckus at this hour couldn't be good. She got up and threw on her fuzzy robe and slippers. The house still had a chill to it, which meant it hadn't warmed up at all outside. Racing downstairs, Nutty right behind her, she found the dogs at the front door, wooing and barking up a storm. She peeked through the blinds in the hall window. Didn't see anyone. Perhaps Cyril had delivered another paper with his special report on the town meeting. She pulled the door open.

No paper, but there was a package. A regular, manilla envelope, oversized, propped against the door. Stan stuck her head out and looked around. No one in sight. She picked up the package gingerly. It was kind of heavy. She flipped it over. It hadn't gone through the mail, because it was blank. Someone had clearly just dropped it off. She shook it. One piece, whatever it was.

She looked at the dogs. "What do you think?"

Scruffy wagged and stomped her feet. Henry laid his face on her leg. He looked concerned. "It's probably okay," she told him. He sighed as if to say, *Your choice, Mom, I'll support you.* She stepped inside with the envelope and shut the door, then ripped the flap open. Pulled out a large hardcover book, almost unwieldy in its size and shape. A photo of an old map of the town adorned the cover. *Frog Ledge: Connecticut's Revolutionary Headquarters,* by Helga Oliver. Helga's photo, professional and unsmiling, was in the lower left corner. Stan frowned. Someone had left her Helga's book under cloak-and-dagger circumstances. Why not come over at a reasonable hour, ring her bell, and hand her the book? Unless it was part of the upcoming celebration of Helga's life. Betty had said it would be a big deal. Maybe this was the beginning—everyone got a copy of her book. But at six a.m. on a Sunday?

She flipped through it. A notepaper stuck in the middle caught her attention. There was nothing written on the paper, but the story it marked gave her a chill: "Death of a Boxer," by Helga Oliver. Coincidence? Doubtful. Plus, there were way too many coincidences going on around here. No, someone wanted her to read this. Now. Who and why?

She let the dogs out, made coffee, and picked up the book again. Helga's article was a two-page, slightly rambling account of the Felix Constantine saga. The story started at the party where Felix was last seen. Hosted at the former Trumbull Hotel on Main Street, which now housed apartments and shops on the ground floor, the party was "an elegant affair, attracting the who's who of Frog Ledge and neighboring towns." Boxing had apparently been a big-deal sport that brought with it a certain level of sophistication.

Helga described Felix as "strong, dashing, and quite charming," which suggested she'd at least made his acquaintance. Stan scanned the description of the room, the elaborate outfits and the fancy menu. Helga detailed all the "important" people in town who attended—Felix's nationally known coach, the town government officials, even a reverend from one of the local churches. And the boxer Felix was supposed to fight—the Frog Ledge favorite named Tommy Hendricks.

Whom Helga identified as her boyfriend. Stan hadn't picked *that* up from the newspaper articles she'd read.

"Well, well," Stan said out loud to the empty room. "The plot thickens." So Helga had been in the mix the night of the murder. And her boyfriend was Felix's contender. Maybe they'd fought early. Perhaps over a woman.

Stan did the calculations in her head. Helga was eighty-seven when she died, so in 1949 she would have been twenty-one years old. Just because they didn't look like it when they were almost ninety didn't mean they weren't wild and crazy kids in the 1940s. A lot could've happened at that party.

The story wrapped rather abruptly.

> *At some point during that party, Felix Constantine stepped outside for a smoke. He wasn't seen again until his body was found in the basement of the nearby Frog Ledge Library farther down Main Street nearly three days later. No one ever knew what happened to him, but he will always remain one of Frog Ledge's biggest mysteries.*

No mention of murder, or the fact that the case had remained unsolved all these years. No speculation on who did it or why. Just that his body was found. Odd. She flipped through the rest of the book, looking for any other relevant stories. There were none. Out of curiosity she opened to the inside cover to look at the copyright date: 1991. More than twenty years ago. Her eyes fell to the bottom of the page. Someone had written their initials in deliberate, blocky handwriting: *ACP.*

Stan frowned. ACP. Arthur C. Pierce?

Chapter 23

Helga Oliver's "private" funeral services over-flowed into the Figaro & Sons Funeral Home parking lot. Stan shouldn't have worried about her attendance—it looked like half the town had showed up anyway.

"Big crowd," she commented to Jake as they waited to get near the guest book.

"Yeah," he said. "I guess the invites got a little out of hand."

"A little?" His mother appeared at their side. "Hi, Stan." Jake's mother looked more like his sibling than his mother. She had red hair like Jessie, but shorter and wavy, and youthful, cream-colored skin. Not a freckle to be had on either her or Jessie, as some redheads were plagued with.

"I'm not sure what happened here, but I bet Carla took over," Nora continued. "If it was up to Don, it would've just been the immediate family, us, and Gerry's kids. But you know how she is. Everything's for show." She shook her head. "Unbelievable."

"Don't worry about it," Jake said. "Nothing you

can do. If people need to pay respects that badly, let them."

Nora smiled and squeezed her son's arm. "He's good for the soul, isn't he?" she said to Stan.

Stan smiled, feeling her cheeks redden. "He is."

"I saved you two seats," Nora said. "Jessie and Brenna are here already. Come find me." She disappeared back into the crowd.

"She'll fixate on this all day," Jake said.

"Would Carla really do that? Go against what Helga wanted?"

He shrugged. "I don't think she sees it that way. My mother's right. Carla's big on perception. She probably didn't want people saying her family kept folks away. Who knows. There are bigger things to worry about. Like the fact that Helga's gone."

He still looked so sad. Stan wished she could make it better. Instead, she feared she was about to make it worse with the story she had to write. The one she still hadn't told him about. She should just tell him. But that was so inappropriate right now. Maybe right after the funeral? But she had to get to Jessie and do the interview. There might not be enough time.

Guilt had her scanning the room so she wouldn't have to look at him. Doing so, she caught sight of Betty Meany a few people back in line. "I'll be right back," she said, and slipped away.

"Stan!" Betty brightened when she saw her and motioned her to come closer. Thinking she was about to get a hug, she obliged. Instead, Betty hissed, "Can you believe the gall of that girl?"

Bewildered, Stan looked around. "Who?"

"Sarah! Her little show last night at the meeting. Her behavior is so *appalling*. She's worked out a deal with him. It's the only logical explanation."

"A deal with whom?" Stan asked. She felt like an owl.

"That shyster Fox, of course. He had to offer her big bucks."

"You think they staged that? Come on, Betty. I didn't get that sense at all."

"Why has she got her nose in Jake and Izzy's business?" Betty continued, like she hadn't even spoken. "This isn't about her mother. This is about her own interests. Shameful!"

"I don't know," Stan said. "Maybe she can help with the whole ghost thing. Put it to bed if there's nothing to it."

"Of course there's nothing to it." Betty scoffed at the thought. "It's silly. There are no ghosts there. The past is the past. If you ask me, they should leave it alone."

"I don't know, Betty. I disagree," Stan said. "If a story needs to be told, it should be told." *And you should own your part of that,* she wanted to add, but didn't.

Betty didn't like her comment. Stan could tell by the narrowing of her eyes and how thin her lips got, nearly disappearing into her face. "Humph," was all she said.

Char and Ray stepped up in time to fill the awkward silence. Char looked relieved, presumably to see Betty was still alive, then shifted her gaze anxiously to Stan, probably for an assessment of Betty's state of mind. Stan imperceptibly shrugged.

"Hi, sweetie," Char said, enveloping Betty in a Char-hug, nearly cutting off her airways. "How are you holding up?"

"I'm fine," Betty said, disentangling herself.

Char looked hurt but tried to hide it. "Will we see you after at Gerry's house?"

"I doubt it," Betty said. "Lots to do for Sunday."

"Well, now, that's not very neighborly," Ray said cheerfully.

"I don't have time this week to be neighborly," Betty said, and took a step forward when the line moved so she wasn't facing them anymore.

Her behavior puzzled Stan. She'd never seen Betty so snippy. Not even to people who upset the library's equilibrium, like the teenagers who got rowdy or the people who spilled their drinks on books or tables. But especially not to her friends.

Stan glanced back to the front of the line. Jake had nearly reached it. "I'll see you all later," she said, squeezing Char's arm.

"Okay, honey," Char said.

"Are you coming to Gerry's?" Ray asked.

"No, Jake's got to be at the bar early after all and he's dropping me off at home." She didn't mention what she was doing after that—interviewing Jessie Pasquale about her person of interest.

Char and Ray went to the back of the line and Stan headed up front to join Jake in signing the guest book and finding his family. On the way, she passed the hallway leading to the restrooms and decided to pop in and freshen her lipstick. As she exited, she slowed at the sound of voices on the other side of the door.

"You better get out of here." Gerry Ricci's slightly wobbly voice. "You don't belong here."

"Sir, with all due respect—" It sounded like Cyril. Had he come to cover the funeral? Or to pay his respects?

"I said get out!"

Stan pushed the door open and stepped into the hallway. Cyril and Gerry both turned to her. Gerry glared. Cyril looked upset. Gerry looked from her to Cyril, wagged his finger at him once more. "Don't let me see you near that coffin or that grave!" He hobbled away with his cane.

Stan looked at Cyril. "What's that about?"

Cyril shook his head. "Nothing. I'm not wanted here, so I'm going to go. Call me after you do the interview." And he slipped out the side door, leaving Stan staring after him in bewilderment.

She slipped back to Jake's side. "Hey," he said, squeezing her hand. "Everything okay?"

"Fine," she said.

"Let's go find our seats."

Once she and Jake sat, she checked out the rest of the attendees. The War Office volunteers were present, dressed in Revolutionary clothing. Maeve Johnson and Edgar Fenwick were part of that group. Gerry Ricci sat in the front row. He sat ramrod straight, but Stan could see him dabbing at his eyes with a handkerchief. Did he know Cyril was a suspect in Helga's death? Was that why he told him to leave? But how would Gerry know that, if it was still on the down low?

Interestingly enough, Dale Hatmaker sat in the third row. Probably to keep up appearances. Or to do more petitioning for the job. Unless he was responsible for Helga's death and was now coming to see the aftermath. Carla and Don Miller and their two little boys sat in the front row. Stan didn't see Sarah Oliver yet, and the service was due to start in five minutes.

The reverend walked into the room, ceasing all conversation. As he started to speak, Stan saw Sarah slip into the room alone and take a seat in the last row. Stan watched, feeling sorry for her, until Sarah noticed she was staring. She turned around and forced herself to pay attention.

The reverend, a kind-looking man, kept his talk short. He spoke about Helga's commitment to the town, her passion for its history, and her dedication to educating others. "But first and foremost, Helga loved her family," he said. "Not only her two children, her son's family, and her companion, Gerry, but her extended families. Really, she considered this entire town her family, and the town reciprocated."

He spent a few more moments extolling her virtues, then invited everyone to join him at the cemetery. Stan checked her watch as they filed out of the funeral home. Cyril had already stressed her deadline. "We need to go to press tonight by eight," was his last message, urging her to catch up with Pasquale as soon as possible.

Well, Pasquale was here. And she'd definitely go to the cemetery. Stan certainly wasn't going to interview her there, so she'd have to wait until Pasquale went back to her office. Hopefully she wasn't taking the rest of the day off to go to Gerry's house. She certainly didn't want to do the interview there. And she had to get to Dede Richardson's house by four to meet the dogs.

Stan and Brenna gathered outside at Brenna's parents' truck. Nora and Paul were already in the truck. They were all riding to the cemetery together once the hearse was ready to go.

"I'm glad this is almost over," Stan said.

"Me too," Brenna said. "How's Betty holding up?" she asked Stan.

Stan shrugged. "She seems stressed. And sad." That was the truth, anyway.

She nodded. "Understandable."

The hearse pulled around front, hazard lights blinking. Jake's mom knocked on the window, signaling them to get in. They fell into the line behind Don Miller's family and began the slow procession the three miles to the cemetery.

The rest of the service passed in a blur. The pall bearers, including Don and Jake, carried the coffin to its final resting place in the Frog Ledge Cemetery as everyone gathered. Stan let her mind and gaze wander around. Even in the dead of winter, this cemetery was a beautiful place. Stan often rode her bike through here in the nice weather. The spot where Helga would rest was right under a grand oak tree.

She kept one eye on Dale Hatmaker. He stood off to the side a bit, properly solemn, aloof from the rest of the funeral-goers. Betty stood near Jake's parents, her head bowed, as the reverend said his final words. Then everyone lined up to leave a flower on the coffin and began filing away, back to their cars. Stan left her flower, then stepped off to the side to wait for Jake and his family to finish their good-byes. As she stood there, the reverend stepped up to Betty and hugged her.

"I'm so sorry for your loss, Betty," he said. "But know that Helga thought of you like a daughter."

"I know," Betty murmured, wiping a fresh tear away.

"She used to tell me," the reverend continued, "there's nothing I wouldn't do for Alice Donahue and her beautiful daughter. So rest assured, she'll be looking out for you from heaven." With one last sympathetic squeeze, he walked away.

Alice Donahue. The young woman mentioned in the story of Felix Constantine's murder. The one with keys to the library. Alice Donahue was Betty Meany's mother.

Which meant Betty also had a personal connection to Felix Constantine.

Chapter 24

Despite all the jobs Stan held growing up, going through college, all the way up until she landed in corporate America, she'd never actually done any journalism work. She'd always seen it from the other side—the public relations side, as the company spokesperson keeping the nosy media at bay. It had been a fun job. Challenging at times, especially when people misbehaved versus when stock markets or job markets or other externally controlled variables misbehaved, but never boring.

Heck, she should just be honest—she'd loved being a spin doctor. Today she realized just how different the two jobs were as she mapped out her plan of attack to tell Frog Ledge exactly what was going on in the Helga Oliver situation. In her old job, she'd do whatever she had to do to protect the company or person, where now she had to figure out the best way to tell the truth—including whatever down and dirty scandalous pieces the truth was composed of.

This wasn't going to go over well. Her relationship with Jessie Pasquale was tenuous at best, despite her standing with Jake. And now she had to show up and demand answers to a question most people didn't realize was even under consideration. Two, actually. Why was Cyril Pierce a suspect in Helga Oliver's death? And the even bigger question: When and how did this become a murder investigation?

Maybe she should just call Jessie.

Even as the thought ran through her head, she knew it wouldn't fly. Real journalists didn't hide behind their phones. They went out and chased down the story, no matter how uncomfortable that story was. That's why reporting in big cities was probably easier. Or reporting in cities where you didn't actually live. Here, everyone would know by tomorrow exactly what she was doing, and they would all want to pull her aside and ask her questions. Expect her to spill the beans. Either that or avoid her like the plague. She saw it all the time with Cyril. People either wanted his ear for something stupid or they crossed the street when they saw him walking. Now she'd get to see what it was like.

On the bright side, since moving to Frog Ledge, she had a lot to add to her résumé in case she ever needed to look for work again. Now she could add journalism. If she was ever in the market for another corporate job, maybe she could apply to CNN.

After Jake dropped her off from the funeral, Stan went upstairs and dressed in her newly designed reporter outfit: jeans, a black turtleneck shirt, a sweater, and black boots. She didn't have a long black trench coat like Cyril. Not that she wanted one. Personally, she thought it made him look like the Unabomber. She pulled her knitted black cap over her hair, put a pair of hoops in her ears, and regarded herself in the mirror. She could probably pass for a college student, although she wasn't sure why it was necessary to look like a college student to have a reporting gig. Probably because of the salary.

She threw all her stuff, including the new package of steno pads Cyril had given her with the assignment (he refused to use technology like iPads when reporting), into the messenger bag she'd bought a few years ago for a trip to California. She'd used the bag only that one time. It wasn't the approved corporate America bag. She'd held on to it with a feeling it would come in handy again someday. Slinging it across her body, she took one more look in the mirror. Henry, watching her, thumped his tail.

"You think it's okay?" she asked him.

He whined in answer. Scruffy heard him and raced over, *woo-wooing*. She hated to be left out of anything.

"I think she's going to throw me out," Stan said. "But that's okay. If she wants to look bad in the paper, that's her choice." She was kidding herself, really. No one took the *Frog Ledge Holler* that seriously, despite the work Cyril put into the paper week after week. But if this really had turned into a murder investigation and other news outlets got ahold of it, Pasquale would have to get real serious about her responses—or at least her superiors would. It would be good practice.

"I'll be back soon, guys. Wish me luck." She grabbed a jacket and her car keys, and headed to the garage. She backed her Audi out of the driveway and headed toward Main Street and the town hall. It struck her that most reporters probably weren't driving Audis. She'd never seen Cyril drive anything but his bicycle. It made her feel like a fraud.

She reached the town hall in her usual three minutes. It was nearly two. This way, she'd given Jessie time to regroup and eat lunch after the funeral ended. She parked in the nearly empty parking lot out back, scanning it for the cruiser. She was in luck. There it was, parked in its usual space. Stan got out, checking one last time for her notebooks and a pen, and walked toward the building. As she reached the door, Cyril popped into view on the other side and pushed it open for her.

"About time you got here," he said, swinging the door wide. His self-imposed "newsman" uniform was back in place, and he looked a thousand times better than he had that morning at the funeral parlor. He even wore a jaunty fedora. It looked worn and tired, kind of like the old-time newsmen who made them famous.

Stan stepped in, eyeing him suspiciously. "What are you doing here?"

"I thought you might need some last-minute coaching." Cyril leaned close to her ear. Stan resisted the urge to recoil. "Trooper Jessie is in her office with the door shut. She just got back. Perfect timing, actually." He rocked back on his heels and regarded her with a somber look. "So, tell me what you're going to ask her."

Stan sighed. "I'm not in the mood to role-play, Cyril. And I think I can handle asking a few questions. You wanted me to do this, remember? I'm the only one and all that? Not that I don't think it's a conflict of interest for me, too. After all, I am dating her brother."

Cyril squinted at her, then waved her concern away. "Unless he's got something to hide, that doesn't matter. It's not just about asking questions. You have to ask the right ones. So tell me what you're going to ask when you go in there."

"I'm going to ask her if she's looking into Helga's death as foul play."

"No."

"No?"

"You're going to ask her WHY she's looking into Helga's death as foul play. That way you're not giving her the opportunity to shut you down with a one-word answer. Like 'no.'"

"How can she say no?" Stan asked. "She's been questioning you!" She lowered her voice as a woman walking past gave her a strange look. She couldn't help it. He was such a strange man. The potential murderer thing notwithstanding.

"Yeah, but she hasn't arrested me, so that's not public news yet. If she doesn't want to answer you, she will find every way in her power to evade you. She's very good at being a police spokesperson. They love to give you a 'no comment' until the PR guy can figure out his positioning statement. Sorry," he said when her eyes darkened. "I know you were a PR person. No harm meant."

Stan exhaled loudly. "It's fine, Cyril. I'm going to go in there and get the best story I can. Is there anything else you want to coach me on?"

He thought about it for a minute. "Show me your tools."

"My *what*?"

"Your tools. Notebook? Pencil?"

"You gave me notebooks," she reminded him. "And I have a pen."

He shook his head. "Always have a pencil."

"Why?"

"What if you have to chase her outside and question her in the rain? Or the bitter cold? Your pen will freeze."

She stared at him. "It's sunny out. And I'm not chasing her outside anyway."

"Fine, fine." He thought for a minute. "I guess you'll be okay," he said, finally.

"Thanks for the vote of confidence." She started to walk away, then looked back when he called her name.

"You'll need this," he said, handing over a press pass with her name typed neatly on it. "Otherwise, she won't even say hello."

Chapter 25

The door marked RESIDENT STATE TROOPER, with an additional plaque below reading JESSICA K. PASQUALE, was shut tight when Stan approached. She could see a light on underneath the door, though, so she rapped on it and waited.

The town hall workday was in full force. The city clerk's office, across the hall, had a line of five people. Behind the tax window, Luisa Riley, town tax collector, was engaged in an animated story one of her coworkers told. The young woman's arms flailed in the air, bracelets jingling, as she described her daughter's antics with the training potty, which the little girl had apparently stuck on her head and couldn't dislodge. Luisa, leaning against the counter, was laughing. She waved at Stan when she saw her watching.

Then Pasquale's door flew open, startling Stan back to the task at hand. Her expression didn't change when she saw Stan there, but Stan could imagine the inner sigh.

"Hi," Stan said. She was never sure whether to call

her "Trooper," "Jessie," or something else altogether. Especially when she saw her in an official capacity.

Pasquale raised her eyebrows. "Hello."

"Do you have a minute? I have a few questions. Oh, I should probably show you this." She fumbled around in her pocket for the press pass Cyril had so thoughtfully provided her, and produced it.

Pasquale glanced at it, then did a double take. Her eyes slid to Stan, then back to the pass, then returned. "Press?" she said, her voice tinged with black humor.

"Yes, I'm helping Cyril with the *Holler*." Stan shifted uncomfortably from one foot to the other, then corrected herself. She couldn't let Pasquale sense she wasn't feeling all that confident. Even if she wasn't. "I'd like to talk to you about Helga Oliver." She watched the other woman's jaw set.

"Come in," Pasquale said through clenched teeth. Stan stepped through the door and flinched when it slammed behind her. "I don't know what you think you're up to, Stan, but there's nothing to talk about. Does my brother know you switched occupations?"

Stan flushed and ignored the question. "According to Cyril, there *is* something to talk about," Stan said. "I'm not *up to* anything except bringing the story to Frog Ledge citizens. I'd like to know if . . . er, why you're now considering Helga Oliver's death a murder."

"No comment."

"Jess—Trooper, we're writing the story anyway." Stan stood up a bit taller and uncapped her pen. "You may as well help me get it right."

Pasquale glared at Stan. If looks could kill, she'd

be as dead as the late Helga Oliver. "We have reason to believe foul play might have been involved in Mrs. Oliver's death. We are conducting an investigation and as such, I can't comment on an ongoing investigation. We don't believe there is any danger to the public at this time. That's all I have to say."

Stan scribbled furiously in her official steno pad. She was getting into this. "When did you first come to this conclusion?"

"We opened the investigation earlier this week."

"Like on Sunday? After her death? Or later?"

"No comment."

"Why did you open it? What prompted that action?"

"No comment."

"Did anyone tip you off?" *Like Betty Meany?*

"No comment."

She couldn't resist. "Have you thought about asking Sarah Oliver to connect you with Helga through her psychic abilities?"

Pasquale stared daggers at her and said nothing.

Stan decided to throw her a curve ball. "Speaking of ghosts and communing with the dead, do you have any thoughts on the ghost hunters coming to town?"

"No."

Apparently it wasn't such a curve ball. Stan hissed out a frustrated breath. "If at first you didn't believe Mrs. Oliver's death was foul play, was the crime scene compromised?"

Pasquale made a sound of complete indignation. "What do you think this is, *CSI Frog Ledge?*" She stalked around her small office once, then again. "Ever since you moved to this town things have been upside down. You know that, right?"

Stan managed a smile. "Good to know my black cloud is dedicated to following me wherever I go."

"Off the record." Pasquale waited, her face stony, until Stan flipped her notebook closed. "You know I was at the crime scene. I heard the call on the scanner about an accidental and headed over for two reasons. One, because I know Helga spends— spent—most of her time there, and two, because I always check out accidentals. Because sometimes they're not so accidental. I followed the appropriate procedures once I arrived and recorded everything. Unfortunately, there were people traipsing around inside before I got there"—she looked pointedly at Stan—"and I hope nothing was disturbed. But I don't have any reason to believe the crime scene was compromised."

"Why is that off the record? People are just gonna ask anyway."

Pasquale made a frustrated noise that was half moan, half growl. "It's off the record because I said so! I am the police here. I get to call the shots, not you."

"I'm just trying to write a story," Stan said, holding her hands up in defense. "I want you to be placed in the best possible light, too. Did you remove any evidence?"

"No comment."

Back to this again.

"Why did you question Cyril Pierce? What evidence points to him?"

Pasquale groaned. "No freakin' comment."

"Can I name him?"

"Absolutely not. I never went on the record stating who we questioned. Does he *want* you to?"

At Stan's shrug, Pasquale stopped pacing and sat on the edge of her desk. "He's crazy."

"All in the name of journalism. You know how those guys are. Truth-tellers."

"Aren't you one of them, too?"

"Just for today. I'm the one usually spinning the story. Now I just bake dog treats."

The sound that left Pasquale's mouth could've been a laugh. Stan was encouraged. Sort of.

"Listen. That's all I can tell you right now. We're looking into Helga's—Mrs. Oliver's—death more closely." Stan saw the cloud pass across her face. It must be hard to treat this like any other case when the victim was basically your family. "It's an ongoing investigation. When—if—we have more, we'll have a press conference, as appropriate."

May as well drop a bombshell and catch her off guard. "What about Dale Hatmaker?"

Pasquale cocked her head, but not before Stan caught the surprise that flickered across her face. "What about him?"

"I don't know. Seems he had plenty of reasons to want Helga out of the picture. Her job, for one. Certainly more reasons than Cyril Pierce would. He was in the museum this week, poking through everything and talking about getting rid of pieces. Maeve Johnson looked kind of scared of him. Have you checked to see if he was around early Sunday morning?"

"Are you offering a tip on a possible murder?" Pasquale asked, her tone cold.

"No, I'm simply making an observation."

Pasquale said nothing. Her face had returned to pure cop.

"So, did you?" Stan persisted.

"Did I what?"

"Check to see if Hatmaker was around the museum early Sunday? Or anyone else who shouldn't have been, for that matter?"

"I'm sorry, but when did you take over my supervisor's job?"

Stan flushed a little but held her ground. "It's worth asking."

"I am quite competent on how to conduct an investigation," Pasquale responded, her words clipped through her gritted teeth. "I think we're done."

Stan flipped her notebook shut. "Have other media outlets been alerted yet?"

"No one's called me. And I'd like to keep it that way."

"I can't help if they pick something up from our story," Stan said.

"No," Pasquale said. "You can't. But you can make sure that you're not reporting something just to put the newspaper out."

Stan flipped her notebook closed and capped her pen. She slid them both back in her purse and looked at Pasquale. "I don't know Cyril that well, but I sincerely doubt anything he does is just to 'put a paper out.' He strikes me as somebody who really believes in what he does, and wants to serve the community. And given the fact he's the person you're questioning, I highly doubt he's trying to sell a newspaper."

With that, she left Pasquale's office and closed the door behind her, leaving the other woman staring after her. She smiled, aware that for once, she'd finally gotten in the last word with Jake's sister. And she would still be on time to meet Dede, with her pet food chef's hat on. They had a wedding to discuss.

Chapter 26

Stan pulled into Dede's driveway a few minutes early, but the front door immediately opened. Dede leaned out, waving.

"Hello, Stan!" she called. A gorgeous Irish setter stuck his head out the door next to Dede's leg. Stan saw his tail waving behind him. It reminded her of Nutty's plume.

"Hi, Dede. I hope it's okay I'm early." She walked up the front steps to the little yellow house. The dog squeezed past Dede to get to her, sniffing and licking her hand.

"He knows exactly who you are. How cute is that?" Dede hugged her. "Your timing is perfect. Come in."

Stan stepped inside Dede's little house and immediately felt at home. It was small but cozy, with the kind of furniture her gram would've loved and the smell of baking cookies filling the air. Stan's stomach rumbled. Lunch had escaped her again. Everyone else had gone to Gerry's after the funeral for a catered meal.

"This is Gus." Dede motioned toward the setter,

who sat at Stan's feet, tongue hanging out, smiling at her.

"Hi, Gus." Stan petted him. Gus stood up and licked her face. Stan laughed. "He's friendly, eh?"

"He's a love. And this"—Dede pointed at a little white puffball with black ears and a black stripe down her back perched on a kitchen chair—"is Lila."

"Aww. Hi, Lila." Stan reached out and let the dog sniff her hand. "She's adorable."

"Isn't she?" Dede picked the dog up and nuzzled her. "I don't have her groomed with the straight hair like the Shih Tzu show dogs. She doesn't really like that hairstyle."

"Well, she's a rescue dog. She's probably more down to earth anyway," Stan said. "I don't have my schnoodle groomed like a schnauzer. She likes having her own hairstyle."

"Exactly. I knew you'd understand. I made coffee and cookies. Please, sit."

"That sounds great." Stan pulled out a chair. "It's been a long day, with the funeral and all. I saw you at the cemetery but didn't want to interrupt."

"Oh, my goodness, you should have." Dede brought over a plate loaded with gooey chocolate-chip cookies. "I thought about rescheduling our meeting because we'd both be so drained, but then I thought, what better time to focus on beautiful animals? And look. My other babies have come to meet you. They heard you were baking them a special treat."

Two cats peeked around the corner, eyes fixed on Stan. The black and white one seemed braver—he? she? advanced cautiously into the room, sniffing the air around Stan. The other, a long-haired buff-colored cat, remained in the hallway, content to let the other cat take the lead.

"That's Mittens," Dede said, nodding to the black and white cat. "If you couldn't tell from her feet." It was true. Her body and legs were mostly black, but her feet were white, as was the middle part of her face.

"She's so pretty." Stan reached down to pet her.

"And that's Diamond." Dede nodded at the shyer of the two. "He's hiding from you, but when he gets comfortable and comes out, you'll see the diamond on his head. They're my other babies." She waved at Diamond. "You can come out, sugar," she crooned, making kiss noises at him. He watched her with thinly veiled contempt. Stan recognized the look. Nutty had perfected it.

"Did you know Helga well?" she asked, unable to keep her eyes from straying to the cookies. "And, was her maiden name Cross?"

"Why, yes, it was! Helga Cross." Dede smiled. "I haven't heard that name in a long time. Yes, I did know her well. My big sister, God rest her soul, was very good friends with Helga. Go on, eat them," she urged. "How do you take your coffee?"

Stan dug in gratefully. "These are divine," she said around a mouthful. "What was your sister's name? Oh, and black coffee is fine. No sugar."

"My sister? Donna Cook was her married name. Rochefort, before that. Yes, there was a whole group of girls who used to congregate at our house." Dede smiled at the memory as she poured coffee from her small pot into two cups and added a dash of milk to hers. "Donna, Helga, Maeve Johnson—she was always

Maeve Johnson, she never married, you know. Alice Donahue. Jackie Kelly. Donna was always snotty when I tried to play with them, like big sisters usually are, but Helga and Jackie always let me. Jackie's gone, too." Her eyes clouded. "So's Alice. Maeve is the only one left now. Helga, though, my, was she a lot of fun. Such a daredevil. Never afraid to do or say anything, and she said a lot. Usually got her in trouble, too. I remember once she was downtown at the candy store. You know, where the flower shop is now?" She carried the mugs over and set them down.

Stan nodded.

"She was studying for something, carrying this big, heavy textbook with her." Dede demonstrated the width of the book with her hands. "Saw Ronald Morrison, Jackie's boyfriend at the time. They got in a shouting match. Helga seemed to think Ronald was being, well, unkind to Jackie, and she wasn't having it. But old Miss Swenson who owned the candy store threw them both out for causing a ruckus. Ronald walked out first, dismissing Helga. Well, Helga followed him out; then she charged down the street after him, jumped in the air like a basketball player, and bashed him on the head with the book so hard he went down like a lead balloon." Dede demonstrated the bashing with the imaginary book in her hands.

"You're kidding." Stan giggled.

"I am not kidding!" Dede laughed, too. "She was a trip. I'll miss her."

Stan tried to appear nonchalant. "So you must remember the murder case from 1949. The boxer?"

"Of course." Dede sat. "That's what all the hoopla is about with these silly ghost hunters. I've heard all about it. My phone has been ringing off the hook all morning after that town meeting yesterday. Did you go to that, dear?"

"I did. I wanted to hear more about it. I didn't see you there."

Dede wrinkled her nose. "That's because I didn't go. It just felt slightly blasphemous, do you know what I mean? I know people like those shows and that's fine. But when it's in our own backyard, I'm just not sure how I feel. Why can't people just leave the past alone?"

Same thing Betty had said. Abbie was right. No one wanted this dirty laundry aired. But why? A matter of principle? A New England thing, like Char had said? Or something more sinister than that? "It must've been hard for that man's family, to never get justice for him," Stan said.

"I suppose you're right," Dede said. "And not many people are left who remember it, anyway. But my sister and her friends, they were all there that night, at the party. Helga's boy, oh, what *was* his name . . . ?"

"Tommy," Stan supplied.

"Right! Tommy was the other fighter, so they were all invited. I remember it like it was yesterday. They were all dressed up, so excited. And to have it turn out so horribly. What a tragedy.

"And Alice, of course, found the poor man's body. The way Helga told the story—because Alice never spoke about it—she went down to retrieve some old cards from the card catalogue, a once-a-month project, and there he was. It deeply affected her. She really wasn't ever the same. And Tommy, either. All the girls liked Tommy, you know. But he only had eyes for Helga. Until all this. He left town a few days later and was never heard from again. Which sent Helga into a bit of a tailspin. She had a difficult time after that, too." Dede sighed. "Never stopped looking for him. Death touches a lot of lives, doesn't it?"

"It certainly does," Stan said. "No one ever heard from Tommy again?"

Dede shook her head. "Not that I know of. It was like he fell off the face of the earth."

"What about Dale Hatmaker?" Stan asked.

Dede blinked. "What about him?"

"Was he involved in that mess?"

"Hmm. You know, I don't think so," Dede said. "He's too young to be part of that crowd. He would've been just a boy when that happened, and besides, I don't think he's lived here all his life."

Well, that killed Stan's theory that Hatmaker had a personal stake in the boxer's murder, or the solving of said murder. Which didn't, in her mind, remove him as a suspect in Helga's murder because of his thirst for Helga's position. But this diverged him from the Felix Constantine path.

"So . . . Alice Donahue was Betty's mom. She died young, right?"

"Very young," Dede said. "Such a sad thing. Cancer, but I was convinced it was her mind. Like I said, she never recovered from that man's death. Betty was barely twenty. Just when she needed her mother most. I still think if Alice had been alive, Betty never would have married that good-for-nothing Burt Meany."

Burt had a great reputation. "What about Betty's dad?" Stan asked.

Dede sniffed. "He was not the nicest man. He went on with his life, no problem. Once Betty went to college, he moved away. I don't think she sees him much even today. She really was gypped in the parental department, poor thing."

"But Helga took over because she and Alice were so close."

Dede thought about that, then nodded carefully. "I suppose in a way, yes. But Helga, well, I loved Helga, let's get that out of the way. She did have a difficult streak. She expected a lot from people. Especially people she felt responsible for. I always joked that both her husbands had died to be free of her expectations. She had to have mellowed, because Gerry, her boyfriend, had no problems. But she was tough on a lot of people. Family, friends, everyone. Even Maeve had distanced herself these last months. Especially after the card games dwindled. Forty-fives." She winked. "Maeve was the reigning champ. They played every week, with partners, for money. With most of the group gone, the card games barely happen anymore. They used to have such fun. And fight to the death about it. But when Arthur stopped playing, it skewed the numbers."

"Arthur?"

"Pierce, yes. Cyril's dad. They were all friends. It's harder for him to be social, since he moved. He lives at Knotty Pines now, and he has to rely on the senior center bus to get around. And I just heard about his recent diagnosis, poor man. What a terrible shame. He just told us about it last week when he came over to the senior center for a card game. He didn't have his usual oomph, that's for sure. He used to have such a temper about his card games. He would throw the cards and storm out if he lost. I'm surprised they all lasted the past fifty years playing together."

Arthur Pierce. Not just a reporter, but a friend.

This web grew wider and more intricate with every conversation. It probably wasn't unusual to have so many connections in such a small place, but with everything else going on, it was taking on a life of its own. Stan's brain felt like a rapidly regenerating spider's web, and she was having a heck of a time linking all the names where they needed to be. "So, Maeve and Helga weren't as close anymore either? What happened?"

"I'm not sure. I couldn't put my finger on it, but something didn't seem right between them over the past month or so." Dede took another cookie. "They used to go to Bingo together, too, every Sunday, and Maeve started showing up alone. And Maeve didn't even go to Helga's last talk on the new exhibit at the museum. Usually she was the first one there, supporting her friend. Selfishly, I was too busy with my babies to give it much thought." She stroked Lila's fur. "Speaking of my babies—not that this hasn't been a lovely trip down memory lane—what kinds of fun wedding things do you have to show me?"

Stan turned her attention to the upcoming canine nuptials and gave Dede an update on her progress, but her mind kept wandering back to Helga. A lot of things had changed in Helga's life after Felix Constantine's murder—her friend Alice, who'd discovered the body and suffered irreversible trauma, the abrupt departure of her boyfriend, Tommy. That event seemed to be a consistent black cloud that followed her and her friends for years. It clearly had stuck with her.

The more Stan learned, the more convinced she was that Felix Constantine's death sixty years ago was somehow the key to Helga's death. She was just having trouble making that key fit into the right lock.

Chapter 27

Stan pulled into her driveway. She didn't notice Cyril sitting on her front porch steps until she'd gotten out of her car. His bike stood neatly to the side of her porch. He had an orange cat with him. The cat sat right next to him, at attention, watching Stan as she climbed the steps.

"Who's your friend?"

Cyril pointed to the cat's collar. There was a piece of paper clipped to it. "I'm not sure who this is. He was just sitting here when I got here. But he has a note. I didn't read it. Didn't seem to be my place."

"Hmmm." Stan regarded the cat, then stooped to pet him. He immediately purred and smushed his face against her hand. "I don't remember seeing you around before. Do you have a house? Are you just here for a treat because someone told you it was the place to go?"

Cyril watched her curiously but didn't say anything. Inside the door, the dogs barked. The cat wasn't fazed.

"Let's see what this note says." Stan took the piece

of paper off the cat. He watched her with interested green eyes.

"Dear Stan," she read. *"My name is Benedict. My mommy just died and I need a home. Can you help? I heard you have good food. XO, Benedict."* She looked at Cyril. "What the . . . Who does that? And why does that name sound familiar?"

He shrugged. "Your reputation precedes you." He glanced at his watch. "We have a story to write. Can you give the cat a home or not?"

"I can't just take someone's cat! Who left him here? Are you sure you didn't see anybody?" She looked around, as if the perpetrator might be hiding behind one of her trees. She couldn't quite place the name but felt certain she'd heard it recently.

"I'm telling you, no one was around but this cat."

"This is nuts." She sighed. "Well, come on. I'll set you up in the guest room until we figure out who dropped you off on my doorstep." She scooped the cat up. He purred again and rubbed against her chin.

He was adorable. Stan had always been partial to orange cats, not that she could admit it to Nutty, who certainly wasn't going to be thrilled.

"Come on in," she said. "I was actually looking forward to telling you how it went with Pasquale."

"Really," Cyril said. "That's good news." He followed her inside, stopping briefly to pet the dogs.

"Come sit. I'm going to put the cat upstairs." She snuck up to her guest room as stealthily as possible without letting Nutty see their guest. Luckily she had an extra litterbox. She hurried to the basement, filled it up, and brought it to Benedict's room. She set up a blanket for him, then went downstairs to fetch some food and water as Cyril paced her kitchen. Nutty watched her suspiciously as she added a couple of treats to the bowl.

"Relax," she told both of them. To Nutty, "I'll explain later."

When she returned, Cyril sat, pen and notebook out. "So what happened with Trooper Pasquale?"

Stan recounted her conversation with Jessie while she made a new pot of coffee.

"Thank you for defending the newspaper. But you didn't get anything on why they think it's foul play."

Stan frowned. Maybe she hadn't done so well after all. "She wouldn't comment."

Cyril paused in his pacing and tapped his fingers on the counter. "I'm not surprised. She always plays things close to the vest."

"Shocking, considering her personality." Stan made a face, then reminded herself she was talking to a real reporter. About Jake's sister. She was losing her PR edge. "I still don't get why she's after you. Unless there's something you're not telling me." She eyed him, wary again. "People would tell me I'm crazy, having you, a murder suspect, in my house."

He shrugged. "I'm only a person of interest so far. I didn't do anything to Helga. I think there's more to this than Pasquale is letting on. She told me I was seen in the vicinity."

"And that person thought, gee, Cyril looks like he's off to murder someone? None of this makes any sense," Stan said. "Didn't you and Helga get along?"

"We got along swimmingly," Cyril said.

"Swimmingly?" Stan rolled her eyes.

"Hey, did you get voices?" Cyril asked, changing the subject.

"Voices? What do you mean? Isn't that Sarah Oliver's department?"

"Real people. Reactions to the news."

"No, that wasn't part of the deal," Stan said.

"It's always part of the deal. It's how you write a story." He glanced at his watch. "There are people at the War Office tonight for special tours in honor of Helga. Can you run over and ask them? Those are her friends anyway. They'll be good choices."

Stan opened her mouth to protest when the doorbell rang. "Hang on," she muttered, and headed down the hall, the dogs at her heels.

Jessie Pasquale stood there, dressed in full uniform, face grim. "Stan. Is Cyril Pierce here?"

Stan stared at her. This couldn't be good. His bike was right outside—and it was distinctive, with that silly basket on the front—so she couldn't say no. "Why do you—"

"Cyril Pierce?" Jessie called out, stepping past Stan into the hall. Henry and Scruffy started barking their nervous barks, Henry's coupled with worried looks in Stan's direction.

"Shh, guys," she said, grabbing their collars as Cyril appeared in the hall.

"Yeah?" He didn't seem fazed that the resident state trooper was looking for him.

"Can you come with me, please?" Jessie asked.

"Where are we going?"

Jessie sighed. "Cyril, just get in the car."

He crossed his arms. "I'm sorry, Trooper. I need to know what this is about."

"Fine, then." Pasquale didn't look at Stan. "You're under arrest for the murder of Helga Oliver."

Stan's mouth dropped. What was Jessie doing? "Jessie. You can't—"

"Be quiet, please," Jessie said, eyes still on Cyril. "Let's go."

Cyril acquiesced. "May I get my coat?" he asked.

"Go ahead."

He went into the kitchen, returned a minute later with his coat and hat. "It's fine if you need to hand-cuff me," he said.

Pasquale rolled her eyes. "Let's go."

As he walked by Stan, he said urgently, "Get the voices and finish the story. I left you an e-mail address on the table. E-mail it there by eight and it will get printed. And don't worry. The truth will prevail," he said in a louder voice, as Jessie Pasquale took his arm and led him out the door.

Stan watched helplessly as Pasquale led him to the squad car. This made no sense. Why wasn't Pasquale looking at others with more motive? Unless there really was something Cyril wasn't telling her, he wasn't it.

Was he?

Chapter 28

Stan regretted not having more compassion for the reporters she'd dealt with in the past. Not that the stories they'd been writing on her previous firm had been life and death matters, but still. She remembered days of pushing them right to their deadlines—even past them—because of corporate red tape and revision after revision of a two-sentence statement, demanding approval rights for quotes, insisting they change the slant of the story because it could be construed as slightly unfavorable.

She offered up a silent mea culpa to the journalism gods, then got out of her car and hurried to the door of the War Office. Before she could push the heavy wooden door open, it opened in front of her. A woman who had to be Helga's age or pretty darn close to it smiled at her. She wore a full-bodied light blue dress with an apron and corset and a bonnet over gray braids. Her bright red lipstick made her look like a corpse. "Good evening, child! Please, come in. Welcome to the War Office, headquarters of the Revolution efforts."

Stan stepped into the room onto the gray slatted floor, uneven from years of heavy boots traipsing through, and took it in. Another place she'd never been to, just like the historical society and the museum. She felt terrible about that. Especially since she was only here now to get a quote. It wasn't that she had no interest; rather, she'd simply never made the time. When the volunteers had been part of other events out on the green, she'd enjoyed their tributes to the Revolutionary War, but a visit to learn about the town's war efforts wasn't anything that had occupied her mind as a must-do.

"Thank you," she said to the bonneted woman, who struggled to close the heavy door behind her without letting it slam. "I'm Stan Connor."

"Millie Simmons. Thank you for visiting the War Office." She clasped her hands together and smiled. "Let me get my cape and I'll give you the tour." Millie hurried through a doorway into another room.

Left alone, Stan observed her surroundings. The house was larger than it appeared from the outside. She took a few steps until she was in the center of the room next to a small, wooden card table with a matching folding chair. On the table was a feather pen, some sheets of paper, and a small lantern. An old-fashioned writing desk was pushed up against the wall. The floor next to it was a trapdoor. The rest of the room was filled with supplies, most likely for events: drums, whiskey barrels, toy rifles and wooden cutouts of rifles, pieces of costumes, and white cloth bags filled with something Stan couldn't identify. The fireplace looked like it was used regularly. Stan supposed it was—there probably wasn't any heat in here, and if there was, who would pay the bill? Revolutionary War weapons decorated the walls—muskets, rifles, all kinds of nasty-looking swords.

Millie returned from the other room. She wore a long blue cape over her dress. "Well, then, let's show you around!" she exclaimed. "This is our main room, where the war officers strategized and kept watch over what was happening. It was a dark and dire time, and our soldiers and leaders worked tirelessly—"

"Um . . . Ms. Simmons? I hate to interrupt."

"Don't be silly, dear. Ask whatever questions you have."

"I'd love to hear all about the War Office, but I'm here because I need to talk to one or two of Helga Oliver's friends."

Her smiled flickered a tad, but remained in place. "We're all Helga's friends here. What did you want to talk about? Other than how we miss her so, and this place is a bit worse with her absence."

Stan nodded somberly. "I understand that. But I'm here as a reporter. To talk about a new development in her death."

Millie faltered. "You . . . reporter? Development? Whatever do you mean, dear?" She sat down heavily on her folding chair, as if she were afraid the conversation would be too much to bear standing up.

Stan pulled her steno pad out of her pocket, already feeling like the devil. This reporting thing was difficult. "I'm writing a story for the *Holler.* Someone has been arrested in Helga's death." It sounded so surreal, to say it out loud. "The police think her fall wasn't an accident. Would you care to comment?"

Millie's face went deathly white. Alarmed, Stan took a step toward her, afraid she might faint. Before Millie could say anything, the door swung open again and a man, also in full costume, entered, his heavy boots rattling the floor. Despite the funny hat, Stan recognized him. Edgar Fenwick, the ghost-hater. "Millie? Oh, hello there. I love to see visitors!" He adjusted his pants over his big belly as he walked over to Stan and pumped her hand. "Edgar Fenwick. Pleased to have you here."

"Mr. Fenwick, hello. I'm—"

"Edgar," Millie interrupted. "She's not a visitor. She's . . . a reporter." Her lip quivered.

Edgar took a good look at Stan, squinting slightly. "Reporter, eh? With whom? Not the local. Cyril wouldn't know what to do with the likes of you." He chuckled.

"I'm writing for the *Holler*. It's about—"

"Helga. It's about Helga," Millie cut her off again. "Edgar, you'll have to talk to her. You won't believe what she has to say." She rose from her folding chair and fled into the other room, where Stan suspected she was hovering in the doorway listening.

"Helga, she says? What do you need, young lady?" Edgar took the chair his counterpart had vacated.

Stan stifled a sigh and began her spiel all over again. "Trooper Pasquale has made an arrest in Helga's death," she finished. "I'd like to get some reactions on that."

"Arrest?" Edgar echoed. "What in blazes are you talking about, young lady? And where is Cyril?"

Stan sighed. "The police think someone killed Helga," she explained again. She let the second question go unanswered.

Fenwick's eyes opened wide as saucers. "You're joking." Around the corner, Millie made a sound like a baby bird screeching.

"I'm afraid I'm not."

He stared at her. Millie came back into view, wiping tears away. "Who . . . who did it?" she asked in a wobbly voice.

"I can only tell you who was arrested, not who did it," Stan said. "Since everyone is innocent until proven guilty, right?"

They both just looked at her. She sighed. "They arrested Cyril Pierce. I'm not sure why."

Millie's hand fluttered to her throat. "I feel sick," she said, and fled from the room.

"Cyril?" Edgar looked shocked. "You must be mistaken."

Stan shook her head. "I'm looking for some comments from Helga's friends about that news." Hadn't she said that about three times already? "How does it feel to hear that?" Kind of a silly question, in retrospect.

Edgar stared past Stan, out the small window into the night. "I warned her," he said, so softly Stan had to strain to hear him.

"Excuse me?"

He focused on Stan again, as if he had just remembered she was there. "I said, I warned her."

Stan shivered, just a bit. "Warned who?"

"Helga, of course," he said. "Not that she ever listened to reason."

"Warned her about what?"

"Not to stir up the past. You know what they say about those sleeping dogs." He nodded, slowly. "They say let them lie."

Chapter 29

"He wouldn't tell me what he meant. Just that he warned her to let sleeping dogs lie." Stan toyed with her latte cup. It was the second one of the day already. A folded-over copy of the *Holler* was strewn on the chair next to her. Her byline mocked her under the above-the-fold headline: *Arrest Made in Town Historian's Death.*

She'd been at Izzy's pretty much since her friend had turned the lights on this morning. In the back booth. The one Izzy had termed the "break-up booth," because it wasn't in the café's main traffic line. Stan didn't want to attract attention due to her new byline, but she didn't want to be home alone either.

"Sounds menacing," Izzy said. "Do you think he meant the boxer's murder?"

She'd been coming over to hear the story in bits and pieces as the ebb and flow of customers allowed. Stan wanted to talk it out but had to be careful— there was so much she couldn't reveal yet. She also needed an opinion on how to approach the subject with Jake, who had certainly seen the paper by now, but she didn't know if Izzy's would be unbiased enough. But she had to figure something out soon. She needed to go talk to him. She hadn't seen him since Helga's funeral yesterday.

"I can't imagine what else Edgar would've been talking about. But he clammed right up. And the web of people who were close to that boxer's murder is getting overwhelming. I can't imagine why anyone would want to be a journalist, if they have to deal with this kind of thing all the time. It's so frustrating." She flipped the paper over so she didn't have to look at it. "I don't know what to think anymore."

She'd been up half the night after returning from the War Office and finishing her story. Truth be told, she'd been slightly freaked out about Edgar Fenwick's reaction and spent a lot of time in her den pondering his words. They were familiar, at this point: Don't stir up the past. Although Edgar Fenwick hadn't elaborated on what was to be left in the past, Stan felt like he had to be talking about the ghost hunt. Everyone was so antsy about that. But from Edgar's statement, it sounded like he'd linked it to Helga's death. Just like Stan had. She might be grasping, but her gut told her she wasn't.

Despite all the unanswered questions, the *Holler* had waited on the front porch first thing today. Her byline, followed by the disclaimer "*Special to the* Holler" seemed way bigger than it needed to be. Cyril's bike still stood on her front porch. She still had this poor, orphaned orange cat in her guest bedroom. Benedict. He didn't seem to feel poor, though. Or even orphaned. He purred a lot when she'd brought him food, and he gave her lots of head butts. But she still needed to figure out who he was and where he might belong.

And that was only the immediate list.

I just can't believe . . ." Izzy picked up the paper, glanced at the headline, and shook her head. "Do you really think Cyril killed Helga?" she asked in a low voice. "Why on earth would he do that?"

Stan shook her head miserably. "I don't think he did at all. I feel like there's a huge piece of the puzzle missing. And I'm not sure that the police are looking for it now that they have their guy. Or so they think."

"What possessed you to agree to get involved—er, write this story? And is he actually paying you? I didn't think the *Holler* made any money." Izzy glanced at the line forming at her counter and sighed. "I have to go make some drinks in a second."

"Fifty bucks a story." Stan cracked a smile. "But I don't think he can write checks from jail, so I'm probably out of luck. Trust me, I didn't want to do it, but you know me. I'm horrible at saying no. I really didn't need the fifty bucks that badly."

Izzy laughed. "Want a double chocolate-chip muffin or something when I come back?"

"I would love one. Or two."

The chimes rang, signaling a new customer. Stan glanced up and saw Sarah Oliver walk through the door. She was alone. She didn't look their way as she went to the counter, ordered a coffee, and took it to the bar facing the street.

Izzy saw her, too. She looked at Stan. "Think she saw the paper?"

"No idea." Stan watched Sarah settle onto a stool,

adjusting her ever-present flowy skirts around her. Something besides sympathy—and the lyrics from "Dreams"—niggled in the back of her brain, but she couldn't quite grasp it. "But I'm sure her brother or sister-in-law filled her in."

"Isn't she a medium?" Izzy asked. "She should know all this already if she is. Heck, she should know if Cyril did it! Why don't you go ask her?"

"No! You go ask her," Stan said.

"I have lattes to make."

"Sure you do." Stan rolled her eyes. "She's supposed to join the investigation tonight, though, remember?" Tonight was the big night. Adrian Fox and team were doing their ghostly investigation at the murder site. "I wonder if Jake will show up. I haven't talked to him about it."

"Oh, no way," Izzy said. "He's not really into this."

"Plus, he's probably seriously mad at me," Stan said.

Izzy frowned. "Why?"

"The whole reporting on this story thing without telling him they were looking at Helga's death as a murder," Stan said.

"You didn't tell him beforehand?"

"I didn't have a chance. The only time I saw him yesterday was at the funeral, and it wasn't the place."

"Wouldn't he be mad at his sister?" Izzy asked. "She could tell him. Why is it on you?"

"I doubt she would tell him, because it's an ongoing investigation. So he would have to hear about it from me. Except I chickened out of telling him."

Izzy raised her eyebrows. "Given his moods lately, I'd say you're screwed. I really need to go help Mya. The line's getting longer and she's giving me dirty looks. I can feel it. Hey, before I forget. Can I get some new treats for the dogs? They've been mad at me for the hours I'm keeping. I haven't been able to bring them down as much." Izzy lived in the small apartment above her shop—same setup as Jake and his place over McSwigg's. Her three dogs, Baxter, Elvira, and Junior, were regulars at the café, and Scruffy and Henry's good friends. "You know how picky Elvira is," she added.

"I have some treats in my . . ." Stan paused as a thought clicked into place in her brain. She could almost hear the *ding, ding, ding* of the right answer. Benedict. Picky eater. Sarah Oliver's comment at the Groundhog Day celebration: *My mum is a fan of your cat treats. Her Benedict is a picky eater.* "You have got to be kidding me," she muttered. Sarah had dumped Helga's cat on her porch?

Izzy stared at her with open concern, but before she could ask what her new problem was, the door to the café banged open, sending the chimes on a frantic dance. Frank Pappas walked through the door. Well, walked was an exaggeration. More like stomped. He scanned the café, eyes finally settling on Izzy at their table, and strode over.

Izzy stood. "Hey. What's up? Everything okay?"

"No, everything's not okay." Frank glowered at her.

"What's wrong? And tone it down, honey. You're scaring my customers." Izzy kept her tone light, but Stan could see annoyance dancing in her eyes.

"How do you figure I can work on a building when I have gawkers lined up on every side of it? And morons trying to break in to do their own ghost hunt? This is all because you didn't send those scam-artist Hollywood types away. I'm going to be behind schedule, and you're going to be paying a lot more for this job. Do you get that?" He was almost foaming at the mouth, jabbing a finger into the air. A woman with headphones on who was working on a computer two tables away packed up her stuff.

Stan recognized the look on Izzy's face and thought about ducking under the table for cover. Izzy's eyes went to slits. When she opened her mouth, daggers flew out along with words.

"Your own people told you they were having problems there, so don't point fingers at me. And if you want to continue this conversation, you'll do it back there," she said, pointing to the back of the café, her hand shaking with fury. "Otherwise, you can leave, or I can have you removed."

With one last, nasty look at both of them, Frank stalked to the back of the café. Stan heard the door to the office slam.

"I'll catch you later," Izzy said, shoving her chair against the table. Ignoring Mya and the growing line, she marched to the office behind Frank.

The door slammed again.

Chapter 30

With no evidence of bloodshed from Izzy's back office after twenty minutes, Stan focused on Sarah Oliver, still sitting across the room with her coffee. She wanted to get to the bottom of the Benedict mystery. At least that one might be easier to solve than the Helga mystery.

Sarah still sat on her stool overlooking the street. She had a book open in front of her. Stan weighed her options. She didn't know if Sarah read the paper, or got a message from her mother, or somehow had heard that Helga's death was now being considered a murder. If she knew, she would likely be devastated. If she didn't know, Stan didn't want to be the one to tell her.

Either way, it would be difficult to be upset with her. If Stan was right about the cat. But she needed to know.

Stan approached her. "Sarah, do you have a minute?"

Sarah glanced up from her book. Stan glimpsed the cover. *Discover Your Psychic Type.*

"Hi, Stan. Of course. Do you want to sit?" She picked up her bag, but Stan shook her head.

"No, thanks. I only have a second. Are you doing okay?"

Sarah shrugged. "It's hard. But I felt at peace at the funeral. My mum was there."

"Oh." Stan decided not to mention the murder thing, if Sarah wasn't going to. "Did you by any chance leave your mother's cat at my house?"

She didn't know what she expected—an admission of guilt, a plea for forgiveness, something that would suggest Sarah understood what an inconsiderate thing she'd done, both for Benedict and Stan. She certainly didn't expect the bizarre reaction she got.

Sarah clapped her hands. "So it worked!"

"Worked? What worked?"

"My test." She beamed. "I knew Benedict would know if he was meant to stay with you. If he wasn't, he would've left. But I specifically asked him to stay and wait for you if it felt right to him."

Stan wished for more coffee. Preferably with a shot of strong alcohol in it. "I'm glad he waited for me. I'm not sure what you want me to do, though."

Sarah looked at her blankly. "Give him a loving home, of course. I can see how you treat animals. He'll feel like a king with you."

That was flattering to hear, but still. "I don't think I can keep another cat. I already have a cat, and two dogs. It would've been nice to be asked first. Before leaving a house cat outside on my porch. What if he'd wandered off?"

And, of course, Sarah burst into tears. Unlike most people who cried in public places, she didn't seem to care if anyone heard her. She cried loudly, making gasping noises like she was being strangled, too. Stan wanted to hide under the table as people turned to look. Now she was responsible for upsetting a newly dead, possibly murdered woman's daughter. *Way to go, Stan.*

"Sarah." She cursed inwardly but tried to make her voice gentle and soothing. "Don't cry."

Sarah continued to cry. Stan fumbled in her purse for her packet of tissues, pulled a few out, and handed them to her. Sarah blew her nose, loudly, then quieted down some. Once she'd resorted to exaggerated sniffles and the other patrons had mostly gone back to their business, Stan tried again.

"Look. I'm sorry. I didn't mean to upset you. It's just . . . I don't know if it will work out. He seems like a nice cat and all—"

"He *is* a nice cat." Sarah's eyes started to well again. Stan braced herself, but Sarah kept it under control. "My mum loved Benedict. Probably more than me. He's named for Benedict Arnold, you know. My mum was one of a small group of people who believed Benedict Arnold wasn't all bad and still deserves his place in our history. Anyway, I didn't know what to do with him. I can't have him because I'm allergic, and he likes your food, and no one else will take him. My brother doesn't want him, and Mum wouldn't trust just anyone." She let out a shaky breath. "And I asked my friend who's an angel reader—"

"A what?" Stan asked.

"An angel reader. She gets messages from the angels."

This was getting a little too woo-woo for Stan. "You asked her . . . ?"

"I asked her how to tell if you and Benedict would be a good match. She said Benedict would know, and that's why I sent him to you. But I understand if you can't keep him." She swiped one final tear from her cheek, then stood up. "Should I come get him now?"

"I . . . what would you do with him?" Stan asked.

Sarah shrugged. "I guess I'll have to bring him to the humane society."

"No! You shouldn't do that," Stan said. "Not unless you know for sure it's a no-kill shelter."

From the blank look Sarah wore, Stan figured she didn't know what that meant. She resisted the urge to pull her own hair out and run screaming from the café. She asked herself the same question as yesterday: *How in the world do I end up in these situations?*

"Look," she said, finally. "I don't want you to rush to a decision and then regret it. I was just struggling with where he came from and if he really did belong to someone. I didn't want to steal someone's cat."

"That's why I left the note," Sarah said.

"Yeah, okay. I get it." Stan sighed. "Why don't we do this. I'll see if Benedict can get along with my cat and dogs, and if he seems to like it there. Right now he's in my guest bedroom. If it looks like everyone can get along, then he can stay. Deal?"

"Deal!" Sarah got up from her seat, all smiles, and threw her arms around Stan. "You are a wonderful lady. I knew Mum was right."

"Your mother thought I was wonderful? I didn't even know her well."

"She told me." Sarah winked. "Just yesterday. Please let me know how Benedict is doing. I'll see you tonight for the investigation." With that, she picked up her coat and bag, and exited the café, her skirt swirling in the wind gust outside the door.

Stan watched her go, not sure whether to laugh or cry.

After she left Izzy's, Stan took a quick detour down the street to McSwigg's. It was nearly eleven-thirty, so Jake and some of the staff would be getting ready for lunch. She'd tried Brenna on her cell earlier to see if she'd made any headway on the "rings" for the bride and groom, but got no answer. Maybe she could track her down in person.

Plus, she couldn't avoid Jake forever. Even though she kind of wanted to. For a while, anyway. She paused at the front door of the pub, took a breath. Smoothed her hair. Found a box of Tic Tacs in her coat pocket and popped a few in her mouth. When she couldn't find anything else to procrastinate with, she pulled the door open and went in.

No customers yet. Jake and one of his bartenders, Larry, were behind the bar. They both turned to look when she entered. She smiled, hoping her nervousness wasn't shining through.

Larry lifted his hand in a wave. Jake didn't. He glanced at her. His gaze lingered for a second, two, then he looked away. No smile. No sexy head tilt. No nothing.

Stan's stomach dropped. She'd been expecting some negative reaction, but not this blatant snub. Unless she was reading it wrong. She had a tendency to do that. Maybe he was just engrossed in whatever he was talking about and hadn't really registered her presence.

Sure. And maybe Helga really had talked to Sarah yesterday about how wonderful Stan was.

She squared her shoulders, pasted her smile on, and headed to the bar. "Hey," she said, pulling out a stool. Duncan, hearing her voice, shot out from under the bar like a rocket and propelled himself onto her lap. At least he looked happy to see her. She leaned down for some kisses. The dog happily obliged.

"Hey there," Larry said. He glanced at Jake, clearly wondering why he wasn't speaking, then took the cue. "I'll go get that box," he said, and fled into the kitchen.

Jake crossed his arms and leaned back against the bar. Stan played with Duncan's ears to keep her hands occupied—and so he wouldn't see them shaking.

"What's up?" she asked, trying to sound nonchalant.

"Nothing," Jake said. "You looking for a quote?"

Ouch. "No, I'm not. But I guess you saw the paper," Stan said.

Jake nodded. "You are a woman of many talents."

Stan frowned. She couldn't actually tell if he was mad. His tone was even and his face was neutral. He didn't look like he had when he and Frank were arguing the other day, and he certainly didn't look like he did the night he and Izzy were "talking." Then again, he didn't look like he normally looked when she sat at his bar and flirted with him, either.

"Cyril asked for help," she said. "And I clearly don't know how to say no." She tried for a smile. It was a no go. "Can we go upstairs and talk?"

He paused as if weighing the answer. Finally, he nodded. "We can go in the kitchen. I have a few things to do and I think Brenna is upstairs."

She untangled herself from Duncan and rose from her stool. Dunc padded anxiously behind them as Jake led her through the double doors into the kitchen. Larry made a quick but discreet exit when they came in.

Jake pulled out some potatoes and began slicing. "So, what's up?"

"I thought you might want to talk about the article." Stan leaned back against the counter and watched him work. She wondered if her backup oven would be off the table now.

"Not much to talk about. It looks like there were some developments. Even though not many people knew there was actually a case." Jake's knife sliced cleanly through the Russet potatoes into french fry–sized chunks, making her mouth water. "I don't really know what to say about Cyril. About any of it. To think someone would kill her . . ." He shook his head.

"Cyril didn't kill Helga."

"Looks like my sis—the police think he did."

"Why would he do that?"

"Why would anyone?" Jake asked. He dumped his excess potato peels into the trash and started a whole new batch.

"I don't know. It's likely related to the murder at your building. Are you sure she never talked to you about it in detail?"

Jake sighed and put the knife down. He rubbed his hands over his stubble. He looked like he hadn't slept in days. "Are you working on a story? Or investigating on your own? Because I'm not going to help you with either."

"I'm not doing either," Stan said, stung. At least not the first one. The investigating part, well, she was just asking questions. No harm in that. "But I think it's wrong that Cyril is in jail."

"I think it's wrong that Helga is dead. How long have you known about this?"

"Cyril came to me Wednesday night to ask for help."

"Wednesday." He shook his head and looked around the room, as if he might find a script somewhere that would help him continue this conversation. "And today's Friday, and you let me find out in the newspaper. So I guess what's bothering me the most is, you don't trust me."

"That's totally not true!" Outraged, she stood up straight, hands on hips. "Not fair. Cyril got arrested, and it . . . threw a monkey wrench in everything. I didn't know how to tell you because you were so sad, and this would've made it worse. And then I ran out of time." It sounded lame even to her own ears, but it was the truth.

"What am I supposed to think?" Jake asked. "I'm not saying you have to tell me everything. But with something like this, it would seem like you'd want to confide in someone. Like, the person you're supposedly closest to. This is pretty heavy stuff, no?"

Stan narrowed her eyes. "Of course it is. And I know how much she meant to you, so I didn't think it was something you would want to hear." What was he up to? She couldn't tell if he was really angry, or hurt, or what was going on here. But she knew it didn't feel good.

"Of course I wouldn't want to hear it," he said. "That doesn't mean I couldn't have talked it out with you."

"I don't know what you want me to say. I made a bad choice, I guess."

"I didn't say you made a bad choice," he said. "I just wish you trusted me."

"You really think I don't *trust* you? Are you kidding?" She couldn't even believe what she was hearing. Was he crazy? She wouldn't bother dating him if she didn't trust him. But maybe he was used to women behaving differently.

But instead of getting defensive, he simply shook his head. "No, I'm not kidding. Let's be honest, Stan. There's a part of you that doesn't completely trust me. Or anyone, I don't think. I'm not saying it's right or wrong. I'm just telling you what I see."

Furious tears plucked at her eyes, but she used every ounce of willpower she had to not cry. Jerk. Who did he think he was? She didn't owe him any explanation about how she gauged the level of trust she had in people. She trusted him. Probably more than anyone, except for maybe Nikki. He didn't see that. And she clearly wasn't doing a good job of demonstrating it. As she tried to figure out the best way to answer him, the kitchen door swung open.

"Hey, Jake, where'd you put the—" Brenna stopped abruptly when she saw Stan.

"Hey," Stan said, trying for a smile and not succeeding well.

Brenna frowned. She said nothing. Then she

turned and went back the way she'd come. The door slammed behind her.

Stan looked at Jake. "You've got to be kidding me. She's mad at me, too?"

"I'm not mad at you. I don't know what Brenna is. Maybe disappointed, too."

Whatever. "You know what, fine. She can be mad all she wants. You can both be mad. Or disappointed. I was just trying to help. Maybe you should try being mad at Jessie, too. *She's* the one who started investigating. *She's* the one who questioned the 'person of interest.' And *she's* the one who could've given all of you a heads-up before any of this happened. It's not *my* job to run around and tell everyone what Trooper Pasquale and the state police are doing. But I'm sure she'll get off easy, as usual, because her job is *confidential*. Whatever." She slung her purse over her shoulder and headed for the door.

Then she stopped and turned back. "And I have news for you. I *do* trust you. Like, one hundred percent. And I'm sorry you can't see that."

She left him standing there over a counter full of potatoes, staring after her. Too bad the heavy front doors were constructed so they wouldn't slam, because it would've given her great pleasure to make the whole building shake on her way out.

Once she hit the sidewalk, she paused for a long moment, part of her hoping he'd come after her. But he didn't.

Chapter 31

The temperature couldn't have been more than thirty degrees, but Stan was boiling hot. She took the long way home, walking down Main Street and around the far side of the green before finally arriving in her driveway. She should've gotten the dogs and gone for a real walk to expend some energy, but she didn't even feel like doing that. Somewhere along the way, her mad turned into sad. She noticed a few tears on her cheeks. But it could have been the wind whipping in her face.

Who was she kidding? It wasn't the wind. Jake and Brenna were both mad at her because she hadn't shared her knowledge of the alleged murder. Not just mad, either. Jake had looked . . . hurt. He'd already been annoyed with her about the ghost hunt, but this was the icing on the cake.

And speaking of cake, she had a wedding to worry about, and now she didn't have an assistant to help her. Cyril had been arrested. Helga had been murdered. The town was divided over a ghost hunt, which may or may not bring the spirit of another

murdered man to light. And her mother had been
radio silent since Stan had gotten mouthy with Tony
Falco.

All in all, a crappy week.

She climbed her front porch. A package waited.
This one had a return address label, at least. She recognized the name of the kitchen company where
she'd ordered her cake pans. At least she could practice her wedding cake recipe. She picked up the
box, went inside, and locked the door behind her,
stooping to hug the dogs. Now she did let herself
cry. That's what dogs were for, right? To offer comfort and support no matter what was going on.

Stan let herself have a few moments of self-pity
and doggie licks; then she pulled herself together.
There had to be a way to resolve this mess. All of it.
She just needed to figure a few things out. Armed
with a purpose, she went into the kitchen, deposited
her new pans on the counter, turned the coffee on,
and grabbed a notepad and pen. Time to make a
list. One of her favorite things to do when she felt
lost and overwhelmed.

She titled this list "What I Know" and numbered
it. Then she jotted things down.

1. Helga fell or was pushed down the steps
   and died.
2. Betty said she was murdered, because she
   never would've gone walking without her
   cane.
3. Betty wouldn't tell anyone else her theory—
   not even police.
4. Dale Hatmaker wanted Helga's job.

5. Sarah is allegedly a medium and can talk to Helga.
6. Someone called the ghost hunters.
7. A boxer named Felix died at Jake and Izzy's building sixty-something years ago. He was supposed to fight Helga's boyfriend.
8. Jessie Pasquale arrested Cyril Pierce for Helga's murder, which no one else seemed to know was a murder.
9. Edgar Fenwick told Helga to let sleeping dogs lie.
10. Betty's mother and Helga were close friends, and Betty never bothered to mention it.
11. Helga wasn't nice to Betty (allegedly) or Sarah. Or most anyone, apparently.
12. Mom's mad about me not coaching (or being nice to) Falco.
13. Dale Hatmaker was moving things out of the museum.
14. Someone left a book on my porch about the boxer's murder. Maybe Arthur.
15. Arthur covered the murder and was friends with the whole group.

Ugh. Stan shoved the notebook away. There wasn't even a good way to put these in order, save for number one. How was she supposed to make any sense out of this mishmash of information? Stan stared out the kitchen window into the distance, trying to force her brain to get its act together.

There had to be a better way. Stan got up and

paced her kitchen. Scruffy followed her. The little
dog seemed to know she was upset. Henry, however,
was happily napping. Stan wished she had the ability
to tune life out that way.

Nutty, however, was also in rare form. Stan had a
hunch it was related to the extra cat upstairs. Even
though Nutty hadn't seen Benedict face-to-face,
he'd been spending an awful lot of time sniffing
around the door to the guest room and meowing.
Demonstrating all-around bad behavior—like right
now. Meowing and rubbing all over her legs, he
then proceeded to jump on the wrong end of the
counter—not his designated eating area—and a pile
of mail and other items, including her new cake
pans, went crashing to the floor.

"Nutty! What's wrong with you?" Stan bent to pick
everything up. "If these pans are dented, I'm going
to be very angry at you." She pushed the mail into a
neat pile. As she redeposited it on the counter, she
noticed the green edge of the certified envelope
she'd taken on Helga's behalf at the historical society earlier this week. "Aargh. Amara needs to come
get this. Thanks for reminding me, Nutty."

She dialed Amara again. Voice mail. This was getting annoying. She couldn't be that concerned
about it, if she wasn't calling her back. Stan left another message, then hung up and pondered her
next move. She needed to have another conversation with Betty. Betty, who had alerted Stan to the
possible murder before even Jessie Pasquale came to
that conclusion. Betty, who hadn't offered any other
theories since then and seemed to be avoiding even
her closest friends.

It didn't make sense.

Stan checked her watch. Only twelve-thirty. She didn't have to meet Izzy and the ghost hunters at the bookstore building until eight. Plenty of time to make a few rounds. First, she'd stop by the library to talk to Betty and see where that led her. And she'd bring Scruffy as an icebreaker. No one could resist her little schnoodle. Henry was popular at the library, too, but right now he looked more concerned about his nap than the investigation.

"Scruffy! Want to go make some friends?"

She did, of course. Henry rolled over lazily and kept snoring. She bundled Scruffy in her new winter parka. One of the best things about Frog Ledge was its dog-friendly atmosphere. Most places didn't blink an eye if anyone brought their dog, as long as he or she was well-behaved. Jake had been largely responsible for starting that trend. Duncan was a McSwigg's regular.

Thinking about them made Stan sad again, so she focused on her task. The sooner she got to the bottom of whatever was going on, the sooner she could address her personal life. If there was a personal life left.

Stan drove over to the library, relieved to see Betty's Mazda in its usual spot. She gathered Scruffy's leash and they hurried inside. She found Lorinda at the front desk, talking to one of the staff.

Lorinda waved at them. "Hi, Stan and Scruffy!"

"Hey there," Stan said. Scruffy strained at her leash until she could get to Lorinda, who leaned down to accept her kiss.

"What's shaking?" Lorinda rose, balancing perfectly on her typical five-inch heels. Today's were a snazzy purple snakeskin pattern.

"I'm looking for Betty."

Lorinda pointed up. "In her office. Locked away. Came in and went straight upstairs. Haven't seen her all day."

"Really?"

"Yep, I worry that she's taking Helga's death too hard." Lorinda shook her head. "It's so sad. She'll love to see you, I'm sure."

Stan wasn't too sure about that, but she didn't say anything.

"Anyway, can Scruffy go visit the children's library while you go see her?" Lorinda asked.

"She would love that." Stan handed over Scruffy's leash.

"Excellent. This will be a huge hit." Lorinda winked. "Take your time, honey." Scruffy trotted happily away with her. She loved visiting the library.

Stan climbed to Betty's second-floor office. The door was slightly ajar. Betty was on the phone, speaking in what sounded like terse tones to whoever was on the other end. Stan couldn't hear what she was saying. She stepped up to the door and knocked, pushing it open. "Betty?"

Betty looked startled. She held up one finger, then said, "I'll have to call you back."

Stan waited until she'd replaced the phone, then stepped in and took a chair in front of her desk. "How are you?"

"I feel fine," Betty said. She certainly looked better than she had even at the funeral yesterday. Her spiky hairdo was back, and she had added a teal scarf to her simple black dress for some color. "It's hard, but I had to get back. Things were piling up, and with the event Sunday . . ." She trailed off and shook her head. "Life goes on, doesn't it? So what's going on?"

"You tell me," Stan said.

Betty frowned. "What do you mean?"

"Did you read the paper this morning? I'm sure you've heard by now either way. About Cyril."

Betty picked up a bottle of water from the corner of her desk. "Yes, I heard," she said.

Stan waited. "And?"

"And what?" Betty sipped her water. "Of course I was shocked. But Jessie must have found something to bring her to that conclusion."

Stan threw up her hands. "Come on, Betty. You knew before Jessie Pasquale that Helga was murdered. You dropped that bombshell and then stopped talking about it." She leaned forward in her chair. "I think you know who did it. And you know it's not Cyril."

Betty managed to look horrified. She rose from her chair, went over to her door, and closed it. "I beg your pardon, Stan!"

"You don't need to beg my pardon. I think you need to beg Cyril's. If you know who did it and you're letting him take the fall, that's wrong."

Betty fiddled with a pen on her desk. Stan noticed her hand shook.

"I don't know who did it. But I also don't know why on earth Cyril would kill Helga."

"I don't think Cyril killed anyone," Stan said. "Unless my gut is way off."

Betty didn't say anything.

"Tell me about Dale Hatmaker. How badly did he want Helga's job? Did he bribe the mayor or something so he could get it if Helga suddenly became unable to do the work?"

"I don't know. Dale's a slime ball," Betty said. "But I haven't figured out if he's capable of killing anyone."

"Are you working on figuring it out? If you are, that could be dangerous." Not that she should talk.

Betty still didn't answer. Stan sat back. "Why won't you talk to me? You trusted me enough to tell me your hunch in the first place. What changed?" Inwardly, she cringed, hearing herself have a similar conversation from the other side. Trust. It seemed to be lacking in Frog Ledge lately.

Something flickered in Betty's eyes. "I do trust you," she said. "But I have nothing to tell you."

Frustrated, Stan changed direction. "Why didn't you tell me your mother was Alice Donahue? The Alice Donahue who had keys to the library the night of the Constantine murder, and found the guy's body later?"

Betty's hand froze. "Why are you bringing my mother into it?"

"That's common knowledge. It was in all the reports. It just took me longer to connect the dots with your maiden name since I'm new to town." She managed a smile. "You should at least give me props for doing my research."

Betty's face remained stony. Guess she didn't appreciate the joke.

"Listen. The way I figure it, either Dale Hatmaker or someone associated with the Constantine murder killed Helga, if Jessie Pasquale is indeed right and she was murdered. Those were the two things that stood out after she died." Stan held up a finger. "Hatmaker greased someone's palms for a job"—she held up a second finger—"and the ghost hunters came and stirred up this murder. Do you agree?"

Nothing.

"What do you know about the Constantine murder? What did your mother know? What was Helga doing that Edgar Fenwick told her to 'let sleeping dogs lie'?" Stan fired the questions off the way she presumed a real journalist would. Although she did wonder about leaving time for the person to answer.

Betty shoved her chair back and stood up. "I have no idea, and I'm insulted that you're insinuating any such thing. I also don't appreciate my mother's name being thrown into this mess. That incident happened over sixty years ago. Most people associated with it are dead. I don't know why you're feeding into this tabloid frenzy to bring it up all over again so people's relatives can suffer. If Trooper Jessie thinks Cyril killed Helga, well, my heart is broken because I'm fond of Cyril. But again, she must have her reasons to think that. Now, if you'll excuse me, I have work to do. We need to be prepared to celebrate a wonderful woman's life."

Stan remained seated. "Trooper Jessie didn't have a lot of reasons to suspect me last year either, but she did."

Betty didn't respond. Instead, she walked to the door and opened it.

Don't let the door hit you in the behind. She had been

dismissed. Again. Her plan hadn't worked so well, and she wasn't any further along gathering information than she had been. But man, was she tired of being the bad guy.

She pushed herself out of the chair. "Fine, Betty," she said. "But if an innocent man goes to jail and you could've stopped it, you'll regret it for the rest of your life."

She went to find Scruffy, leaving Betty standing next to her door. She looked smaller than ever.

Chapter 32

Stan rounded up Scruffy from the children's area of the library, much to Scruffy's chagrin, and hustled her outside. Scruffy had mastered the classic puppy-dog eyes. Accented by her long eyelashes, the look left most humans helpless. But not today. Today Stan was on a mission.

Stan drove Scruffy home and dropped her off, despite her protests, then drove back to the town hall. Pasquale's police car was parked in its usual spot. The sight made her fume. What was she doing sitting around in her office? There were murders to solve around here. She parked haphazardly in a spot near the door and strode inside, straight to Pasquale's office. Not bothering to knock, she flung the door open. Pasquale and Tony Falco looked up, startled, from what appeared to be a serious conversation across her desk. Pasquale muttered something that sounded like, "For the love of God."

"Excuse me," Stan said. "But we need to talk."

"I'm in the middle of something," Pasquale said, but Falco rose.

"Not at all, Trooper. I'd like for you to be available to our citizens." He rose and turned a gracious smile on Stan. "Kristan, good day. Please take your time. I'll check in with you later," he said to Pasquale, and left, closing the door behind him.

Stan resisted the urge to spit at him as he walked by.

Pasquale turned her Icy Stare of Death on Stan. "What is it now that couldn't wait?"

"I need to see Cyril Pierce."

"Sorry. He's in custody. Waiting for a judge to set bail." Pasquale turned back to the papers on her desk.

"Great. I can still talk to him, can't I? His father can't make it, so he asked me to check in on him," she lied.

"I didn't know you were such close family friends with the Pierces," Pasquale said.

"You don't have to be snotty," Stan said. "I know you're just doing your job, but no one questions you. It's me everyone gets mad at all the time, even when I'm only trying to help. So since I'm already in trouble with everyone, and Jake's disappointed in me, can't you cut me some slack? This once?" She was mortified to hear her voice waver, but it was too late. Tears began to prick her eyes. *Do not cry in front of her. Do not cry in front of her.* She channeled the first song she could think of into her mind. Unfortunately it was Stevie Nicks's "Fall from Grace." Her tears started to bubble into hysterical laughter, so she covered it up with a coughing fit.

Pasquale's face finally showed some concern. Stan figured she was more worried about a civilian having a breakdown in her office rather than said civilian's personal problems, but at least it got Pasquale out of her chair.

"Stan. Sit." Pasquale pulled out the chair Falco had vacated and shoved her into it, a bit more forcefully than necessary. "Here." She pulled a bottle of water out of a small refrigerator next to her desk, opened it, and placed it in front of Stan.

Stan drank, grateful for the time to get herself under control. When she felt like she could speak without crying, laughing, or singing, she put the bottle down. "Thanks," she said.

"Listen." Pasquale perched against the side of her desk. "My brother isn't disappointed in you. Are you kidding? He's crazy about you. But he's just really upset. He loved Helga. Our whole family did."

Crazy about her? Pasquale was the crazy one. It was no use. The tears started to bubble up again. Of all the people in this town, why did she have to lose it in front of Jessie? "You're wrong. He is disappointed right now," she said. "And I think he's mad at me." She sniffled, searched in her purse for tissues. "Why can't he be mad at you? You're the one investigating."

Pasquale smiled a little sadly. "He is mad at me. That's nothing new, though. I'm just more used to it." She rose, walked slowly around the room. "Why are you involved in this? You don't want to be. Trust me."

"I didn't want to be involved." Stan swiped angrily at her eyes, grateful she'd worn her waterproof mascara today. "But I'm really bad at saying no to people. And Cyril was pathetic enough that it was extra impossible." She shrugged. "So now I'm in it. May as well see it through."

"Seems rational to me for someone with no investigative skills, no badge, and no gun," Pasquale said. Her sarcasm was not lost on Stan.

She chose to ignore it. "Do you really think Cyril would hurt Helga? Why, Jessie? Why would he do that?"

Instead of getting a smart response, or a blank cop stare, Pasquale thrust her hands into the pockets of her trousers. "I don't know," she said. "That's what I'm trying to find out."

Stan recovered quickly from the shock of Jessie's honest, no-sarcasm-involved answer. "Maybe I can help you," she said. "Please let me talk to him."

Pasquale looked at her for a long time before she spoke. "You tell anyone, I'll throw you in jail, too. Meet me at the barracks in half an hour."

Entering the state police barracks from the rear did not bring back fond memories of her own experience as a murder suspect. But she had no choice. It was the only way Pasquale would let her in to see Cyril.

"You coming?" Pasquale asked impatiently. She held the door. Before she let Stan pass, she held out her hand. "Cell phone."

"Why?"

"Because I'm not supposed to let you in there in the first place. I'm not going to let you hand him a cell phone, too."

Stan handed it over and followed her through the dark hallway, past doors with keypads next to them. She knew one of the closed doors led into an interrogation room. She'd been there before. She followed Pasquale into a stairwell. The holding cells were in the basement. They were as sparse and ugly as she'd imagined. Luckily, her experience had ended in the questioning phase.

The first two cells were empty, which seemed like a positive. Maybe recent arrests had been minimal. As if reading her thoughts, Pasquale smiled. "They're only empty because the criminals got moved to the real jail. No bail money."

Excellent. Stan almost bumped into her when she paused abruptly in front of cell number three. She peered inside. Cyril Pierce sat on the cot. He blinked when he saw Stan.

"Fifteen minutes," Pasquale said, and went back the way she'd come. Stan heard the door slam behind her and had a sinking feeling she'd just been locked in here.

"What are you doing here?" Cyril asked, as if she'd just showed up at his office unannounced rather than came to visit him in jail.

"Coming to visit. You're welcome," Stan said.

Cyril missed her snarky tone. "Nice of you, but I didn't think I could have visitors."

"I can be convincing when I want to be. And I needed to talk to you. You're not telling me the whole story."

"The whole story? The whole story about what? Nice story, by the way. One of the cops brought it to show me."

"Thanks. But stop trying to distract me. The whole story about why you got arrested!" Stan paced the small hallway. "You told me Pasquale tagged you because you were hanging around near the green and the museum early Sunday morning before the celebration. It sounded lame to me when you said it, because *hello,* you're a reporter. That's what they do. But now I'm really not buying it." She ticked points off on her fingers. "One, Helga sounded like a difficult person, from what I'm hearing. Two, Betty Meany immediately thought Helga had been murdered, but swore me to secrecy about it. Three, Edgar Fenwick said he told Helga to let sleeping dogs lie, but she didn't listen. And four, people don't get arrested for being in the neighborhood unless there's a darn good reason. There were plenty of other people around, too." She knew she had more reasons than that but couldn't remember them all right now.

"Wait. Betty thought Helga had been murdered? Before I got arrested?"

"Way before. And that's off the record."

Cyril frowned. "Did she think it was me?"

"No. Well, she said she didn't know who it was. I don't know if that's true or not, but I didn't get the sense it was you." She searched her pockets for her cell phone to see the time, then remembered Pasquale had confiscated it. "Did you see Dale Hatmaker around the museum early that day? He's hot for her job, you know."

Cyril shook his head. "Dale Hatmaker was doing a cemetery tour that morning. I know because he asked me to cover it, but I didn't have time to do both."

"He was? With witnesses? You're sure?"

"Positive. I saw them on my way to the green," Cyril said.

That killed her theory about Dale's desire for Helga's job being strong enough that he would want to kill her to get it. Which left her no choice but to believe Felix Constantine was the answer. "Well, that narrows it down. What do you think Edgar Fenwick meant about telling Helga to let sleeping dogs lie?"

Cyril gave her a blank look. "I have no idea."

Stan didn't quite believe him. "Tell me about your father. That's what I've been wanting to ask you for days now."

"My father? Why?"

"Because he was the reporter on the Constantine murder. I wanted to know if he remembered anything about it. He—"

"Leave my father out of it," Cyril interrupted. His tone changed from matter-of-fact to angry.

Stan stared at him. "What?"

"I said, leave my father be. He's not well, and that was a long time ago. He wasn't even there that night. He just covered the murder. I doubt he'd remember much about it anyway." Cyril turned and walked to the back of his cell, his back to Stan. "Listen. I appreciate you helping me. I didn't kill Helga. I don't know if anyone killed Helga, or if she really did fall. But that's not your problem. Just forget about it, okay?"

Forget about it? Both he and Betty had, in their own way, dragged her into this mess, and now they wanted her to bow out gracefully and go on with her life? Too late. The stakes were too high. "Cyril, I can't just forget about it," she started to say, but then Pasquale's footsteps sounded on the stairs.

A minute later, she appeared. "Time's up," she said, motioning to Stan. "You're done."

Stan had no choice but to follow her. She glanced back at Cyril one more time before she walked away. He still had his back to her.

Chapter 33

Knotty Pines, the senior living center where Arthur Pierce resided, was just over the border of Frog Ledge's neighboring town on the west side. When Stan drove up, it struck her that it was larger than some college campuses. There were three different buildings in the sunny yellow community, all branching out from one main building where the offices were located. The complex had three components—the assisted living facility, the independent living area where folks maintained their own apartments, and the full-time care area. The construction looked new and the grounds out in front looked as good as they could look in the middle of winter. Unsure where to park, Stan looped around the driveway and found herself behind one of the buildings, near a covered bridge over a small pond. Seating areas with benches overlooked what must be flower gardens in the nice weather.

But she still had no place to park. She backed down the narrow driveway and circled again before coming across a small parking lot about a quarter-mile away from the main office. Residents must not get that many visitors, if this was all they offered. Which was sad.

She'd been up most of the night contemplating this visit. Benedict, her new friend, had helped. She'd spent some time with him and told him her dilemma over a bowl of chicken, rice, and carrots. He'd agreed she should seek Arthur out, though he hadn't offered her any clues about what might have happened to Helga, based on his proximity to her in the days before her death. So here she was.

She parked and walked briskly through the chilly air to the front door. A large desk with pamphlets was positioned next to the door. No one manned it, though, so she walked through the entryway into a larger waiting area. Three hallways branched off in front of her. No main desk. No one in sight. So much for security.

Stan chose the direction that looked like it might lead to people and found an office directly on her left. A woman with her hair in a bun and glasses perched on the edge of her nose looked up from some paperwork and fixed an unfriendly stare on her.

"Yes?" she asked, her voice dripping with boredom.

"Hello, I'm looking for Arthur Pierce," Stan said in her friendliest voice.

The woman sighed and yanked her glasses off. "Go back the way you came and take a right. The nurse's station is there and they can direct you. I'm the facilities manager."

Good for you. At least they don't normally let you talk to people for a living. Stan bit her tongue and smiled.

"Thanks so much." She turned and headed in the other direction.

This time, she chose the right hallway and found a much more cheerful nurse behind the desk. "Arthur? Sure thing. He's in apartment 409. The independent living area, that way." She pointed down the hall where Stan had encountered Ms. Personality. "Walk all the way to the end and take the elevator to four, make a right, and you'll find him a few doors down. If he doesn't answer, knock on the door to the right. He spends a lot of time at his neighbor's."

Stan thanked the nurse and doubled back the way she'd come, breezing by the nasty manager's door without looking inside. She couldn't help but peek into the rooms she passed. Habit. She'd always been the kid who loved to look into people's windows at dusk while she walked her grandmother's dog Sabrina, just as the sky was turning shades of navy and the rooms already lit seemed so bright. She would imagine the lives of the people inside the houses. Create stories for them. Were they married? Kids? Having a fight? Or, on days when her imagination was in overdrive, she thought maybe they were spies, planted in the neighborhood to keep an eye on an international criminal. People in the neighborhood had probably thought she was a crazy Peeping Tom.

Here, the stories carried by the rooms seemed sad. She was in the nursing home area, judging from the setup of each room and the hospital smells wafting down the hall. She was cheered by the sight of a fluffy tortie cat sitting on one resident's bed, all curled up in a ball like cats did. At least these folks could have their pets, or get visits from pets. Maybe they even had a resident cat or two. It was a positive thing to do, especially for people who were ill or immobile. Stan couldn't imagine one day without her animals. This was especially true when half the world was angry at her. Her pets still loved her. Even Benedict, who didn't know her well. They didn't care what mistakes she made.

She finally reached the end of the hall and the elevator bank. After waiting for what seemed like forever, the elevator doors finally creaked open. She gingerly stepped in and hit the button for the fourth floor, hoping for the best. It took a while, but the elevator finally released her unscathed. The walk down the wallpapered hall felt endless. She scanned both sides of the hall on her way, reading the numbers on each door. When she got to 409, she slowed. The door was wide open.

Stan peered inside. Her mouth dropped. The place looked like it had been ransacked, and she could only see the hallway leading to a kitchen. Correction—she couldn't actually *see* the hallway. Piles of newspapers, shoes, and jackets were strewn about in various stages of disarray. He couldn't be a hoarder, in a place like this. Could he?

"Hello?" She rapped with her knuckles, waited. Nothing.

"Mr. Pierce?" she called, stepping inside with one foot, gingerly nudging aside a yellowing newspaper.

A loud yell and a crash made her jump a foot. "You're incompetent!" she heard a man's voice shout from the other side of the wall.

Whirling around, she realized the room right next to Arthur Pierce's was open, and the loud voices were coming from that direction. At least this was a trusting environment. Remembering what the woman downstairs had said about Mr. Pierce's tendency to visit his neighbor, she moved over to the door to the right of Arthur's apartment and knocked.

The voices stilled. Then, as if on cue, two heads appeared in the doorway. One was a shiny cue ball, with just a little white fuzz above each ear and a mustache. He had a hammer in his hand. The other head belonged to the man she'd seen Sunday with Cyril. He had a cigar clamped between his teeth again, too. She'd only gotten a quick glimpse of him then, but now she saw how closely his son resembled him. Stan figured once he released his grip on the smelly cigar, she would see the same bad teeth that plagued Cyril.

Don't be a jerk, Stan. She shook off her inner conscience and smiled. "Mr. Pierce?"

The balding guy looked at his friend and whistled. "How'd you get a hottie like that to come see you?"

Arthur Pierce frowned at him and stepped out of the apartment into the hallway.

His friend rolled his eyes. "I'll hang my picture on my own. Maybe then it will stay on the wall." He disappeared and slammed the door.

Pierce turned his attention back to Stan. "Yeah, that's me."

"I'm Stan Connor. I live in Frog Ledge with your son. Well, not *with* your son," she corrected, horrified. "I mean, we live in the same town."

"I get it, Ms. Connor," Pierce said in the same deadpan voice Cyril used. "Let's go over to my apartment." He shuffled slowly past Stan to his open apartment, motioning for her to go first. He followed her in, closing the door behind him—and closing her in with him. The stale smell, coupled with the narrow, crammed space, made her throat constrict. She hoped nothing dead lurked underneath all these piles of things.

Stan took a few careful steps inside, then turned, not wanting him to come up too close behind her. Instead, she found him watching her curiously from the doorway.

"How can I help ya, young lady?" he asked.

"I'm sorry to interrupt your afternoon—"

Arthur chuckled, which caused him to wheeze. He pulled a handkerchief out of his pocket and blew his nose loudly before folding it and returning it to his pocket. Stan's stomach clenched. She never understood why anyone would want to put what was effectively dirty tissues in your pocket and carry them around all day. And reuse them, to boot. He cleared his throat. "You're not interrupting. What can I do for you? You here about my son?"

Stan hesitated, not sure how to answer. The old man had to know—didn't he?—that Cyril had been arrested.

"I read the paper," he said. "I know what happened." He waved his hand impatiently, urging her forward. "Go. Sit."

Obediently, she proceeded through the tiny kitchen into a living room that had two chairs and an ottoman. Beyond the living room, she could see a bedroom and bathroom down another small hallway.

Stan had still never seen Cyril Pierce's office in Frog Ledge, but she'd always imagined it had that true newsroom vibe, despite its one-man staff.

Arthur Pierce's apartment gave her the confidence that she was correct, if his son was anything like him. Piles of newspapers, old and new, were stacked on every available surface in the living room. An old-fashioned typewriter sat on a table by the window, with blank paper stacked next to it. Stan got the sense that the machine was actually used. She half-expected to hear the burps and buzzes and static of a police scanner. She chose the chair with the least amount of newspapers piled on it and sat on the edge.

"You can throw those on the floor," he said. "I have a reason to have all of these, you know."

"I'm fine," she said, but he was already off on a tangent.

"Everyone's always trying to clean up after me, but I like my apartment this way. I know I should put my shoes away, but still. Even my wife understood. She said, 'Once a newsman, always a newsman.'" He looked sad. Abruptly he got up, went into the bathroom, and returned with a handful of pills, then searched for some water.

Stan spied a glass on the crowded coffee table to the left of her chair—right next to a bottle of Scotch. She picked up the water and handed it to him. He nodded his thanks.

Once he'd swallowed his pills, he threw a pile of stuff off his other chair and sat. "So, what about my son? He didn't kill no one, you know. 'Specially not her."

"I don't think he did either, Mr. Pierce. That's why I wanted to ask you a few questions."

Arthur stuck his damp cigar back in his mouth and chewed, waiting.

"Do you remember the murder of Felix Constantine? The boxer from 1949?"

Arthur blinked once. Twice. Rolled the cigar in his mouth. "Sure I do," he said, finally. "I covered it. Why you wanna know about that?"

So much for Cyril's theory that he didn't remember. "Because I think it might have something to do with Helga's death."

Arthur didn't speak for a long time. When he did, though his face remained unchanged, Stan detected a tremor in his voice. "Why'n the world would you think that, young lady? And what do you know about her dying?"

Stan spread her hands wide. "All I know is that suddenly it's a murder investigation and your son is sitting in the state police barracks. If it has nothing to do with that, what would it have to do with? Why else would anyone want to kill an eighty-seven year-old?"

"Except no one killed her," Pierce said. "I think it's all just a big mistake."

"That's quite a mistake."

"The police have been known to make them."

"Did Helga have any enemies that you knew of?"

Pierce smiled slightly. "You mean besides the people who didn't do what she wanted them to do? Nah, everyone loved her."

"Mr. Pierce, I'm serious. This is important."

"I gathered that when my son went to jail," he said.

Stan leaned forward. "Did you leave a book on my front porch?"

Arthur frowned. "Why would you think I know where you lived?"

"Your son knows where I live. Someone left me the book Helga wrote back in the nineties. It has the initials *ACP* inside it."

Arthur didn't respond.

"It was marked to the piece Helga wrote. About Felix Constantine."

Still nothing.

"Is there something in there that's a clue? That could point us to Helga's killer and help Cyril? Help me understand, Mr. Pierce."

"Young lady, if I had a clue that could help my son, I'd surely give it to you. But I'm 'fraid I don't."

Stan gritted her teeth in frustration. "Have you heard about the ghost hunters who came to town to look at the old library building where Felix died?"

"Yup."

"Then you know they're looking into paranormal activity there. They got an anonymous tip. Which seems convenient."

Arthur stuck his nasty cigar in an ashtray and picked something off his tongue. "Don't pay much mind to that kind of nonsense. What're you gettin' at?"

"It seems like a coincidence that Helga died and the state police are investigating it as a murder, and at the same time there's a ghost hunt going on in the building where this other murder occurred. It might sound crazy, but I feel like the two are related, and you're the one who would have all that insider knowledge."

Stan felt like she was starring in her own amateur episode of *Cold Case*. If she'd known any songs popular in the 1940s or 1950s, they'd certainly be playing in her brain right now. Since she didn't, her brain instead chose to play "The Chain" in a continuous loop. She wondered if she'd ever hear anything besides Stevie Nicks in her head again. Good thing she was a fan.

Pierce remained silent. He took off his glasses, rubbed them on his sleeve, and readjusted them on his face. Stared at Stan.

"You reported the story," she tried again. "What do you think happened to Mr. Constantine? Did you have a theory on who killed him?"

"How would I know that? The police never figured it out. Damn straight we woulda wrote about it if they had." Pierce waved his cigar. "Someone like him, who knows? He wasn't a local. Any number of folks coulda been after him. Followed him here. Who knows." He pointed the cigar at her. "Way he operated, wouldn't surprise me. Slick, he was. That wasn't no upstanding profession, boxing. Just 'cause you're a smooth character. B'sides, the coroner couldn't find nothing for a weapon. That was something that didn't get a lot of press. Could be, the drunken fool fell and hit his head. Maybe that's why they never pursued it."

His words barely hung together. Stan's brain hurt trying to follow his logic. "So, what would all that have to do with Helga? Would someone kill her because of something she knew about Felix's death?"

Silence. Then Pierce shook his head. "Helga was my friend. Much as I wish it hadn't happened, she took a bad spill. All this hoopla—well, it's just that. Hoopla." Arthur got up and went to a leaning pile of stuff on his counter. He perused it, then pulled out a cigar box and selected a new one. Lit it, puffed, and returned to his seat. Stan had a troublesome vision of what would happen if Arthur fell asleep with that cigar lit around all these newspapers.

"Mr. Pierce, with all due respect, what if it isn't hoopla? What if there's something to this theory? It's the only way we're going to be able to help Cyril," she said. "Helga seemed like she wanted to remember Felix. She wrote a whole article in her book. I would think you did a lot of work on that story. Can you please just think about it and let me know if anything comes to mind?"

Pierce regarded her with no expression, chewing incessantly on that cigar. "Listen," he said, finally. "There's only one way you're gonna be able to figure out what happened to that boxer."

"There is?" Stan's heart started to pound. He knew something. Now they could move forward, figure this out, get Cyril out of jail, and restore Frog Ledge's sanity. "How?"

"Sir Arthur Conan Doyle." Pierce nodded, looking immensely pleased with himself. "He's got all the answers."

"Sir Arthur . . . I'm sorry, Mr. Pierce. What do you mean?"

He looked at her like she was an incredibly stupid woman. "Just what I said. Doyle. He's got the answers."

"But he's dead," Stan pointed out.

Pierce shook his head. "You young folks. No imagination at all." He laid the cigar in an ashtray and picked up the television remote. "Young lady, I have a show to watch. You'll excuse me, won'tcha?"

With that, he turned the TV on. The volume had to be at thirty or higher, because the sound nearly blasted Stan out of her seat. Resigned, she thanked him, hoped he heard her, and let herself out, wondering how much Scotch Pierce had downed before her arrival.

Stan took the elevator back to the first floor. As the door opened to let her off she almost bumped into Carla Miller, who was waiting to get on.

"Hello! We meet again," Carla said with a bright smile.

"Hey, Carla." Stan stepped off and held the door so it wouldn't close. Carla got on, her bright smile remaining in place until the doors closed between them. Stan watched the buttons until it stopped. On the fourth floor.

Chapter 34

Stan didn't know where else to go but home. Her bright idea of confronting Betty had resulted in one more person angry with her. Her visit with Arthur Pierce hadn't gotten her anywhere but smelling like old cigar, armed with a drunken suggestion to ask a dead author for help. Fabulous. Just like the rest of the week.

She pulled into her driveway and headed inside just as her cell phone rang. Fumbling around in her purse as she tried to get the door open and keep Nutty from running outside, she saw Brenna's number just as it went to voice mail. Hope filled her chest. Maybe Brenna had decided she was being silly and wanted to tell Stan she wasn't angry anymore. That she was on her way over to help with the wedding cake. She waited impatiently for her voice mail alert to sound, then pressed Play.

And felt her spirit deflate as Brenna's voice filled her ear, cool and aloof and not friendly at all.

"Stan, it's Brenna. I wanted to let you know that I'm resigning from Pawsitively Organic. I've accepted a full-time job and I think it's best if we part ways now." A slight hesitation, then she spoke again. Stan could hear a faint quiver in her voice. Or maybe she just hoped to hear it. "Thanks for letting me work with you. I learned a lot." *Click.*

That was it. Over. Stan felt tears prick her eyes. Just like that. She was on her own. Stan leaned against her door and allowed more tears to come. Seemed like all she'd been doing today, aside from making people mad, was crying. The dogs ran over to greet her. They looked concerned. Scruffy jumped up and held her paw out, sensing Stan was upset. Stan smiled through her tears and took the dog's paw.

"Thanks, honey. Okay, I have to get myself together. Lots to do. I can't change it, right? If Brenna doesn't want to work with me, there's nothing I can do to make her change her mind."

She shooed them down the hall and shrugged off her coat as the doorbell rang behind her. She cringed. Now what? More bad news? She didn't know if she could take it.

Cracking the door, she peered out. Amara was on the front step. "Bad time?" she asked, noting Stan's red eyes.

"Don't ask." Stan pulled the door wide. "What's up?"

"You've been leaving me voice mails to stop by. About the DNA thing."

"Right. Yes, come on in."

"Sorry I didn't get to call you back sooner." Amara stepped in and shut the door behind her. "This last inspection for the clinic is killing me." She stopped and looked at Stan. "You look like you're having a great day."

"You don't know the half." Stan led her to the kitchen. "A cat showed up at my house last night. Apparently he was Helga's cat. Sarah dumped him on my porch. Did some *woo-woo* thing that if he was meant to be with me, he'd stay. So I lectured her about it and she cried, and then I caved and said I'd try to keep the cat. Apparently Helga told her— just yesterday—how wonderful I am. Then I went to see Jake. Which didn't go so well because of this reporting thing. But it went better than it did with Brenna, who actually quit working with me. Just before you came in. Let's see, what else? Betty's mad at me, too, because I asked her about her mother being at the Constantine murder scene. In case you haven't been following, that's been a big story in town." She stopped for a breath and handed Amara the DNA envelope.

Amara stared at her, fascinated. "Wow. That's quite a day."

"That wasn't the end of it, but really, I don't have the energy. Want coffee?"

"No, thanks. I'm coffee'd out. Do you want some of my Rescue Remedy?" She pulled a yellow tube out of her purse. "Great for stress."

"Sure, why not. I'll try anything today." Stan accepted the spray. "What do I do with it?"

"Spray in your mouth." Amara nodded approvingly as Stan sprayed a few squirts, then took the envelope and read the name of the company. "Sounds familiar. I think Helga wrote down for me where she sent it. Let me look." She fumbled in her purse. "That way I won't open someone else's mail by accident. Aha." She pulled out a slip of paper. "Yep, same company. Guess I'm good." Amara ripped open the package and scanned the single sheet of paper as Stan brought her mug to the table.

"I have no idea how to read this," she said.

Stan peered over Amara's shoulder at the five different pieces of paper Amara pulled out of the envelope. One was a certificate stating Amara's DNA had been analyzed by the company. The next two were reports with graphs at the bottom. The final two were maps with lots of swirly lines snaking across them.

"Hmm." Stan took one of the reports and glanced through it. "There's a website where it says you can log in and see your personal page and some of the possible relations."

"Well, that doesn't help me. I don't have a log-in." Amara threw up her hands. "Forget it. I have so many things to do for the clinic. I can't be—"

"Amara. You are way too stressed out. So much for Zen. And Rescue Remedy. Look, you use the kit number and password up here." Stan pointed to the top left corner of the report.

Amara broke into a smile. "You're so smart. Got a computer?"

"Yeah, I'm real smart. So smart the whole town hates me. Here." Stan handed her the iPad. "Have at it."

"The whole town doesn't hate you. Maybe I will have coffee. Unless you're busy. I can do this from home," Amara said.

"No, please. I need something to keep me occupied," Stan said. "At least until whatever mayhem the ghost hunt brings tonight." She got up to pour Amara's coffee.

Amara cocked an eyebrow. "Are you sure you

want to be involved in that? Given everything else going on," she said when Stan opened her mouth to protest.

Stan shrugged. "I may as well do something that I've always wanted to do."

"Good way to keep it in perspective. Besides, this happened before. You thought people were upset with you." Amara shrugged. "It all worked out, remember?"

"Thanks for reminding me that this isn't the first time I've alienated myself from the entire town," Stan said. She brought the mug over and rearranged the papers so she didn't dump coffee on them. As she did so, her eyes fell on the scribbled sheet of paper Helga had written the DNA company name on for Amara. And her eyes widened. "Whoa. Does that say—" She snatched it up. "State Historic Preservation Office. This was Helga's note?"

Amara was barely paying attention. "She wrote it for me, yes."

"But was it her paper or someone else's?"

"I think she took it right out of her purse," Amara said, finally looking up. "Why?"

"Because this is the place that asked Izzy to stop the construction."

Amara stared at her. "You're kidding."

"Nope."

"That's odd. Why did she want to halt the construction?"

"I guess no one knows but her. And maybe Sarah," Stan murmured. Although she had a hunch. "Can I keep this note?"

"Sure." Amara was already back to the DNA. "This is so wild," she said. "I can't believe I can find family members by swabbing spit on a Q-tip and playing online."

Stan chuckled. "I think it's probably more complicated than that. So, what'd you get?"

"Hang on, trying to figure out this website. This is actually kind of cool." She turned the tablet around so Stan could see the screen. "I don't really know the difference between Y-DNA and mtDNA."

"mtDNA is mitochondrial, I think. It was highlighted on the report. And you can look at that specifically." Stan pointed.

"Again. So smart." Amara tapped the icon and scanned the easiest column to read—the one with names. "Most recent match. Carmen Feliciano. Born 1925. No date of death." She looked at Stan. "Is this my relative?"

"Must be. Recognize the name?"

"No, not even sure if it's male or female." Amara sighed.

"Let me see." Stan took the tablet back and perused the site. "Look. That name is under family finder, too. According to this, you have some shared DNA, which makes you somewhere between fourth and remote cousins with this person. And"—she handed the device back triumphantly—"there's an E-mail Your Relative button."

"Huh. Super cool." Amara hesitated. "You think I should e-mail him/her?"

"Well, duh. Isn't that why you did all this?"

"True. I guess I'll go for it." She swiped the e-mail button, tapped out a short message, and hit Send. "There. I guess now I wait. But wouldn't this person be pretty old? You think they're using e-mail?"

"That's such a stereotype! You're terrible. Besides,

look at Helga. She was probably better at technology than we are. You should Google Carmen. See what you can find."

Amara pulled up Google search and typed in her new relative's name. "Hmmm. I have a male Carmen Feliciano from New Jersey who's being indicted for racketeering."

Stan laughed. "You have mob in your family? That's kind of cool."

"You're so weird." Amara scrolled through the hits. "The rest of them are female. And way too young to be my Carmen. Listen to this. Carmen Feliciano on Twitter. 'Dog owner, macchiato junkie, super-sexy double agent.'" She shook her head. "Doubt she's mine. But here are some white page listings." She scanned them. "There is one in Connecticut, but doesn't give the town and it's unlisted. She/he would have to live close by, right? For Helga to get DNA?"

"No idea. The kit could probably be sent by mail. Maybe wait a day or so and see if you get an e-mail back and then you can decide what else to try," Stan said.

"I guess I'll have to." Amara shrugged. "I've waited this long, what's another day?"

"While you're waiting, here." Stan went to the freezer and began pulling out frozen doggie meals. "Why don't you take these home so you have them. And I can get them out of my freezer. I have a wedding to cater and I need the space."

Chapter 35

"You ready?" Izzy had dressed for the ghost-hunting occasion. Or maybe she had dressed for a spy investigation—Stan wasn't sure which. She wore head-to-toe black, including a knitted cap pulled low over her forehead. She still managed to look elegant and magazine-cover ready. Everything she wore seemed to work on her. If Stan didn't like her so much, she might be jealous.

"I'm ready." Stan shifted her weight from foot to foot, trying to stay warm in the would-be foyer while they waited for Adrian and his crew. She'd kept her outfit simple—jeans and a sweatshirt, heavy coat, hat, and gloves since it was still freezing out. And probably inside, too.

Tonight was the night—they were going through the building with equipment and cameras, the next step in proving the Ghost in the Almost-Bookstore was for real. Despite all the bad things going on in town, Stan was excited. Not only had she gotten to meet her hero, but she was going on a ghost hunt with him. This day would definitely go down in

history. Cyril had to be losing his mind that he
couldn't report on this, but Stan wasn't about to add
to her problems by taking that on, too.

Fox and his team had been on-site setting up
since the workers left, and it looked like quite a pro-
duction. There were six of them now, and they were
running around with wires and cameras and other
equipment. They moved quickly and efficiently with
a minimum of conversation, evidence of a well-oiled
machine. Outside, curious citizens—and some Fox
groupies—lined up across the street, hoping to be
the first to hear what they uncovered.

"They're gonna have to lock the doors," Izzy said,
gazing out at the crowd. "These crazies'll be following us inside if they think they can."

"We've got that covered." Fox materialized next to
them. "It wouldn't be the first time we've had a . . .
keen interest in a site. Sorry to keep you waiting,
ladies. Why don't you come right on in," he said,
flashing them his high-wattage smile. "We're just
waiting on one person. In the meantime, I'll tell you
what we've done." He motioned them into the main
room, a mess of concrete, wires, tools, half-cut wood,
and blueprints. "We're working with two kinds of
equipment tonight: infrared cameras and digital
audio recorders, which capture electronic voice phe-
nomenon."

"EVPs," Stan said.

"Exactly." Fox smiled at her. "You do watch."

Stan blushed under Izzy's scrutiny. She felt like
the teacher's pet all of a sudden. "I do," she said
defensively.

"I think it's great. So. With Izzy's permission, we
connected the cameras on all three floors." Stan

noticed he didn't mention Jake's permission. Fox walked them around the room, pointing out cables and cameras of various sizes. "Our focus is on the basement area, because based on our research that's where the body was discovered. But we don't want to limit it to just this floor, because we've had worker reports that evidence has occurred on other floors as well. Tools missing, voices when there's only one person working, that sort of thing."

"Does Frank know about the worker reports?" Stan asked Izzy in a low voice.

Izzy shrugged. "No clue. I think they banded together and compiled it after he ignored their complaints."

Stan was about to ask her what happened after Frank stormed into the café, but one of Fox's crewmen walked in followed by Sarah Oliver.

"Ah, Sarah. Delighted you could join us." Fox stepped forward and gave her a hug. "Sarah offered to be here tonight to see if she can help us uncover activity."

Sarah beamed. She looked a little like she'd been drinking, or maybe it was the high heels she wore while trying to balance on the uneven flooring. She wore her usual flowy skirt, this one black lace, and a matching top. Her black hat had a lacy veil that covered her eyes, giving her an eccentric old-movie-star look. "And tell my mother's story. The hat is my mother's," she explained. "She wore it often back then. I'm getting the feeling she wore it on the night of the party."

Izzy caught Stan's eye and raised an eyebrow. Stan shrugged.

"Okay," Fox said, with a nod to his crewman. "Val, let's secure the doors and get going."

Val nodded and went off to follow orders. He returned with the rest of the gang.

Fox made the introductions. "Wolf and Val are running cameras. Max has recorders for EVP. Andy over there is using the dowsing rods." He produced a notebook and pen. "Me, I'm in charge of taking notes and making sure we capture everything. Izzy is our building owner, Stan is a friend of hers who loves the show"—he winked at her—"and our medium, Sarah."

"Yo," said Max, flipping an unruly piece of too-long hair out of his eyes. He was the guy Stan remembered driving the van when they first came to town. He chewed gum incessantly and wore a shirt featuring a tiger looking down the scope of a rifle. "Let's get this party started."

Chapter 36

They started on the top floor. Stan wondered if that was on purpose. A buildup of the excitement as they made their way to their final destination—the basement.

Wolf held the video camera, Val the digital. Max carried his recorder at the ready. Andy did something in the next room. Fox turned quiet. Serious. He consulted his notes, then turned to Izzy. "Anything on this floor you noticed?"

Izzy shook her head. "I didn't spend a lot of time up here. I wasn't exactly sure what I wanted to do with this space, so I didn't pay it much mind."

Fox nodded. He walked slowly around the room with his flashlight. Motioned to Max, who pressed a button on his recorder. "Is anyone here?" he asked.

Nothing. Nothing that Stan could hear, anyway. She leaned forward, listening intently. On the show, there was always some crackle or static noise that they later deciphered. Max shook his head. Wolf did a slow pan of the room with his camera. Then they moved into the next room.

"Try the rods," Fox said. Andy nodded. He pulled out two copper-colored wands. They glowed in the crew's lights, shooting off flashes of gold around the room.

Andy focused on the rods for a few seconds, then closed his eyes. "Felix. Are you here?"

Stan held her breath. Waited. Next to her, Izzy grabbed her arm in anticipation.

The rods didn't move.

"Is anyone here? Does anyone have a message for us?"

This time, the rod in Andy's left hand moved, ever so slightly, to the left.

Izzy peered at it. "What does that mean?"

"That means yes," Andy said. Izzy gasped.

"What's the message?" Stan asked.

"How are you going to get a message with the rods?" Izzy asked.

"It's more to determine yes or no answers," Andy said. "We just got the answer that someone is here, and there's a message. Adrian—want to try with the recorder?"

Fox nodded. Max wagged the recorder and hit his button.

"What do you want to tell us?" Fox asked the room.

Nothing. Izzy relaxed her grip on Stan's arm.

"Who are you?" Fox tried.

Nothing again.

"Dude. You sure you weren't moving the rods?" Max asked. Wolf snickered. Andy sent him a nasty look.

"Behave," Fox said, before Andy opened his mouth. He looked around. "Val, snap a few shots."

Val obliged. Wolf panned the room again. Fox noted a few things on his pad. Sarah floated around, eyes closed. Stan envisioned her getting tangled up in the wires with those heels and taking the whole operation out. She stifled a giggle. Izzy looked at her curiously.

"Next floor," Fox said.

They descended on the main floor. In the northeast corner of the main room, near the spot where Izzy said one of the guys had told her they'd heard some knocking, the camera caught some kind of orb.

"Bingo," Wolf said.

"What does that mean?" Izzy asked anxiously.

Wolf shrugged. "Hard to say. This part is all about capturing the evidence. The next thing is to watch the hours of footage and see what we're really getting, and listen to the recordings. You guys are seeing all the glam." He winked at them.

Izzy started to ask something else, but then from the other side of the room, an audible gasp. All heads turned to see Sarah, standing near the window, hands on her head as if she suddenly had a raging headache. Stan remembered her similar show at the Groundhog Day event, and what happened next. She did not want a repeat performance.

"Sarah?" Stan hurried over. "Are you okay?"

"My mother," Sarah murmured. "My mother is trying to tell me something."

Stan looked at Adrian, unsure what to do. She couldn't tell what he thought either. But Sarah didn't seem to care what either of them thought.

Eyes still closed, hands on her head like she was in some sort of weird trance, she moved away from Stan. Glided over the floor, her heels miraculously not getting caught up in tools or cables, and headed straight for the stairs leading to the basement.

"She said it was an accident. All of it was an accident." She paused, opened her eyes, and looked around at them. "She wants to show us." She vanished through the door onto the steep wooden staircase. Stan heard her heavy heels clunking down the steps.

Stan felt a little thrill. Was she really talking to Helga? Right now? Was this endeavor actually going to reveal something? Was Sarah for real? The opening bars of "Rhiannon" played in a back corner of her brain. Peering after Sarah, she balked at the narrow black space ahead of her. Sarah hadn't even waited for a flashlight beam.

"Holy cow," Izzy muttered. "This is weird."

Adrian motioned to Max. "Let's go."

"On it." Max headed down behind Sarah, recorder on. Fox turned to Stan and Izzy, who brought up the rear of the party. Izzy was dead last, holding on to Stan's arm. "Be very careful on these stairs," he warned them over his shoulder before starting down. "The workers told me they haven't done much to shore up the basement structure. They're old and very steep."

Stan craned her neck, trying to see past him into the darkness that had swallowed Sarah. She could still see Max's outline, but not hers. The walls on both sides of the stairs looked like they could crumble at the slightest touch. There was no railing.

Adrian stepped onto the staircase, his heavy boot echoing against the old wood.

She turned to see if Izzy was behind her. She was, and she looked eerie in the glow of the spotlight Fox's team had set up near the camera. It cast a strange glow over everything on the main floor. Stan couldn't tell if the shadowy shapes dancing around the room and down the steps were real or her mind played tricks on her.

"Mom?" Sarah's voice called from the dark.

Stan took one step down just as she heard some weird static noise echoing back from below. Max's excited voice echoed back to her, though she could no longer see him. Then a creaking noise drowned out any further words, followed by a crack that sounded like the entire floor had broken in half below them. Then, a thunderous crash, a scream, and silence as Max vanished from their view in a cloud of dust.

Stan felt air beneath her feet and braced for impact. Instead, she felt herself being lifted and propelled backward, hitting the floor with a thud. Her breath left her in a *whoosh* as Adrian Fox ended up on top of her. From somewhere above her she heard Izzy yell. She lay there for a second, stunned, until Fox scrambled to his feet and pulled her up with Izzy's help.

"Are you okay?" he asked urgently.

"Fine," Stan said, rubbing the hip that had taken the hardest blow. "What just happened?"

Max, Val, and Wolf ran over from various spots in the building when they heard the chaos.

"What the—" Wolf looked stunned. "Where's Max?"

"Stair collapse. Call 911." Fox grabbed the giant

flashlight out of Wolf's hand and turned back to the now-gaping hole in the stairwell as Val made the call. "Max! Sarah!" he hollered.

Stan, holding on to Izzy, held her breath and prayed for a response. She didn't know if Sarah had been on the stairs, too, or if she had been on solid ground when Max fell. Minutes ticked by that seemed like years; then she heard Sarah's voice, faint but there.

"I'm here. Max is hurt."

Fox cursed. "Are you okay? Can I get down there?"

Sarah's voice was remarkably calm. "I'm fine. I was already on the ground. I wouldn't try to come down. The stairs have pretty much collapsed down here. Are you all okay?"

Stan nudged Izzy and pulled her forward so she could hear better.

"We are. Is Max conscious? How bad are his injuries?" Fox asked. He knelt at the top of the stairs and shined his own light down. "Can you see? Can you grab his flashlight?"

"Hang on." A brief silence as Sarah presumably hunted around for Max's light. Then a second beam of light shined on. "Got it. His leg looks broken. Max? I think he's coming around," she called.

"Was this a ghost thing?" Izzy asked, eyes wide. "Did he do that to Max?"

Fox ignored her question. "Is there a door outside that goes into the basement?" he asked, his tone urgent.

"There is." Izzy snapped to attention. "I'll show you."

"Hang tight, Sarah. I'm going to come around the back," Fox yelled down.

"Okay," she called back. She was so calm. Stan was impressed, because her own heart was going a mile a minute. She followed Izzy and Fox out the front door and around the back of the building, trying not to alert the crowd lined up across the street that anything was wrong. They'd know soon enough. She hoped the police showed up, too, to keep the scene calm.

Izzy took the flashlight from Fox and shined it along the wall. "It's here somewhere," she muttered to herself. "Aha!" She pointed the flashlight beam triumphantly at a narrow door, old and probably rotting. She stepped forward and tried it. Locked. "Crap." She rapped on it a couple of times, probably hoping to lead Sarah to it so she could let them in.

Adrian Fox lifted one black-booted foot and kicked the door in. The ancient lock popped off on the first try. The wood buckled and splintered. Fox kicked one more kick for good measure, then pushed the door in. "Wait here," he told them. "I don't know how safe it is in there."

Despite the severity of the situation, Stan had a moment of pure admiration as her original stereotype of the big, bad ghost hunter came to life in front of her eyes.

"Well," Izzy said after he disappeared into the basement. "That's one mad ghost." She pulled her phone out. "I gotta call Jake before he hears this from someone else."

Stan didn't respond. Was it a mad ghost? Or the perils of traipsing around in an old building? She heard sirens as two ambulances roared to a stop out front. One of the guys must've directed the EMTs to the back, because soon they rushed around the corner. She and Izzy stood off to the side and watched. Stan felt numb as the EMTs did their thing. This scene had played out in front of her entirely too often in the last week. She thought of Max, his love of Southern food, how fond Char was of him, and sent a quick prayer to whoever happened to be listening that he was okay. She caught a glimpse of his face in the darkness as they brought him out on the stretcher and it looked too white.

As they loaded him up, Adrian Fox strode out of the building, conferred with the EMT, and got in the back of the ambulance with him. Sarah emerged a minute later, in the midst of a heated discussion with another EMT who was clearly trying to get her to the hospital, too.

"I don't need to go," she insisted. "I didn't even fall!"

The EMT clearly disagreed. They were about to get into a brawl about it when Sarah spied Stan. She jerked her arm away and raced over, hiking up her long skirt. It was a miracle she didn't fall with those heels. When she reached Stan, she took her hands and leaned in close so no one else heard her.

"My mother spoke to me. Did you hear what I said inside? That she said there was an accident here?" she asked.

Stan nodded. "Was Felix Constantine's death an accident? Is that what she meant?"

"She wants to help." Sarah took a deep breath and squeezed Stan's hands, so tight Stan almost cried out. "She says Sir Arthur Conan Doyle holds the key. He will tell you what happened."

Chapter 37

Saturday morning, eight a.m. The timer on Stan's oven dinged, jerking her awake. She was embarrassed to find her head on her kitchen table. Her chin felt wet. Had she actually drooled? Gross.

She'd been up since four, baking. She'd never gone to sleep for more than a half hour at a time last night and had eventually given up. After the stairs had collapsed under poor Max and sent the ghost hunt careening off the rails, Stan hadn't felt much like sleeping. Or eating. So she decided to bake. At least the wedding cake was coming along. She'd gotten the taste almost to perfection—enough strawberry to be unequivocally berry-esque, but without being overwhelming. She'd probably need one more trial run before she could declare it final—this time with just a few adjustments to minor ingredients. Henry and Scruffy wholeheartedly approved. Benedict had nibbled, too. Nutty was still pouting about Benedict and had actually turned down the cake. Silly coon cat.

Still, Stan had hope. Nutty wasn't mean to Benedict; rather, he would simply sit somewhere in a far corner of the room and glare at him. Stan could almost see him calculating the food and treats he'd have to give up so the new cat could eat.

Stan tried to be respectful of Nutty's feelings, but even in just a day she'd bonded with Benedict. He was a true gentleman, and very mellow. He was even good with the dogs. Scruffy had tried to chase him down the hall once presumably to play, and he'd stopped and sat and politely let her know that he didn't want to engage in those types of games thank-you-very-much, and given her a gentle tap on the head to drive the message home. Scruffy, embarrassed, had slunk off to tell Henry about the slight. Stan thought it was hilarious.

She wanted to keep him.

She turned back to the task at hand and unloaded her cake from the oven. Now she had to work on the icing. That would probably entice Nutty. She thought a cream-cheese frosting with a hint of strawberry. Maybe a dash of lemon to give it some zing.

The doorbell rang as she began pulling items out of the fridge. She thought about ignoring it, but her car was out in the driveway, so she was clearly home. Not to mention it was barely daybreak. Scruffy and Henry were already at the door barking up a storm. She sighed, deposited her armful of ingredients on the counter, and trudged to the front door. It was probably Char. No one else was talking to her anyway. And Char would want to debrief on the ghost hunt, certainly.

But it wasn't Char. And she certainly wasn't expecting this particular visitor.

Adrian Fox stood on her front porch, messy hair blowing in the wind. He wore a black motorcycle jacket, black jeans, and his trademark black boots. He wasn't smiling. "Stan. I'm sorry to intrude so early. Got a minute?"

"Hey. Sure." Stan pushed the door wide, noticing too late she still had a bar of cream cheese in her hand. She slipped it into her sweatshirt pocket. "Come on in." She glanced out to the driveway. No van or other vehicle. He must've walked from Char's.

"Char said you'd be up. Morning, pups." He scratched Scruffy's ears and petted Henry on the head. "I hope I'm not interrupting."

"Not at all. Just baking. How's Max?" She led him to the kitchen. "Please, sit. I have lots of coffee. Would you like some?"

"No, thank you. I don't drink coffee." Fox pulled a chair out and sat.

"You don't?" She must've looked astonished because Fox cracked his first smile.

"I don't. Just green tea. Max is going to be okay," he said, going back to her earlier question. "He broke his leg in three places. He'll be out of commission for a bit, but he'll manage."

"Thank goodness." Stan remembered the cream cheese and discreetly slipped it back into the fridge, then took the seat across the table from him. "I have some green tea. It's some fancy brand that Izzy sells."

"Sure. Sounds great. Getting ready for a big Valentine's Day party?" He nodded at the heart-shaped cake cooling on its rack.

"Huh? Oh, the cake. Actually, yes and no. I'm catering a wedding."

"Really. You're a caterer? Impressive."

"Well, sort of." Stan smiled. "It's a doggie wedding."

Fox, to his credit, didn't laugh or even smirk. He simply nodded. "That's also impressive. And interesting. How does one dog know he's supposed to marry another dog?"

"It's really more a human thing than a dog thing," Stan admitted. She poured hot water into his mug of tea and handed it to him. "So what can I do for you?"

Fox sobered again. "I didn't expect last night's expedition to turn out that way. I would never put my guys—or anyone—in danger, and I'm devastated that happened to Max. Of course, the media's all over it as a successful ghost hunt."

"The media?" Stan asked with a sinking feeling in her stomach. "What media?"

"All the major channels. Someone leaked the story and it took off. So now, of course, everyone is surmising that this was the work of evil spirits, etcetera. Because that's what sells." He shook his head. "I've already been contacted by a movie producer."

Oh, no. Stan closed her eyes. Jake would be even more livid than he was already. Now he owned a building with allegedly evil spirits. And they wanted to make a movie about it.

"Don't worry," Fox said quickly. "I'm not looking to make a movie. The truth is, I don't think evil spirits had anything to do with what happened."

"That's a relief," Stan said. "And it makes sense. It's a really old building."

Fox didn't say anything.

"What?" Stan asked. "It *is* old."

"That's true," Fox said. The unspoken "but" lingered in the air between them.

Stan narrowed her eyes. "What aren't you saying?"

Fox seemed to be weighing his words carefully. "Listen. Char said I could trust you to be discreet."

Sure, but if he'd already confided in Char, he might have a problem. "Okay," Stan said. "You think someone did this."

Fox exhaled. "I have some concerns about the building."

"What kind?"

"There are people who don't want this particular ghost discussed. And are willing to go to great lengths to keep it quiet. I got a call the other day. After the town meeting. From one of your town councilmen."

"Which one?" Stan asked, but her gut already knew.

"Don Miller."

"What did he want?"

"He wanted to meet. So we did. At a park just outside of town. He offered me money to go home."

"*What?* He bribed you?"

"He didn't bribe me," Fox corrected. "He *attempted* to bribe me. I didn't take the money. Clearly, because I'm here. And I went through with the investigation."

"How much money?"

Fox's lips thinned. "A lot for a town councilman in a tiny town like this."

"What's a lot?" Stan pressed.

"Fifty thousand."

Fifty thousand bucks? Don Miller didn't strike her as the savvy investor type who had that kind of cash in his pocket. But maybe his karate business was more profitable than Stan realized. "Why didn't he want you to do it?"

"He asked me if I would stand down out of respect for his mother and for the good of the town."

"The good of the town. Interesting." Stan leaned back and folded her arms. "What did you say?"

"I told him I appreciated his concern and certainly had the utmost respect for his mother, but that when I spoke with her before her death she was quite insistent that this investigation went forward. No matter what."

No matter what. Chills shivered up Stan's arms despite her heavy sweatshirt. "She really said that?"

"She did. It seemed very important to her."

"She didn't say why?"

"She said it was time for the truth to come out, and I could help her tell that truth. She wanted press. Lots of it."

Stan frowned. "She wanted press? Why?"

"She didn't get into that."

"Did you tell anyone she said that? About how it was time for the truth to come out?"

"You're the first."

"So she was your tipster," Stan said.

Fox hesitated. "Off the record? Promise?"

Stan made a zipper motion across her lips.

"Yes."

Stan nodded slowly. "I had a hunch." She rose and walked slowly around her kitchen. "Helga wanted to talk about Felix Constantine. She wrote about him. She paid tribute to him. I know she tried to stop the building construction under the auspices of a board or committee or whatever it is she sat on. That makes me think she wanted the attention on him that your operation would bring. But the rest of the town seems to want to forget he ever existed." She turned back to Fox. "How did Don react to you turning down his money?"

"He was angry. When I refused to change my mind, he left. But he was not happy with me."

"Do you think he might've . . . taken other action?"

"I don't want to start rumors. You'd need to get an expert in there to look at the stairs to see if they were tampered with. It might be too late anyway. But I thought it was worth putting out there. At least tell someone about the conversation."

"You think a town councilman snuck into a building that's under construction and tampered with the stairs so someone would get hurt? Or worse?" It sounded crazy. But then again, everything happening around town was crazy.

Fox shrugged. "Stranger things have happened. Look. I'm not saying that's it, but it's awfully suspicious that he didn't want me to do the ghost hunt and then this happens."

They were both silent for a minute. "What about how Sarah said her mother was talking about an accident? Do you think that was about Max? Foreshadowing?" Stan asked.

Fox shrugged again. "I can't give you a good opinion on Sarah's abilities. I don't know her well enough. Could she have been referring to Max? Sure. Could she have been referring to something else? Yup. Could she be acting this whole thing out? Of course."

"Maybe she meant Felix Constantine's death was an accident," Stan said.

"Again, your guess is as good as mine," Fox said.

"Do you think he's really haunting that place?"

"I don't know," Fox admitted. "We haven't watched any of our footage, with Max's injury. But there was a camera connected in the basement. We'll see what happened."

Stan refilled her coffee. "This man is the reason Helga's dead. I can feel it." She glanced down the hall as the doorbell rang again. "Excuse me," she said, and went to the door, peering out the side window.

Jake's truck was in the driveway. She cringed. Unless he'd come to break up with her, in which case it wouldn't matter, having Adrian Fox in her kitchen at this time of morning was not going to win her any brownie points. But what was she going to do? She could hardly slam the door in his face. Instead, she pushed it open. "Hey."

"Hey." He gazed at her solemnly. "Can we talk?"

"We sure can." She leaned against the frame. "Let's go for a walk."

"A walk?" He looked puzzled. "It's pretty cold out. And I didn't bring Duncan."

Not seeing any other way out, she stepped aside, wondering how she could spin this. Having Adrian in the house after suggesting a walk would look bad. Jake followed her inside.

"Were you at the ghost hunt last night? Are you okay?" Jake stopped abruptly, his gaze moving past Stan over her left shoulder. Stan looked behind her. Fox was in the kitchen doorway.

"Jake." Fox came down the hall. "Nice to see you. Stan, I'll get out of your way." He started past them to the door.

"Don't worry about it. I didn't mean to interrupt." Jake shook his head. "Sorry to bother you." And he walked out.

Stan watched him go in disbelief. "You've got to be kidding," she said out loud.

"I'm sorry. I didn't mean to cause you any trouble," Fox said. He looked truly upset.

"Don't be silly. Helga's death has been hard on him, but that's no reason for the kindergarten behavior." She raked a hand through her hair, realizing she'd been welcoming all these visitors and hadn't even brushed it yet. She'd been lucky to be wearing yoga pants and not her fleecy pajamas when Fox showed up. "Did you have anything else you wanted to talk about?"

"No, I wanted to tell you about Don Miller. And ask you to be careful." Fox gazed at her. "Whoever doesn't want this story heard is willing to go to great lengths to keep it quiet. I hear you have a . . . tendency to be in the middle of things. I wouldn't want to see you caught in the crossfire."

Chapter 38

After Adrian left, there were no more distractions. Stan had to sit with herself and figure out what to do about Jake. Not to mention the bombshell about Don Miller. Which wasn't really any of her business, but Fox had trusted her with the information. Which meant she should probably call Jessie Pasquale. If nothing else, it might buy Cyril some time if she could successfully weave it into some kind of narrative that culminated in Helga's death.

That was the problem. It seemed like a stretch for a ghost-hunting out-of-towner who had a mishap on an old staircase to have a connection with a woman murdered in a completely different place. Unless she could bring the right evidence to Jessie. Not that she knew what the right evidence was. She wished Fox had recorded his clandestine meeting with Miller. But what would that prove? That he didn't want a ghost hunt. Nothing else. But if she could find something, it would save her the dance of trying to convince Jessie when she clearly was content with her suspect sitting in his cell. Jake and Brenna were both already angry at her, why not go three for three and get Jessie firmly on board, too?

But even thinking Jake's name made her stomach hurt. The look on his face, before the suspicion and anger took over, had been pure hurt. Obviously with everything else going on he would be suspicious to see Fox in her kitchen this early in the morning. Especially after the whole googly-eyed thing when Fox first came to town. But did he really think that little of her, that with one spat she would start cavorting with someone else? Now who didn't trust whom?

That nagging, annoying voice that popped up whenever she needed negative reinforcement was off and running. *You're clearly starstruck by Fox, you never bothered to hide it. He probably thinks you're going to tire of this small-town stuff and look for a life with more flash and pizzazz. And, he thinks you don't trust him.*

"But I'm happy here. I don't want more flash and pizzazz," she argued out loud. Scruffy came over and held up her paw, clearly concerned for Stan's well-being. Stan rubbed her ears. "We love it here. We have a house and a business. And . . . I do trust him. I love him."

Even as the words left her mouth, they shocked her. She hadn't allowed them to even pass through her brain before. It was too soon.

But was it, really? Or was that just an excuse to keep her distance? It had been so long since she'd been in a functioning relationship—her last boyfriend, Richard, was more a convenience thing since they worked together and understood each other's crazy schedules—that she wasn't sure she remembered how a real relationship should be. She'd dated Jake for four months. Why couldn't she love him already? Things didn't have to follow a pattern. Life was crazy. Love was definitely crazy. There was no right or wrong way to approach it.

She had some soul-searching to do, it seemed. Although now wasn't the time to try to sort that out, as Frog Ledge fell apart around her.

But maybe she could help prop it back up. Armed with a new resolve, Stan checked her watch. Ten-fifteen. The Frog Ledge Library was open until noon on Saturdays. And she had a date with Sir Arthur Conan Doyle. And Betty, if she'd speak to her.

The Frog Ledge Memorial Library was hopping today. There was some kind of kids' program going on in the children's section, and every computer on the main floor was in use. The two librarians at the reference desk were running around like crazed chickens. Betty was nowhere in sight.

Stan waited nearly fifteen minutes before a computer freed up. She searched for "Doyle" and, as expected, was sent to the Sherlock Holmes novels. She located the books and pulled out *A Study in Scarlet* first. She read the first page, then flipped through the book, half hoping a signed confession would fall out. Just for fun, she went through each copy of each book in the stack, just on the off chance.

Nothing fell out. No names were written in the margins with an asterisk citing "killer" at the bottom. No key to a secret lockbox with said confessions either. What was she supposed to do, read each book and short story for a clue? This was silly. She sighed in frustration and replaced the book on the shelf. She needed Betty. Maybe Betty would understand the cryptic message delivered by both Arthur and Sarah, and actually speak to Stan to convey it. On second thought, she grabbed one of the Holmes books to check out. It had been a while since she'd read them. What was the harm? Maybe some of Holmes's logic could help her solve her own mystery.

Stan rounded the corner of the aisle and almost slammed into Carla Miller. Carla seemed to be everywhere lately. Fox's story flooded her brain. Had Carla known about her husband's attempt to bribe Fox? Were they in cahoots? It was highly likely.

"Oh, I'm so sorry," Stan said. "Hi, Carla."

Carla fluffed her too-big hair. It looked like she'd had a dye job recently. She had blond streaks shooting through the brown. "Hello there. How are you doing?"

"I'm fine. Getting ready for tomorrow's event?"

"The what? Oh, yes. Of course. The event. So difficult." She nodded at the book under Stan's arm. "Doing some reading?"

"Yep," Stan said. "It's a good weekend for some Sherlock Holmes." Baiting her, just a bit. If her husband was bribing Fox to stay away from Felix Constantine's murder, he had to know something about it. And by default, Carla, too. Maybe they knew what Sir Arthur Conan Doyle was supposed to know.

"Holmes is a character, isn't he?" Carla nodded, as if confirming to herself. "So lovely to see you. I'm sure we'll see you tomorrow. Ta-ta!" And she hurried off, bracelets jingling. Stan watched her go. She didn't know Carla well enough to know if her behavior was strange. But it certainly seemed odd that her mother-in-law's memorial event seemed to have completely slipped her mind.

"Stan?"

She whirled to find Betty behind her. Betty's arms were crossed over her teal blue jacket, foot tapping. "Hey, Betty. I was about to come find you. Got a minute?"

Betty's lips thinned. "Not really. I'm putting together photos of Helga during various reenactments for our slide show tomorrow."

"I can help." She glanced over her shoulder and lowered her voice. "I really need to talk to you."

Betty sighed and dropped her arms. "Fine. Meet me in my office in five minutes. I need to pick something up at the front desk." She turned and marched off.

At least she'd agreed to talk to her. Stan checked her watch. They had just about an hour until the library closed. While she waited for Betty, she figured she'd hit the ladies' room.

Weaving her way through the fiction section back to the main room, she headed toward the back of the building where a nice sitting area overlooked the gardens. The gardens themselves had benches for reading when the weather was nice, but you could still sit inside at the large window and experience some of that Zen. When there weren't fifty screaming children right over your head. Stan ducked into the hallway and through the bathroom door. And heard a voice from one of the stalls.

"I've just changed my mind, and I'd like it removed sooner than next weekend. How about today?"

It was Carla's voice. What was she removing? Stan held her breath, letting the door quietly shut behind her so the outside noise wouldn't filter in. She didn't dare walk to a stall for fear of being heard. Plus, Carla might recognize her bright purple sneakers.

"Yes, Dale, I understand that it's difficult with all the activity going on, but the museum isn't open tomorrow anyway. You need to call Marty Thompson back and tell him he must do it."

Dale? Hatmaker? Had to be. Stan leaned farther into the bathroom, trying to angle her head around the wall that separated the stalls from the little entranceway so she could hear better.

Carla emitted a frustrated sound. "Then by Monday. First thing. I—"

As Stan leaned even farther forward, her cell phone fell out of her pocket and hit the floor with a resounding *smack*. She closed her eyes for a second, then bent and scooped it up. The stall had gone silent. Carla knew someone was there now. Cursing her carelessness—Hadn't she learned yet that she shouldn't carry that stupid phone in her pocket? She always forgot it there and could never find it later—she slipped out the door before Carla exited the stall. Instead of heading back into the main library, she ducked around the nearest corner into the hall where some of the staff offices were located. She held her breath, hoping Carla wouldn't come this way.

When enough time had gone by, Stan peeked out. The coast was clear. She hurried out to the main lobby, but Carla was nowhere in sight.

"Are you coming up?" Betty again, behind her. She held a small box and watched Stan curiously.

"Yes, sure, coming right now." She followed Betty up the stairs to the second floor.

Betty let her in and closed the door behind her. She dumped the box on her desk. "I don't know why I bother to ask other people to do things," she said. "I asked for name badges to be made for all the volunteers and organizers tomorrow with a photo of Helga's book cover. What do they give me? A cannon!" She snorted in disgust. "If I'd wanted a cannon, don't you think I would've asked for one?"

"Of course," Stan agreed. At least Betty was speaking to her, if not blathering on a bit nervously about nothing.

"Anyway." Betty sat. "About the other day. I want to apologize. I was not entirely honest with you."

"You weren't?"

"No, I told you I had no idea why Edgar Fenwick made that comment to you. About Helga letting sleeping dogs lie. But I do."

"Oh?" About time.

"Yes, I'm sure he was talking about this disgraceful ghost hunt. Which I understand put that young man in the hospital. Not that I like to see anyone get hurt, but I hope they've learned their lesson. In any event, Helga was obsessed with this dead boxer. I think she felt that event was a turning point in her life, because so many things fell apart afterward. Especially her relationship with Tommy. I used to hear her and my mother talk. She never got over that." Betty shook her head sadly. "Helga perpetuated this frenzy by speaking to these people in the first place."

"What do you mean?" Stan asked. She didn't want to let on that she knew Helga had been the tipster.

"When they called her, she spoke with them! She encouraged this. Edgar, once he heard, was furious. So I'm sure that's what he meant." Betty sat back, seemingly satisfied that she'd done her part. "Does that make sense?"

"It does," Stan said. So maybe Betty didn't even know that Helga had been the tipster. Unless she was pretending not to know. Betty seemed pretty anti-ghost hunters, too. And her mother did have that connection with the dead man. She wasn't sure she could take anything she said at face value either.

"Well, good. I'm glad I got that off my chest." Betty fanned herself. "This last week has been so stressful. My goodness. I'll be glad when it's all over and things can get somewhat back to normal. Now, tell me, is that boy okay who got hurt last night?"

"He is. Broke a leg pretty badly, but he'll be fine."

"It happened in the basement, I heard."

"The stairs collapsed."

"I'm so grateful we had the remainder of those pieces taken out of there," Betty said. "They could have been badly damaged."

"Pieces?" Stan asked slowly. "What pieces? When were they taken out?"

"The old library materials. We had our original card catalogue down there. Both sets. A through M and N through Z. I believe there were even some very old books. And a few other library-related relics that had been left. The sign for the original library, that sort of thing. We just had them moved a few weeks back."

"Where did they go?"

"To the museum as Helga requested. I know she

had an exhibit in mind. I hope someone is able to take that on. It'll be such a wonderful tribute to Frog Ledge's first library."

"Interesting," Stan said. "I'm sure it would be. Would that exhibit be at this museum? Or another one?"

Betty stared at her. "There is no other museum in Frog Ledge, Stan." Her tone indicated Stan was quite stupid.

"Sure, I get that," Stan said. "So I'm just wondering where Dale Hatmaker is having those pieces moved to."

"Moved to?" Betty repeated. "I'm not sure I know what you're talking about."

"Dale Hatmaker has plans to move the card catalogue for one thing," Stan said casually. "He told me so when I was in there the other day."

"He *what*?!" Betty stood, eyes blazing. "Who the devil does he think he is? Who told him to do that? I've got a good mind to go over there and put my foot right—"

"Betty," Stan broke in. "Listen to me. What does Sir Arthur Conan Doyle have to do with anything?"

Betty's face went ghost white. She sat back heavily in her chair. "Where did you . . . ?"

"Arthur Pierce. And Sarah Oliver. Unless she's a great actress who knows a lot more than people think, she might have some skills," Stan said. "Tell me what it means." She held out the book.

Betty looked at it, then shook her head. "I don't know. Believe me, I wish I did."

"Betty, this is serious. People's lives have been lost. Cyril's future is at stake. And a murderer is on the loose." She leaned forward. "I know you loved Helga. If you know something, tell me. Please."

Betty hesitated. She glanced at her closed office door, as if fearful someone stood behind it, listening. Stan got up, opened it, and checked the hall. "Coast is clear," she said, returning to her chair.

"I don't *know* anything," Betty said. "But . . ." She trailed off again.

"But what?"

"But they talked about Doyle all the time, my mother and Helga. It was like . . . a code word for something. I never could figure it out."

"A code word? That doesn't make sense. Did they talk about it in relation to Felix?"

"They never mentioned his name. But it did seem to be in reference to a past event. I heard my mother and Helga talking once. Before she died."

Stan frowned. "So a long time ago, then."

"Yes." Betty narrowed her eyes. "There's nothing wrong with my memory, if that's what you're thinking."

"It's not," Stan said. "What did they say?"

Betty laced her fingers together and rested her hands on top of the pile of folders on her desk. "My mother was very sick. She was on a lot of medication. It was right before she died, and Helga came to see her. My mother asked her to promise that someday they would tell the story."

"The story about Felix?" A rush of adrenaline coursed through her system. She'd been right.

"That's all they said. 'The story.' Helga promised her they would. She said when the time was right.

But I did hear her say that she would keep the drawer. Always."

"The drawer." Stan jumped up and paced the room. "What drawer?"

"I don't know."

"I doubt she was talking about a sock drawer." Stan thought about it. "Library card catalogues have drawers."

Betty frowned. "Yes."

Stan could hear the implied "duh" in her tone. She ignored it. "And they're in alphabetical order."

"Yes."

"Maybe that's the answer, then." Stan stopped in front of Betty's desk, tapping one finger against her lips. "Maybe they're talking about the D drawer in the old library card catalogue and not Doyle's books. That catalogue is getting a lot of attention these days. It even rated a new space in the museum, you just told me."

"My goodness, I never thought of that," Betty said. "I've been reading Doyle's books for years looking for clues and I don't even like Sherlock Holmes."

"So if Helga and her friends were there in the library basement the night Felix was killed, why would the card catalogue be important? We need to see what's in it," Stan said. Then her eyes widened. "Arthur. Arthur Pierce knew about Doyle."

"They were all friends," Betty said. "Why is that surprising?"

"Because Cyril told me he wasn't there. That he'd just reported on it. But Arthur specifically mentioned Doyle. And, you know what else?" Stan held up a finger triumphantly. "He mentioned Felix, too. He called him 'slick.' It didn't click for me when I was talking to him, but now that I'm thinking about it, how would he have known that if he'd only covered the story *after* Felix was dead? He was there. I wonder if Arthur and Felix had a run-in."

But Arthur hadn't wanted to talk about it. Which didn't make sense, if Helga was calling ghost hunters in to uncover the story. Although, that could mean Arthur had a more sinister reason for not wanting anyone to know he was there.

Had Arthur Pierce killed Felix Constantine? Had Helga known that? Did anyone else?

"Why weren't Maeve and Helga talking?" she asked Betty. "I heard they haven't been as close in recent weeks."

"I don't know," Betty said slowly. "But now that you mention it, I did notice that, too."

Stan sat back, thinking. "We need to get in to see that card catalogue. And we need to stop them from removing it. Do you have a key?"

"No, but I can call—"

"No, don't call anyone. We can't tell anyone about this until we figure out what's in the drawer." Stan wound a strand of hair around her finger, let it fall, wound it again. "We have to get in there tomorrow. I have a plan. But I need help. And you can't tell anyone," she repeated. "Are you in?"

"Tomorrow's the celebration," Betty protested.

"That's right." Stan smiled. "Which means people will be otherwise occupied. So, are you in?"

Betty hesitated for a long moment, then nodded. "I'm in."

"Good. Meet me at my house at eight."

Chapter 39

Stan left the library and slid into her car, her mind still racing, and almost didn't hear her cell phone ringing. She fished the offending object out of her bag. "Hello."

"Stan?" It was Amara, and she sounded excited.

"Yeah?"

"Can you come over?"

"Right now?" Stan glanced at the clock on her dashboard. "What's going on?"

"I got a reply from Carmen Feliciano."

It took Stan a minute to place the name. A lot had happened since that conversation yesterday. "The DNA. Okay, so what happened?"

"You just need to come over."

Now her interest was piqued. "Okay, be there in two."

She made it in one, since it was only halfway down the street. A car she didn't recognize was parked in Amara's driveway—a big red Cadillac. Stan parked next to it and hurried up the front steps. Before she could ring the bell, the door flew open.

Amara looked like she was about to burst. Stan couldn't tell if it was excitement, fear, or something else entirely. "What's going on?"

"You'll never believe this." Amara yanked her inside, then slammed the door and locked it.

"Wow. This is all very stealth." Stan let her friend drag her into the living room.

A very tall, regal-looking elderly woman rose from the sofa. Amara dropped Stan's arm and took a deep breath. "Stan Connor, meet Carmen Feliciano."

"Wow. That was more than just a fast e-mail reply." Stan shook her hand. "Good to meet you."

"And you as well," Carmen said in a steady, clear voice.

Stan couldn't quite peg her age. Maybe seventies? She looked great, at any rate.

Amara was still staring at her like she was star-struck. "Carmen, can you please tell Stan your maiden name?"

"Certainly, dear." Carmen smiled. "I am part of the Constantine family."

It took Stan a second; then her mouth dropped open. "The . . . no way. Not the *Felix* Constantine family?"

"I should say so." Carmen clasped her hands in front of her. "Felix was my big brother."

"I might have to sit down," Stan muttered. "You knew Helga Oliver?"

"I did. We became acquainted some years ago. She found me. Helga has been a lovely champion of my brother's memory. She remembered my name from way back then, when he died. It apparently took her some time to find me with my married name and all, but she did it. And then to discover that we potentially had family ties here, well . . ." Carmen rubbed her arms. "It gives me chills. I'm so grateful she contacted me about doing a DNA test. I knew she was quite involved in genealogy, so when she said she had a potential lead on a relative here, of all places, well, I jumped at the opportunity. I'm so sad to hear of her passing."

Stan looked at Amara, sending her questions via mental telepathy. What did this mean? Could Carmen know something about her brother's death that could help this all make sense? She had to ask.

"Carmen. I apologize for asking this question, but did Helga ever insinuate that she might know anything about your brother's murder?"

Carmen frowned. "No, we didn't talk much about that. Just at the beginning because, you know, it connected us. But as a rule, we tried to stay with happier topics."

That was disappointing.

"Were you and Helga close?" Amara chimed in.

"We tried to get together at least once a month," Carmen said. "We'd alternate the driving. We both recognized we were getting old." She chuckled. "Twenty minutes down the road isn't as simple as it used to seem. But we hadn't seen each other much recently. Although she did ask me to come to her house, quite impromptu, just a couple of weeks ago."

"Really? Did she say why?" Stan asked.

"She said she wanted to talk. It sounded serious, which wasn't like Helga. She was always quite upbeat. But I couldn't make it. I had a trip scheduled, and told her I'd call her when I returned. But I didn't return until Tuesday." She looked sad.

"So you don't know what she wanted to talk about," Stan said.

"No, I know it wasn't to tell me about the DNA test, because I didn't send the kit in until the day I left. I can't imagine what she wanted, but I'm sorry that I'll never get to hear her tell me. I'm so grateful she connected me with Amara. Her last act of kindness." She grabbed Amara's hands and squeezed. "It means so much to me to know that Helga and Frog Ledge never forgot my brother. Now Amara and I get to figure out just how we're related. It's such fun. I'm planning to sign up for one of these genealogy accounts so we can do this properly. But the visit . . . I suppose it could've been something about my brother. She did mention she wanted me to meet a friend of hers."

"A friend?" Stan asked. "What was her friend's name?"

Carmen thought for a moment. "Hmm. Aaron, Arnold—no, Arthur. It was Arthur, because that was my great uncle's name."

Chapter 40

Sunday dawned gray, dreary, and cold looking outside Stan's window. Five-thirty on "celebration" day. Today, a week to the day after Helga died, her life would be celebrated. The entire town would probably attend—whether out of respect for her or curiosity about the murder investigation. Stan was certain there would be an equal number in both camps. As expected for February in New England, the weather was not going to fully cooperate. Snow still covered the green, enough of it that most of the activities would have to take place in the library parking lot. It even looked like it might snow again. It was certainly cold enough.

That wouldn't stop this hearty bunch, though. A little cold and snow never bothered them, especially when they were paying tribute to a loved one. The only sore spot would be the lack of newspaper coverage. Cyril was still being held at the police barracks. The *Frog Ledge Holler,* for the first time probably in a century or more, had ceased operations.

But not for long. Not if all went according to plan.

Stan had been up since two, running scenarios in her mind. At six, she called Pasquale's mobile phone. The trooper answered on the first ring. Unlike Stan, she sounded like she'd already eaten a healthy breakfast and gone to the gym. Stan tried not to resent her for it.

"I need your help," Stan said. "This morning. Can you come to my house at eight?"

"Your house? Why? What's going on?" Pasquale asked.

"I'd rather tell you when you get here. But I need you to pick up Arthur Pierce and bring him when you come. Can you do that? Without your police car?"

"Pick up . . . why? You need to start talking, Stan."

"I will. I promise. Please, just go get him? It's the only way I can think to get him here. This is about Helga. It's important, Jessie."

"I'm a state trooper, not a taxi service," Pasquale snapped.

"I understand that. But your position has more perks. So, will you do it?"

Jessie was silent, but her frustration was palpable over the phone line. "I swear to God, Stan, if you're leading me on a wild-goose chase I'm going to throw you in a cell right next to Cyril Pierce." And she hung up.

Stan smiled. Jessie and Arthur would be at her house by eight. She was certain of it.

Things were falling into place.

By seven, activity was ramping up across the street. Stan could hear the voices and shouts as people descended on the area to set up for the event. The entire day would be devoted to historical reenactments, speeches, tours of the historical buildings, and refreshments at each stop, all as a tribute to Helga. The War Office would be open for special tours, and the historical society would also be open. The museum would remain closed. Which was critical to her plan.

By the end of the day, they'd have more to add to the history books.

At seven forty-five, Stan put the dogs outside to play. Betty arrived a little before eight, looking like she hadn't slept at all either. "So, what's this big plan? I'm a little worried about this, Stan."

"Don't worry," Stan said. "We'll have support."

The doorbell rang again. Stan said a silent thank you. "And there it is." She pulled open the door. Jessie and Arthur Pierce stood on the porch. Pierce looked indifferent. Pasquale looked annoyed.

Betty's eyes widened to the size of saucers. "Why are they . . . ?"

"Hush." Stan motioned them in. "Good morning. Thanks for coming, both of you."

"You didn't really leave us a choice," Pasquale said. "What's all the cloak-and-dagger about?"

"Come in. I have coffee," Stan said. "We'll tell you everything."

"Oh, boy," Pasquale muttered.

"Sorry to get you up so early, Arthur," Stan said.

Arthur looked different without a cigar hanging out of his mouth. Jessie must've forbade it in her vehicle. He shrugged. "It was all just a matter of time."

Pasquale looked at him curiously. Seemed like they hadn't had much conversation on the way over.

"I thought you said we couldn't tell anyone," Betty hissed as she followed Stan to the kitchen.

"I can hear you, Betty," Pasquale said. "I'm right here."

"She's the police," Stan said. "It's okay to tell her."

"This is how I get to spend my day off?" Pasquale asked the ceiling.

"Sorry," Stan said, handing her a mug of coffee. "But you'll thank us later. Arthur? Coffee?"

"Please," he said, as if they were all gathering for a social occasion. "Black's fine."

"Which one of you knows Marty Thompson best? The guy with the hauling company?" Stan asked as she poured.

"I do," Pasquale said. "I went to school with him."

Stan wasn't sure if it was her imagination, or if Jessie's cheeks had turned slightly pink at the mention of Marty's name. "Can you trust him?"

"Of course. What did Marty do?"

"He didn't do anything. I need you to call him and tell him to call Dale Hatmaker. I need him to say he can pick up the pieces they want to get rid of at the museum. Today at one o'clock. And then I need him to drive his truck over and pretend he's going to do that, but he's really not. Can you do that? And ask him to let you know if Dale agrees?"

Pasquale narrowed her eyes. "What's going on?"

"I have a hunch about who killed Helga. I think it was Carla Miller. But I need your help flushing her out today."

Both Betty and Pasquale stared at her. Pasquale spoke first. "That's a big accusation, Stan. You're talking about the wife of a town councilman. And the victim's daughter-in-law, for crying out loud. How, exactly, did you arrive at that conclusion?"

"Can you please call Marty, and then we'll talk about it?"

Jessie sighed, muttered something about getting fired, and made the call. Marty answered right away and was happy to help. He promised to call Dale right away. Stan figured at least some of that was attributable to Jessie's position. Five minutes later, Marty called back. Dale had agreed to meet him at one o'clock.

"Great. Thanks, Marty," Jessie said. "I owe you." She flushed and turned away. "We can talk about dinner sometime, sure." She hung up and pocketed her phone, cop face squarely back in place. "Now. Talk."

Stan turned to Arthur. "Arthur, are you going to help me tell this story? There's a lot of parts I don't know. That's why I wanted you here." She held her breath. *Please don't let him do the whole denial thing again. Jessie will kill me. Or arrest me.*

Pierce looked at the ceiling, then around the room. Nutty, who had sauntered in to see what was happening, jumped on his lap and settled in, purring loudly. Pierce looked at him like he'd never seen a cat before. Just as Stan was about to get up and remove him, he started petting Nutty.

"I guess it's time," he said. "We wanted to do this anyway, Helga and I. Then everything went to hell in a handbasket." He took a wheezy breath, still stroking Nutty. "Helga and I . . . a while back we decided it was time to clear the slate. We wanted to go public with the story of what happened to Felix Constantine."

Betty's eyes widened. "What do you mean? You . . . you knew all this time?"

"We've been walking around with the guilt for years. All of us. And, no, my son didn't know about this," he said to Pasquale. "Helga was gearing him up to write the story, but she hadn't actually told him what the story was yet. He was interviewing her. On background."

"The morning of her murder," Pasquale said. "Is that why he was at the museum?"

"Yep."

"See, he never told me that part," Stan said. "He just told me he was in the vicinity, getting ready for the event."

Pierce shrugged. "My son's good at his job. He was gathering information. Who ratted him out?" he asked Pasquale.

"Gerry Ricci saw him leaving the museum," Pasquale said. "He didn't think anything of it until later. Had himself convinced Cyril had been involved. It was the only lead we had." She looked at Stan. "I knew she had been murdered. The random 'falling down the stairs' story didn't sit well with me."

Stan looked at Betty. "I told you to talk to her earlier."

"Can we get back to me and Helga?" Pierce demanded. "You dragged me out here at this hour, you should at least listen."

"You're absolutely right, Mr. Pierce," Stan said. "I'm sorry. Please, go on."

Pierce looked satisfied. "So Helga and I decided we would tell the story. Only problem was our friends. The ones still breathing. See, we'd made a pact that night. Never to talk about it unless we all agreed, or unless we were dead." He smiled. "'Cept me, of course. I had to write about it. Course

I couldn't tell the whole thing, but I had to cover it. Anyway, all these years later, the rest of them didn't agree."

"Maeve," Stan said.

"Maeve, Edgar." He shook his head. "You think about it, it's pretty amazing we got this far. That's a lotta people carrying this around for a long time."

"What about the one who vanished? Tommy Hendricks?" Stan asked.

Pierce nodded admiringly. "You did do your research."

"And I read the story you left me in the book." Stan met his eyes evenly until he lifted his chin in an acknowledgment.

"Yeah, I left the book. Since you were getting yourself all involved anyway, I figured you could use the facts. Tommy Hendricks died, too. Committed suicide a couple years after that. Helga and I knew about it, but we never spread it around. He'd moved to Florida and it just didn't seem like something we wanted to broadcast."

"Wait." Jessie held up a hand. "Mr. Pierce, I don't know what you're about to tell us, but I would recommend you think very carefully about what you're doing. You have no counsel present—"

Pierce frowned and waved her off. "I'm eighty-five years old. I'm dying anyway. You're free to do what you want to me. The truth is, *I* killed Felix Constantine. It was all me. And I'd do it again tomorrow."

Betty gasped, her hand flying to her throat.

Jessie rubbed her temples as if she suddenly suffered from a major headache. "Mr. Pierce, there is no statute of limitation on murder, you know."

"Like I said," Pierce said. "Do what you want."

"Why?" Stan asked. "What happened that night?"

His gaze turned faraway, like he'd already gone back there. Or maybe he'd never left. "We almost got to tell the story to Carmen. Felix's sister. Helga had befriended her, you know. We had it all set up. Then Helga died." Pierce shook his head.

"Anyway, we snuck away from the big party that night. To our hangout." He looked at Betty. "Alice had the keys. Felix tagged along. He'd set his sights on Helga. Partly because she was beautiful, and partly because he wanted to defeat his opponent before they got to the ring."

"He wanted Tommy's girl," Stan said.

Pierce nodded slowly. "But Tommy was too drunk to notice. A few of us took the party outside to the parking lot. Didn't wanna burn the place down smoking. A while later, I realized I hadn't seen Helga. Or Felix. I went looking for her." Unresolved anger flashed in Arthur's eyes. "Found her in the library basement, trying to fight him off. He was drunk. Not listening to reason. Plus, he was a whole lot bigger than me. So I did what I had to do." He looked at her, willing her to understand.

"I didn't mean to kill him. Just grabbed the first thing I saw—one of the card catalogue drawers—and clocked him with it. Guess I hit him hard enough. Or in the right spot."

"The D drawer," Stan said. "Where Doyle lived." She couldn't imaging what Arthur had lived with over the years, from the incident itself to having to write about the murder he had committed day after day, week after week. What an extraordinary story. Stan wanted to hug him.

Arthur nodded. "Just happened that way. Fitting, all things considered."

"Then what?" Stan asked. Jessie still hadn't spoken, but she listened intently. Betty looked like she was about to pass out.

"When we realized he wasn't gettin' back up, we all sobered up pretty quickly and decided to just leave him there. Swore ourselves to secrecy." Arthur shrugged. "Alice 'found' the body that Monday. The police talked to us—everyone knew we hung out there—but we covered our tracks. Frankly, no one cared that much. Like I said, he wasn't a local. I don't think a lotta effort went into it. But we never forgot.

"Helga never got over it. Neither did I, truth be told. So when she asked me to help her tell the story, I agreed. Hell, they'd just told me I'm gonna croak anyway."

Silence descended over Stan's kitchen as they all processed this information. Finally, Jessie spoke. "So how do we get from this to Carla Miller? I'm not following."

"I think Helga was trying to find another way to tell the story without breaking her promise to her friends," Stan said. "Right, Mr. Pierce? Isn't that why she called Adrian Fox?"

Pierce nodded slowly. "Helga was spiteful," he said with a smile. "One of the reasons I loved her."

Loved her. Stan felt incredible sadness for Pierce. He'd loved Helga back then, and all these years later? And they'd been bound by this terrible secret. It must've been so lonely for both of them.

"She told Maeve and Edgar, fine, be difficult," Pierce went on. "Promised them the story'd come out one way or another. So she thought about it and figured getting the ghost people in was the most public thing she could do. Plus, I think she really believed Felix haunted that place." He sobered. "He haunted her, for sure."

"And she told Don what she was doing, didn't she?" Stan asked.

Pierce nodded. "Don didn't like it either. But I don't think Don killed his own mother."

"Agreed. Carla, on the other hand . . ." Stan looked at Arthur Pierce. "She threatened you, didn't she? When she came to your apartment?"

"Tried to," Pierce said. "She didn't scare me much. Didn't have much to scare me with. My son's already in trouble. He's all I got. I doubt she scared Helga, either, until she shoved her down the stairs."

"You know this for a fact?" Jessie asked. "She told you she pushed Helga?"

"The only thing I know for a fact is what I did all those years ago," Pierce said. "But Mrs. Miller, well, she was adamant that she didn't want this story to come out. It would kill us all, she said. Did she confess to me? No."

"Did she threaten you with bodily harm?" Jessie asked.

"She told me she'd do whatever she had to do to keep our big mouths shut." He shook his head. "Young ladies today have a lot of sass."

Stan looked at Jessie. "She thinks she has a lot to lose. Her status. Her husband's position in town. And she's been pushing Hatmaker to get rid of the pieces from the old library. Including the card catalogue."

"So what's in the drawer?" Betty interrupted.

"Ain't nothing in the drawer," Pierce said. "But Constantine's blood's still on it."

Betty sat back, stunned. "That's why you've all been talking about this drawer for years?"

"We need to get the drawer. That's why we need to pretend the pieces are being moved today," Stan said to Jessie. "I guarantee you, Carla will show up once Dale calls her. To make sure it's done. And then you can arrest her."

"Me too, if ya need to," Pierce said.

Pasquale sighed. "I think I need a new job. Or at least a new town."

Chapter 41

The celebration began promptly at eleven with cannon fire. It nearly scared Stan out of her shoes as she walked across the street. Scruffy and Henry trotted along on either side of her, happy to be included. She planned to hand them off to Lorinda, offering their help for the library programs while she slipped away later. She'd left Benedict roaming the house to see how he and Nutty did together. If they could pass the test, he could stay. If not, she'd have to figure something else out. But today, things were looking up.

In more ways than one.

The Frog Ledge Marching Band had launched into the opening song. Stan couldn't tell what it was. She could see a large crowd already gathered, singing along as they paid tribute to Helga. She led the dogs up the street and to the fringes of the crowd. Scruffy immediately announced her presence by wooing repeatedly until those nearest turned to look at her. Henry looked embarrassed.

"Welcome!" A woman wearing a colonial costume walked up, carrying a large basket. "Would you like a pin?" She held out a big button with Helga's picture on it. A close-up. Not a flattering one, either. Stan wondered what had happened to the cannon but decided not to ask.

"Sure." Stan took it, hoping to slide it into her pocket, but the woman waited, still smiling. Stan took the hint and fixed it to her jacket.

"Lovely, dear. Enjoy the day." The woman walked away with her basket, looking for her next victim.

Stan checked the crowd. There was Betty, wearing a purple coat and matching hat. Helga's favorite color. She walked over and tapped her on the shoulder. "Everything looks great," she said when Betty turned.

"Hi, Stan. It does," she agreed, looking around. "Except for that god-awful pin." She wrinkled her nose. "We're going to have refreshments in the library all day. The dogs are welcome to go in, of course."

"Thanks," Stan said. She scanned the crowd. "Seen Hatmaker yet?"

Betty shook her head. "Not yet. Stan, are you sure—"

"Relax. Everything's going to be fine. Pasquale has our back."

"I hope so." Betty sighed and looked around. "I haven't seen Carla."

"She's around," Stan said. "I'm sure of it. She wouldn't miss the chance to be the star of the show."

* * *

Twelve-fifteen. Almost showtime. Stan leaned against the refreshment table in the library and flipped through the day's program. The proclamation and official ceremony for Helga was happening at twelve forty-five, which was perfect. Everyone would be occupied when Marty drove up at one. She'd seen Pasquale a few minutes ago. She wore street clothes and was engaged in a conversation with someone. Maybe another undercover cop? She took a sip of the Revolutionary Punch offered by a costumed character walking around with a tray. It tasted disgusting. Or it could be her nerves that made it off-putting. Her stomach was twisted up. This had to go off without a hitch or Jessie would kill her. And she'd look like a fool.

God, she'd better be right about this, or she'd be run out of town. Or at the very least, sued for slander. Or libel. She always got the two mixed up. Helga's killer would still be on the loose. And Cyril would perhaps end up in prison for a crime he didn't commit.

No pressure.

She'd seen Jake once, but he'd been busy helping the War Office people haul their weaponry around. He hadn't seen her, or at least he hadn't seemed to. Maybe after this was over they could have a real conversation so she could explain Adrian Fox hadn't been in her kitchen for an unseemly reason so early in the morning. She hoped he would listen.

Her mother was also on-site. Stan had seen her with Falco earlier. Unlike Jake, her mother had seen her. She just hadn't acknowledged her. Which was also a bitter pill to swallow. Stan knew she had to figure something out on that front, especially if her mother was going to continue residing in Frog Ledge even part-time. But right now she had to focus on her plan going off without a hitch.

Which was getting harder by the minute as her nerves wound tighter and tighter. She was concentrating on her breathing in hopes of calming herself when Tony Falco appeared in front of her, looking apologetic. "Kristan, I'm sorry to bother you, but I need a favor and everyone's tied up. Can you assist?"

Leave it to Falco to foul things up. She pushed her annoyance away and pasted on a smile. "What do you need?" she asked.

"Can you go get Helga's cane? We need it for the dedication ceremony and it's still over at the museum. I have to sign the proclamation and take some pictures, or I'd do it. Would you mind?" He held out a key. "You can slip right in the back door so no one thinks the building is open."

Stan glanced at her phone. It was twelve thirty-five. She thought fast. She should be able to run over and get in and out before Hatmaker went to unlock the doors for Marty, and she and Pasquale planned to show up. Plenty of time. She might even get to peek at the drawer herself while she was over there.

"Sure," she said. "I'm on it. Be right back." She grabbed the key and hurried across the street.

Chapter 42

Stan slipped the key into the lock and pushed the museum's creaky back door open, reaching for the light switch. Fluorescent glare flooded the room. Shutting the door behind her, she took a few steps forward and peered around the corner into the main room. Everything appeared to be copacetic. The card catalogue still sat where she remembered it, curbing the irrational fear that Carla and crew had liberated it overnight. Breathing a sigh of relief, she hurried over. And did a double take.

"Oh, no . . ."

There was a gaping hole in the second row of the catalogue. She scanned the letters on the cards. The card below the hole had *E–F*. The card above read *C*. The *D* drawer was missing. Which meant Sir Arthur Conan Doyle had been silenced.

She stared at the empty hole, refusing to believe it. They had been so close. But not fast enough.

Mad now, she let loose a string of curses. How could this have happened? She should've called Jessie last night instead of this morning. They shouldn't have waited. Stan thought she might cry. But she had to get Helga's cane, pull herself together, and walk back out to the party. Then she needed to huddle with Betty and Jessie.

She started back down the hall toward Helga's desk. But she didn't make it far. She heard a noise behind her, suspiciously like a lock turning. Before she could turn to look, something hard—like a two-by-four—slammed into her lower back, sending her sprawling on her face. Stars danced behind her eyes and nausea swirled in her belly. She tried to ignore the pain long enough to flip over to defend herself from the next attack.

Stan raised her hands to shield her head, pulled her knees up into her chest, and rolled away. She opened her eyes and tried to focus in front of her.

She saw boots. Expensive ones. The fancy Burberry winter kind. Stan had looked at a pair last year and passed them up in favor of her Uggs. Now she was glad she had. Her eyes traveled up farther, resting on her assailant's face.

Carla Miller loomed over her, still brandishing her weapon. It looked like a two-by-four. The only difference was the knob in the front, which felt like it had left a dent in her back. It was the card catalogue. Letter *D*, she was certain.

Looked like her theory had been right. Lot of good that would do her now, facing a deranged woman with a card catalogue as her weapon. Not to mention the historical swords and other paraphernalia scattered around the museum. If only she'd been able to grab Jessie before she ran over here. She had at least another twenty minutes before Marty drove up. She'd better move quick, or she might meet the same fate as Felix Constantine. And Helga.

Stan crab-crawled far enough back that Carla would probably miss if she tried to clobber her again, and tried to ignore the throbbing pain in her back. "It's no use, Carla. Everyone knows what you did to Helga. Your own mother-in-law. It's too late to try to cover it up."

Carla chuckled. "You're delusional. I'm the next mayor's wife. My husband has served on this council for years. You think anyone would believe your story? You don't even know what you're talking about." She tossed the drawer on the floor with a resounding thud and reached into her pocket. When her hand emerged, it held a small black revolver.

Stan's head spun as she registered both the gun and Carla's words. Mayor? She had Don running for mayor in her mind? The next election wasn't even for a year and a half. And where had she gotten a gun? *Come on, Marty, Jessie. Wasn't anyone ever early anymore?*

"It doesn't matter if you get rid of the drawer. Arthur confessed to Felix Constantine. He told the police everything, including your threats. It's over, Carla. Make it easy on the rest of your family. Think about your kids," Stan said.

Carla hesitated for a split second, then rage filled her face. "I'm getting rid of this godforsaken piece of evidence that's plagued my family for years. And we'll keep our rightful place in this town. You're not stopping me, that's for sure. You have no idea how hard we've worked to get to this place. I'm not letting anyone stand in our way. Don has a long political career ahead of him, and no one's taking it away from us. Now, get up." She nearly spat the words. The gun jumped with every word.

Stan kept her eyes on it, her throat dry, heart pounding. "I'm not stopping you, but the police will. Trooper Pasquale will be here any minute." Stan hoped. Unsteadily, she forced her legs to move and got up, holding on to the nearest piece of furniture. Her back screamed in pain. She'd never thought about how lethal those silly drawers could be.

"You're bluffing," Carla snapped. "Nobody really cared about what happened sixty years ago as much as my poor, dead mother-in-law thought they did." She chuckled, and the sound sent chills down Stan's spine. "God, I hated that woman from the day I met her. Bossy, demanding, critical battle-ax. You have no idea how satisfying it was to shove her down those stairs, even though technically I wasn't planning on it. Now, let's go. I need to be rid of you before my hauler gets here. They won't find you in the basement for a while."

This woman was stark raving mad. She was going to shoot her in the basement and leave her body there. Where was the cavalry?

"Where's Don?" Stan asked, still trying to stall for time. "Does he know what you did?"

"My useless husband? Probably somewhere in a corner, crying over his mommy, the wuss. His mommy, who made my life a living hell. Always nagging and complaining. Carla, your sauce is bland. Carla, your laundry basket is overflowing. Carla, why do you need another designer bag with my son's hard-earned money?" she mimicked. "On and on and on, every day. And Don never defended me. Never told her to shut her mouth. She was trying to turn my boys against me, too. She's lucky she made it to eighty-seven. Now it's my turn to get some attention."

A sound from outside caught Stan's ear. The unmistakable rumble of a truck engine in the back parking lot. Marty was here. Which meant Jessie wasn't far behind. Carla was toast.

She just didn't realize it yet.

Carla heard the sound, too, and froze. "Move," she barked. "Now. To the basement."

Stan obliged. Carla shoved her forward, the gun jammed into the small of her back, propelling her down the hallway toward the back of the museum. Her mind raced. Her palms were damp with fear. She needed to stay away from the stairs leading to the basement. Carla probably planned to shoot her at the top, let her fall, and shut the door behind her, then fluff her hair and greet Marty.

No way. This full-of-herself, designer-label wacko wasn't going to win. Stan's eyes fell on Helga's purple cane, still resting on its hook, and calculated the distance to it at the same time a rap sounded on the back door. About five feet, give or take.

"Hey, Carla? It's Marty." His voice was muffled through the wood.

Carla hesitated, clearly unsure what to do first. Stan grabbed the split-second advantage. She dove to the ground and flung herself into the space under Helga's desk, flattening herself against the wood. She heard Carla hiss out a breath, heard her footsteps as she moved closer to the door, and then her normal, saccharine-sweet, I'm-not-going-to-kill-anyone voice. "Coming, Marty, give me one second, honey, would you? I'll come out."

Stan inched farther under the desk. She noticed Helga's chair had wheels. *Perfect.*

"Sure thing," Marty called agreeably.

"Great." Carla's voice changed as she focused on her other situation. "Now you're dead."

That's what she thinks. Stan shoved the chair forward with all her might, catching Carla off guard. As Carla stumbled aside, trying to avoid it, Stan leaped up, grabbed Helga's cane off the wall, and brought it down full force on Carla's hand, knocking the gun to the floor.

Carla screamed in indignation. Stan could see her calculating in her head—should she go after the gun or go after Stan?

Stan didn't give her a chance to think about it. She swung again, planting her feet and putting all her power behind it, as Carla rushed at her. This time she hit her in the side of the head. Carla crumpled to the ground, stunned, just as the door opened and Marty, Betty, and Jessie all ran in. On their heels was Dale Hatmaker.

Jessie took one look at Carla Miller on the ground and shook her head. "You can't even follow directions when they're your own?" she asked Stan.

"I didn't mean to mess it up," Stan said. "Tony Falco asked me to come over and get Helga's cane. Which ironically I just used on her. She killed Helga. I was right."

Dale Hatmaker paled. "She did what?"

Stan narrowed her eyes at him. "Don't play dumb. You were in on it."

"Me?" Hatmaker's eyes almost popped out of his head. He held up his hands and looked at Jessie.

"She and Don asked me to help get the museum in order, that's all. I had no idea . . ."

"Go sit over there until I figure out what to do with you," Pasquale told him. She pulled her radio out. "You can send two cars," she said. "Somebody needs to get Don Miller in for questioning, too. And find someone to take care of his kids. Lovely." She shook her head. "Talk about family values." She disconnected.

From the floor, Carla moaned.

"Regardless, I guess my plan worked," Stan said to Jessie.

"Not exactly how it was supposed to," Jessie reminded her.

"That wasn't my fault!"

"It never is." Jessie turned as her backup, Trooper Lou and another guy Stan hadn't seen before, raced into the building. "About time, folks. The murder suspect is over there." Jessie pointed to Carla, who was trying to sit up, still dazed. "And take him in for questioning." She indicated Hatmaker, still sitting on the floor, face ashen. Stan watched as they cuffed Carla and took her out of the building. She was glad it was over, but for the Millers, it was just beginning. Those two little boys, Donald and Derek, would have a long road ahead of them.

Jessie turned to walk out, then paused and looked back at Stan. "Thank you."

Stan glanced over her shoulder. "Me?"

"Yes, you," Jessie said impatiently. "You brought Helga justice. Thank you." And she followed her colleagues out the door, leaving Stan with her mouth open.

Chapter 43

The weather had finally started to turn around. It felt like spring even though it was a tad early. Thankfully, the snow had mostly melted with the recent warm spurt, so they could reach the gazebo on the green. Winter could stick around for another month or more, if it wanted to be a jerk. But this Valentine's Day was beautiful.

Stan stepped back and admired her work. She had spent the morning setting up for Gus and Lila's wedding. The gazebo on the green was decorated with white streamers and bows. A high table inside it held the strawberry-flavored, heart-shaped wedding cake, which had come out even better than awesome, if she did say so herself. The triple-decker cake had three sizes of hearts, the bottom two slightly raised on cake stands so they could all have the fancy ribbon frosting. A plastic Shih Tzu and Irish setter dressed in wedding clothes stood on the top layer. Stan had taken about a thousand pictures of this cake for her Pawsitively Organic Facebook page. Eating it would be a shame. Two smaller tables sat on either side of the wedding cake table, one with an assortment of her best pupcakes, the other with a platter of regular treats, also in assorted flavors. A smaller platter held cat treats for Dede's felines, Mittens and Diamond. Lastly, a table set slightly apart held a platter of fruit, cheese, and crackers for the human guests.

Now, if only the dogs didn't go racing in there and knocking everything over.

"This is the bomb," Izzy said, jumping off her stool. Stan had coerced her into helping set up, and she'd just finished tying white balloons on the fence a couple of the town maintenance staff had put up for the event. No one wanted any dogs running off, but they also wouldn't have as much fun on leash the entire time. "Where are they going to exchange vows?"

"I think right in front of the gazebo." Stan glanced around to check the space out and saw Brenna standing by the fence, alone, watching them.

"Who's reading them?"

"Dede, most likely. She has some doggie reverend coming." Stan ignored Izzy's snicker and glanced at her watch. "Can you hold down the fort for a minute while I get my dogs? I just want to make sure nothing happens to the cake."

Izzy grinned. "Are you going to let anyone eat it later? These guys are just waiting for their chance." She indicated her three dogs, sitting like angels in the grass, watching carefully. They fully understood that special treats were in their near future.

"Maybe." Stan winked. She walked over to where Brenna stood. "Hey."

"Hey." Brenna shifted from one foot to the other

and shoved her hands in her pockets. "It, uh, looks great out here."

"Thanks. It does, doesn't it?" Stan nodded in approval. "How are you?"

"Crappy." Brenna took a miserable breath and blew it out. "I'm sorry, Stan. I acted like a jerk. I shouldn't have gotten upset at you."

"Bren, it's okay," Stan said. "I should've told you guys about the investigation. I chickened out."

"I'm still sorry," Brenna said.

"Okay. So am I." Stan hugged her.

"And we owe you one. You brought Helga's killer to justice. Thank you," Brenna said, stepping back.

Same thing Jessie had said. "It wasn't just me," Stan said.

"You cared enough to figure it out, though."

"Of course I care." Stan looked away. "I care a lot. About all of you." And right now it was killing her that she and Jake weren't back on secure footing yet.

"I didn't really take the job, you know," Brenna said.

Stan smiled. "No?"

"Nope, so I, uh, wondered if I could have my job with you back?" Brenna asked hopefully.

"Can you start today?" Stan asked, and Brenna smiled, her first real smile since they'd started talking.

"You bet."

"Good. Go help Izzy, then. I'm just running home to get the dogs."

Brenna obliged and Stan hurried across the street to her house. She'd just clipped the leashes on her dogs' collars when a van pulled up in her driveway. Curious, she looked outside. Adrian Fox got out and walked to the door.

She opened it. "Hi."

"Hi. I wanted to tell you we're leaving."

Stan wasn't sure how she felt about that. "Come in for a second. No ghosts?" she asked as he stepped inside.

Fox hesitated. "There's something on those tapes. But with everything that's gone on, I'm going to sit on it for a while. We'll reach out to Izzy in a few weeks and see what she wants to do."

Stan nodded. "That's nice of you. It was really great to meet you. I always wanted to go on a ghost hunt. Thanks for making that happen."

Fox smiled. "Anytime." He paused, then muttered something that sounded like "screw it" and pulled Stan into his arms. He skillfully kissed her, then let her go, leaving her staring at him in shock. He cocked his head. "Anything?"

Stan thought about that for a minute, then shook her head. "Nothing."

Fox smiled. "Worth a shot. Take care, Stan." And he slipped out the door, to his car, back to his superhero bad-boy world.

Stan watched him go. Meeting him had been amazing. And while he had some superhero traits, he was really just a regular guy. Nothing like Jake, who was way better than a superhero. And a better kisser. Now she just had to make everything right with him. As soon as this wedding was over, she would tackle that.

"Come on, guys, let's do this." She hurried back across the street with the dogs just as Dede drove up. Stan waved at her as she parked on the street and got out of her car, the bride and groom trotting obediently after her.

"This is lovely!" Dede breathed, taking the scene in. "Here, I just have to get the cats." She handed the dogs to Stan.

They looked adorable. Lila wore a white tutu with a beaded collar that resembled pearls. Gus wore a black jacket with tails. "Where's his top hat?" Stan asked.

She was joking, but Dede reached into her front seat and pulled it out. "He throws it off, so we'll have to just put it on for pictures."

Dede leaned into the car again and returned with two cats on leashes. Mittens and Diamond didn't look fazed in the least, as if they did this all the time.

"Wow. Nutty would not be happy with me if I had him on a leash," Stan said. "How do you get them to do that?"

"I've been taking them on leashes since they were babies," Dede said. "They'll have a great time. And I didn't invite any dogs that don't like cats. Now, show me the cake. I can't wait to see it!"

Stan brought her over to the masterpiece. Dede *oohed* and *aahed* appropriately, then whipped out a smartphone and began taking pictures. "I have to put this on Facebook," she said.

Facebook? Stan smothered a giggle. Who said seniors weren't progressive? She welcomed the publicity—they'd complement her own page nicely.

Guests began arriving in droves. It looked like the entire town's dog population had been invited. The "reverend," one of Dede's good friends who was a real-life justice of the peace, arrived and huddled with Dede to get ready for the vows. Scruffy and Henry were playing with Izzy's dogs, so Stan didn't have anything to do until it was time to serve the cake. She couldn't keep the smile off her face. Who knew a doggie wedding would make her so happy?

She grabbed a seat and took a quick break. The ceremony was just about to begin when Jake slid into the seat next to her. He had Duncan firmly on a leash, which was why she didn't get advance notice that he was there. Duncan tried to jump into her lap. Jake reined him in. He settled for dropping his chin on her leg. She bent down for a kiss. Duncan obliged. She wondered if Jake would.

"How's it going? Everything looks great," Jake said.

"Thanks. It's going well. Almost time for the ceremony." He'd sought her out. Did that mean he forgave her? They'd barely spent any time together after Carla's arrest, largely due to her wedding planning, but also due to the awkwardness that had popped up between them that neither of them knew what to do with. She was also giving him space as all the news following the arrest flooded the town.

Arthur had confessed on the record and he was on "house arrest" while they figured out what to do with him. Stan suspected he wouldn't spend a day in prison. Carmen Feliciano had spoken with him, and while no one knew the details of that conversation, both had seemed at peace with the outcome.

Cyril Pierce had been released from prison and was writing stories like crazy, at his father's request. It could be a big break for his career. Reporting on a sixty-year-old cold case involving one's own father was a journalistic goldmine. What Cyril chose to do with that remained to be seen.

Even though Don Miller had resorted to bribery—not sabotage, said a structural engineer Jake brought in to inspect the basement stairs in the old library building—to protect his mother from implicating herself in the Constantine murder, he'd been cleared of any suspicion in his mother's death. Carla had acted alone and the murder was being called a "crime of passion." Which left Don a single father trying to explain to two young boys why their mommy wasn't coming back. All around, a sad story.

But Frog Ledge would move past it with steely New Englander resolve. Today, at least, was a happy day. And Jake was here, sitting with her, so maybe things were going to be okay with them, too. She could only hope.

"So what are you doing later?" Jake asked.

The hope bloomed brighter. "I don't know," she said. "Why?"

"I was hoping we could go out for Valentine's Day. Like on a date." Jake pulled his baseball cap off and rubbed his forehead. "God, do I sound stupid or what? I don't know what it is about you that makes me act like a teenaged fool."

Stan laughed. His nervousness was cute. "I would love to go out for Valentine's Day."

He breathed a sigh of relief. "Cool. I was gonna set up the gazebo out here for us, but I figured it would be too cold. We'll have to save that for the summer. Or at least spring. So I made us reservations at that place you've been saying you wanted to try. The Italian place down by the water in Mystic."

"Really?" She clapped her hands. "I'm so excited!"

"Good. I'll pick you up at six?"

"Sounds perfect." She looked up as Dede motioned for her to join them in the gazebo. "Time for the ceremony," she said to Jake. "I'll be back."

Once the doggie vows had gone off without a hitch, she and Dede served up the cake. Stan was relieved that all the dogs who sampled it loved it—and the pupcakes were a hit, too. A lot of them came back for seconds. As she served up the last few pieces, someone tapped her on the shoulder. She turned to find Sarah Oliver smiling at her.

"I heard you were running this shindig today, and I wanted to come down and personally say thank you," Sarah said.

"Please, Sarah, don't thank me. I wish things could've turned out differently."

"It's okay," Sarah said. "My mother is at peace now. All she really wanted was to get her story told. You helped with that. And with Benedict. Everything's good."

Touched, Stan hugged her. "Thank you for coming by."

"You're welcome," Sarah said. She blew Stan a kiss and turned to go. Then she stopped and turned back. "By the way, Frannie's really proud of you. She says Sabrina's trying to find a way back so she can sample your cooking."

Stan felt chills whistle up her spine. She'd never told anyone in town her grandmother's name, and she knew for a fact she'd never talked about Sabrina, her gram's first dog. She opened her mouth to ask Sarah how she could possibly know that, but the other woman was already walking away, skirts swirling around her. Stevie's song "If You Ever

Did Believe" played in Stan's head, a soundtrack for the moment.

"Everything okay?" Jake materialized at her elbow.

"Yeah, fine," Stan said, still staring after Sarah.

"Was that Sarah?"

"It was. She came to thank me." Stan turned her full attention to him. "Here, Dunc. Seconds?" She offered him a treat, which he wolfed down.

"More like thirds," Jake said. "But it's a special occasion."

Dede joined them in the gazebo, all smiles. She threw her arms around Stan. "This was such a wonderful day! I can't even begin to thank you enough. This is fabulous." She dabbed at her eyes. "So wonderful I could cry."

"Thank you, Dede," Stan said. "It was great fun."

"And it looked like a great success," a voice from behind Stan said. They all turned. Stan's mouth dropped open. It had been almost a year, but she'd recognize Sheldon Allyn anywhere. The famed, flamboyant pastry chef and TV star had been interested in Stan last year when he'd heard of her talents, but circumstances had killed the opportunity. So what was he doing in Frog Ledge now?

He looked the same, that was for sure. Today he wore a silver suit with a neon pink tie. His brown hair was still feathered, but a tad longer than she remembered. He wore full makeup, including a shade of eyeliner that Stan immediately coveted— a nice slate green.

"I've been following your business on social media," Allyn said, air-kissing the space next to her cheek, as if their last encounter hadn't been contentious. "You're even more fabulous. I want to make you a star. Or at least get you set up in a bakery. This wedding clinched it for me. I have a shop in mind for you in Boston. Right on Newbury Street. Imagine?" He closed his eyes as if indeed imagining, then opened them and focused on Stan again. "So, what do you say?"

RECIPES

Growl-nola

1.5 cups oat flour
1 cup old-fashioned oats
2 tablespoons oil (vegetable or canola)
⅓ cup honey
2 eggs
½ cup unsweetened apple sauce (or mashed apple)
⅓ cup water

Mix dry ingredients and then add wet ingredients. Place in 8 × 8 pan, sprinkle oats on top of batter. Bake at 325°F for 25 to 30 minutes.

Breakfast Bones

    2 cups wheat flour
    1 cup white flour
    ½ cup wheat germ
    ½ TBLS instant dry yeast
    2 dashes cinnamon
    1 TBLS honey
    2 eggs
    1¼ cup water
    2 TBLS oil (vegetable or canola)
    ½ cup bacon

Mix all wet in stand mixer, add flour and then add
other dry ingredients. Lastly, add bacon. Knead in
mixer for about 4 minutes. Roll out dough to
¼"—½" and cut with a bone shaped cookie cutter
in the size of your choice. 3" bone cutter is recom-
mended. Convection bake at 350°F for 20–25
minutes.

Dehydrate treats for 10 hours for longer-lasting
freshness.

Tail Waggers

1 cup oat flour
1 oz minced dehydrated beef liver (could also
    use dehydrated steak)
3 small minced carrots
2/3 cup rye flour
1 cup water

Mix all ingredients in stand mixer. Squeeze dough through reusable pastry bag with large star tip dropped at the bottom of the bag (this will create the "wagging" effect!). Make approximately 6" sticks. Bake at 350°F for 22 minutes then check. When you shake tray some of the sticks should move, if not, bake a little longer. Dehydrate for 10 hours for a longer lasting freshness.

—Recipes courtesy of The Big Biscuit,
Franklin, MA

Acknowledgments

As always, it takes a village. This time even more so.

Thank you to John Talbot of the John Talbot Agency, Inc., for believing in this series, and to my editor, John Scognamiglio, and the rest of the folks at Kensington for making sure the finished product is worthy.

Sherry Harris, my Wicked Cozy sister and first editor, gets a lot of the credit, as always, for making this book what it is today and keeping me sane during the process. She and our other Wicked Cozy blog mates—Edith Maxwell/Tace Baker, Barbara Ross, Jessie Crockett, and J. A. (Julie) Hennrikus/Julianne Holmes—are my biggest supporters and best friends. I love you all very much.

Thanks to Jim Chianese of the CT Paranormal Research Team and Chris D'Addio, who both lent me their expertise on ghost hunting and all things paranormal. I had a lot of fun with this topic.

Vanessa Sealey at The Big Biscuit, your recipes are to die for. Thanks for helping me provide high-quality treats for dogs everywhere!

Special thanks to Keith Golembiewski, my genealogy expert, for educating me on this process and all the cool ways you can find family members these days and trace history. Fascinating!

I was honored to use the name Dede Richardson in this book in honor of the real Dianne "Dede" Richardson. Thank you to Myron "Mikie" Richardson, her husband, who bid on naming rights for a character at an auction for animals and asked me to use his wife's name. Dede and their cats, Mittens and Diamond, are all named in this story.

And my rescue organizations of note: The Greater New Haven Cat Project, Inc. in New Haven, Connecticut, for your amazing work with feral cats; Angel Capone Pitbull Rescue in New York for getting the word out about how great this breed really is; the East Coast Maine Coon Rescue in New Jersey for saving coon cats like Nutty every day; and the Woodstock (NY) Farm Animal Sanctuary, which does amazing things for abused, neglected, and abandoned farm animals. Thank you to each of these organizations and all their dedicated volunteers and staff for being animal advocates. The world needs more of you!

Doug and Cynthia Fleck, my biggest thanks as always for your support, love and unconditional acceptance of my writerly quirks. Love you guys. And Kim Fleck, you know I could never do any of this without you. Thanks for being my biggest champion and the best social media expert around! Love you to the moon and back!

And to the readers, booksellers, and librarians, without whom there would be no authors. Thank you all.